Whose Curious Stars

By
C. Marcus Parr

et

Et Cetera Press
2009

Designed by C. Marcus Parr
Set in Garamond

et
Published by Et Cetera Press
Sandy, OR 97055

Author's Note
The author composed all prose herein except for the Monty Python "Universe" song and where noted.

ISBN: 978-0-578-01840-9
1. Fiction—coming of age—Oregon. 2. Teenage delinquency—pregnancy out of wedlock—drug use. 3. Astronomy—fetal alcohol syndrome.

For Peter Hays

If I address you whose curious stars
Climbed to the tops of their houses and froze
It is in hope of no
Answer, but as so often, merely
For want of another....

"To My Brother Hanson:
B. Jan. 28, 1926, D. Jan. 28, 1926"
W. S. Merwin

Human beings invented Original Sin because
the alternative hypothesis was worse. Better to
be at the centre of the universe whose terrors
are all a direct result of our own failings,
than to be helpless victims of random and
largely malevolent forces.

A. S. Byatt

Chapter 1

On a rainy September day in 1993, the year I turned fifteen, my mother married Robin Stanley on the banks of the Rogue River near Medford, Oregon. My kid brother and I stood off to the side under a golf umbrella. I held my brother's hand and glared at Robin Stanley and wished he'd drop dead before the final vows.

Self-righteous churchmen and their wives raised black umbrellas against the downpour, reminding me of mourners at a funeral more than guests at a wedding. The wind came up and the preacher's words were lost. I could hardly hear "I now pronounce you man and wife." My brother and I made a run for it before Robin Stanley could kiss the bride.

They held the reception beneath a white revival tent that dripped from condensation and where the rain found holes in the fabric. I spent a good part of the day babysitting my brother and avoiding my stepfather's reproach whenever Jesse knocked over a drip bucket. The buffet was homemade by Presbyterian church ladies—potato salad, cold cuts, white bread, Jell-O squares for dessert. No cake. They toasted the bride and groom with diet cola in paper cups. The guests were from the Living Faith Congregation, Robin Stanley's church in Medford. Only Jesse and I represented the bride's side of the family.

My mother first met Robin Stanley at a religious retreat, three months before the wedding. A week after they met, she introduced him as her fiancé. I wore disapproval on my sleeve that day, and he and I quarreled from the get go. My stepfather's complexion was like flour paste, and his hands were bone cold. His eyes ran away from you when he spoke, and were red rimmed with worry. He was unlike my father—my *real* dad—who practiced law down in San Francisco. Dad has confidence to burn, and people say I take after him. Unlike Robin Stanley, who showed all the poise of a house of cards.

My mother recognized my foul mood and came up to me. "Danny, aren't you happy for me?"

"Sure, Mom." How I really felt was plastered all over my face.

"Why aren't you smiling?"

I took a breath. "Congratulations, Mom." I tried to put sincerity behind my words but they tasted like soot.

"No," she corrected, "you're supposed congratulate Dr. Stanley. Give the bride your best wishes." I kissed her on the cheek and offered up a thin smile.

While the day wore on, Robin Stanley had a heart-to-heart with my brother and me. The three of us walked away from the reception, to talk privately out of the rain. We settled on my mom's old Buick. Jesse and I sat in the backseat with Robin Stanley in front, stinking up the air with his aftershave.

"From now on, Daniel," he said, "I want you to call me *dad*." He reached over the seat to put his hand on Jesse's shoulder. "Do you understand? I'm your dad now."

My brother is an imperfectly formed five-year-old. He is about a decade younger than me. The difference in our ages happened because my mother couldn't make up her mind whether or not to save her first marriage. Then came the day, after years of uncertainty, the pregnancy strip turned blue.

There has only been one dad in Jesse's life, and so when Robin Stanley tried to gain favor, my brother looked to me for an answer. He didn't have a clue what Robin Stanley was going on about.

My brother and I have a way of speaking without words. I could say something poetic, that we were linked through our hearts or something, but that's not how it was. Jesse relied on me to be his big brother, to always be there for him. His trust created a bond between us that nothing could break.

On that day his eyes crinkled in a smile when I signaled it wouldn't hurt to call Robin Stanley *dad*, at least for the time being. But my stepfather was not a stupid man. He wasn't blind to our conspiracies, even back then. My bad manners were making a mockery of his appeal for a truce. I think he realized on his wedding day that he'd bought into something bigger than he bargained for.

"*Jess!*" he said. "Did you hear me?"

Jesse pressed his mooncalf face against the back window, trying to ignore the question. Tears squeezed out of him like juice from an orange. Jesse's blubbering had nothing to do with Robin Stanley's tone of voice. The thing is, Jesse cried over just about anything.

Six years earlier, my parents' marriage was falling apart because Mom drank too much. Every night, before Dad came home from the firm, she would fix herself a Manhattan. Later, as Dad unwound with a martini, she joined him for another, and the booze worked like a razor between them. By the time dinner was served, their conversation usually deteriorated into argument. They fought over a lot of things but mostly about her drinking. No dishes were thrown. Dad was not physically abusive, but voices were raised and tension filled the house like poison. On some nights I was afraid to breathe. Mom would often end up on the front room couch and wouldn't get up until I left for school the next day. I remember the morning she got sick to her stomach. I figured it was the booze until her gynecologist confirmed it: she was three months along. After that, she quit drinking altogether, but by then the damage was done. Jesse had Fetal Alcohol Syndrome.

From the back of the Buick I said, "You don't understand, Robin. You're scaring him."

My stepfather brushed a flake of lint from the sleeve of his one good business suit. He smiled to pretend to keep his temper. "I am not scaring him."

"He doesn't understand, Robin."

For a moment I saw something in him that nearly took me a year to figure out. My stepfather's eyes were like lifeless holes in a mask. You couldn't tell what he was thinking, probably because he wasn't thinking about much. But as we locked stares in the Buick, he dropped the pretense and showed me who he really was, a selfish prig. A boy my age can't hide his feelings all that well, and Robin Stanley could easily read the hate in me. He shifted his weight against the steering wheel and looked off toward the reception tent where the wind got caught in the door flaps and made the afternoon distant and gloomy. When he glanced back at me again, his eyes were black from all the darkness that day.

"I'm not scaring you, am I?" He patted Jesse on the shoulder.

My brother howled. Once started, it usually took a good five minutes for him to stop. Robin Stanley resigned to wait it out. But Jesse's sobs came in waves and troughs. Tears dribbled from his eyes as he struggled to regain a sense of calm only to explode with more of the same. Robin Stanley grew annoyed at each whimper until his patience finally gave out.

"Well," he said, "I know what you need, the two of you. Church school."

He opened the car door and left me with my kid brother, who was full of snot and sniffles.

"It's okay, Jesse," I told him and leaned over and gave him a hug.

*   *   *

Later, on the drive north from Medford to our new home, Robin Stanley told us about his two sons from a previous marriage. It was a revelation, the first of many. Back then I knew next to nothing about my stepfather. His talk about his kids was news to my mother as well. She had the look of shock on her face. "Does this mean I'm the mother of *four* children?" she asked.

He tried to suck up to us in the backseat, snickering self-consciously like the fraud he was. He said, "Don't worry about it, Karin. We boys won't gang up on you." He laughed. But when he saw the reflection of my contempt in the rearview mirror, the fun drained clean out of him. Robin Stanley turned to my mom. She would never meet his kids, he said, and I had to wonder why not. "Still," my mother remarked, turning to look out the window. "You could have told me." Robin Stanley went silent for over an hour, and I watched his bloodless hands clutch the steering wheel like he was wringing somebody's neck.

The more time I spent with Robin Stanley the less I liked him. During their brief engagement when Mom arranged for a run of get-togethers, I made an effort to talk to him, but Robin Stanley showed no interest in sports, what I was interested in. He never played football or baseball in school. "Bowling's my game," he said. On those few occasions before the wedding when we were alone, the silence between us was awful. Although we had only known each other a short time, it was clear that I could never, as my mom hoped, "grow to love Dr. Stanley."

I already had a father.

Robin Stanley brought us to his parents' farm in the rolling hills of nursery stock farms, southeast of Portland. As we approached, I leaned forward to get a look at the place when Robin Stanley took a turn up a gravel driveway, off the county road. I had expected something picturesque—a red barn, white farmhouse with wraparound porch, lazy chickens behind a picket fence. There was nothing of the kind. Through a thicket of raspberry canes, I saw a doublewide-trailer set on a square of gravel overgrown in weeds. An ancient pick-up truck was parked off to the side, and a ramshackle pole barn was surrounded in fields of scrub and bramble. On this scrap of dirt a few miles outside of Strand, a town of five thousand in the foothills of Mt. Hood, my stepfather's parents—Eve and Virgil Stanley—had farmed for decades, only to end up broke and worn out. Seeing this desolation for the first time, I wanted to run in the opposite direction. I fell back against the seat as though the air had been knocked out of me. I could not hide from my mother the bitterness I felt.

In a tone that tried to cover up a deep sense of regret, she said, "Isn't it wonderful?"

Eve Stanley greeted us from the front of the doublewide. My mother lined us up against the car while she took a snapshot with a plastic camera, to commemorate our arrival. The flash brought bellyaching and whining from my kid brother. Eve Stanley rubbed Jesse's ears and turned to her husband. "Would you look at 'em?" she said. "Like a sugar bowl." Jesse had what the doctor called "railroad track" ears. They were misshapen and funny looking, and they stuck out like radar scanners. Jesse broke down in wet slobbers and hid in my mother's Laura Ashley wedding dress. The old lady had no idea my brother was mentally retarded. Her son had kept Jesse's handicap a secret as well.

Virgil and Eve Stanley wore clothes more suitable to an earlier epoch. They looked like migrants in a Dorothea Lange photograph. Virgil had a sandstone face, rutted with a downcast mouth and gullied beneath the same lifeless eyes of his son. I lived with the Stanley's for nearly six months, and in all that time, I never saw Virgil smile. His wife was his opposite, and it seemed to me, there was less of Eve than Virgil in Robin Stanley. She filled out the apron that she wore over a faded dress. She was a large woman with docile features, and had a face like risen bread dough and hands softened by baking flour. She had been defined by her role on the farm. Eve's mannerisms told the story of a woman who had lived a life of disappointment, pledged to duties that had gained her little and robbed her of all promise.

The Stanley's looked as though they had little to spare and no keenness to do so. I stood looking at them and wondered, how is it possible that my stepfather brought us here to live on their worn-out farm? The doublewide trailer was hardly big enough for two old people let alone an extra "family" of four. Still, Eve Stanley clucked behind us like a mother hen and ushered us into the house. They put up Jesse and me in what had been a storage room. When Virgil Stanley showed us our new digs, he pointed to the pile of boxes in the corner. "I'll get them outta here tomorrow," he said. In all the months that followed, my brother and I shared that miserable room with those damn boxes.

But compared to my mother's bedroom—Robin Stanley's old room—ours was the royal suite. To get to her room, Mom had to pass between Virgil and Eve Stanley's recliners in the living room, near the woodstove. From my new bedroom, I watched as she grasped the situation and stopped dead cold. Her back was to me, but I could see the discontent that tightened her shoulders. She slouched through the door, defeated, it seemed to me, by Robin Stanley's broken promises. For over two hours, she shut herself inside that bedroom and refused to come out. She was too afraid to face us in her current mood should she suddenly become unable to carry on the fraud of hopefulness and show us how she really felt.

Eve Stanley helped Jesse carry his boxes of toys to our new room, and when all was packed away, she leaned down and said to him, "You can call me Granny, if you like." Jesse freely hugged the old lady. He rarely showed affection to strangers, but he ended up calling her "Gammy." I, too, was grateful for her hospitality and warmth. She offset the stony exterior of Virgil Stanley and her holierthan-thou son. Here was some relief in the spare hopelessness of the landscape.

She fed us lunch at the rough-cut kitchen table and treated us to freshly baked raspberry pie on chipped plates with cups of hot chocolate. It was the last of sweetness and light for a long time to come.

*   *   *

If you stood my dad up against him, Robin Stanley would lose big time. Three of him tied together would hardly make a real man.

My stepfather had the look of a trapped animal. He was nervous around people he didn't know, and he always seemed afraid something bad might happen. Mom explained that he had been electrocuted as a boy. She said the accident had stunted his growth. I don't know much about electrocutions. I'm more familiar with death by drowning or a sudden blockage in the arteries of the heart. When he was about my age, Robin Stanley nearly died from an alternating current of two hundred and twenty volts of electricity delivered into his hand, up through his head, and down through his shoes.

"Tore the sneakers off my feet," he told me.

In the hour following lunch on our first day at the Stanley farm, the two of us spoke inside the barn where he faked a childlike enthusiasm to show me around. A shaft of light through the barn door prettied up the dust in that dismal place. The interior was vacant of industry, gutted like the shell of scuttled ship. The hulks of a tiller and brush hog were mislaid beneath stacks of fruit trays. Robin Stanley pointed out the electrical socket that had nearly killed him. The armored electric cable and utility box dangled from a nail in the support post where the mark of a flash fire spoiled the wood.

I walked over to it and ran my fingers down the ridges to count its age. It must have been an ancient tree. There were irregular thick and thin bands in the flesh that told of wet and dry seasons before its harvest. For a hundred years that tree had survived forest fires and drought until men with chainsaws came to cut it down.

"Two-twenty current. You don't know what that is, do you?"

Rather than admit, I said, "I know it."

"When I was your age I used to wear corrective lens," he said, standing beside a stack of crates. "But I don't need them anymore. Not after getting shocked. God corrected the defect in my sight." He laughed. "In more ways than one. The doctors told my mother I was dead. I saw God, you know."

I turned away because I could not stomach another word about Jesus and all the rest of it. On the drive north out of Medford, I had listened long enough to his lessons from scripture. We had suffered through his saying grace in a fast food restaurant while our burgers went cold. And now, as Robin Stanley lectured us about the nature of the afterlife, I thought about how much I resented his telling us we should call him *Dad*. I thought about his threat to send me to church school. My fingers traced a line in the wood alongside the cable. In spite of all my stepfather's hand wringing about Heaven, the future looked bleak as far as I could tell. The town of Strand was no more than a spur track off the logging road, a broken-hearted relic of a town without promise. A cruel fate had snatched me out of the paradise of California and pitched me into purgatory. I made a resolution then and there that I would not accept Robin Stanley's beliefs or pretend to believe in his supernatural hoodoo. I decided that I hated the man.

"Daniel, you listening to me?"

I faced him. "I heard you."

He cocked his head as if to digest my mockery. "Daniel...you're not one of those boys who..." He puckered his lips as he searched for the right word. "You don't *abuse* yourself, do you?"

I made no response.

"You know what I'm talking about, don't you? *Masturbation*."

I took a breath. "I don't see how that's any of your business."

He cast his eyes downward, but I could see the trace of victory in his face. As though he'd caught me at something shameful and grim.

"The Lord will punish you for spilling your seed on the ground. It's in the Bible. The Story of Onan. He was slain by God, do you know that?" His self-satisfied smirk seemed to say that I was beyond "saving."

I pushed past him, out of the barn.

I suppose, it's natural for stepsons to hate their stepfathers. This kind of conflict is something you read about in fairytales. But I felt justified in my hatred—Robin Stanley was a tyrant. It wasn't that he beat my brother and me. He barely laid a hand on either of us, but tyranny can come in different forms. My stepfather practiced a tyranny of cheerlessness. My best friend, Hitch McDonough, said that Robin Stanley could "suck the daylight out of the sun and turn it dead black." My stepfather's greatest sin was that he was a colossal bore. To a fourteen-year-old who had led an exciting life in San Francisco, the man was boredom made flesh.

He was not a real doctor, not a Medical Doctor, but an optometrist. He insisted that his customers call him *Doctor*. He had the salutation printed on thank-you notes: *Dr. and Mrs. Stanley wish to thank you for your thoughtful gift....* When they were dating, he gave my mother the impression that he was a successful physician. I think she agreed to marry him for his money and professional standing, if the truth were told. He didn't bother to correct her assumptions until a few days before the wedding. Instead of explaining that he lived with his parents on their deadbeat farm, he promised her "a house in the country." This was another lie in a long run of deceit. My mother deserved better than Robin Stanley with his false claims and uneasy smile of apology.

On the day we moved into the Stanley doublewide, my mother was shaken by this sudden "change in circumstances," as she put it. As far as I could tell, she had agreed to marry a make-believe husband, someone she thought was a respected professional man with a house in the country. The truth can sometimes sting like a slap in the face. She stayed locked up in the bedroom for hours and turned a deaf ear to Robin Stanley's raised voice at the door. He rapped until his knuckles were red.

"Karin, are you coming out?"

She cried that she wanted to be left alone.

"Unlock the door this instant. Let me in."

Eventually, the latch came unlocked, and they had words in private.

An hour later my stepfather gathered us into their bedroom to explain our state of affairs. My mother's eyes were sore from crying.

She sat on the bed covered in a quilt whose stitching had gone ragged. The loose patches of blue and corn-yellow fabric fluttered like the wings of dead butterflies in her hands. Behind her on the wall, a Thomas Kincade poster was tacked to the paneling at something off plumb. The artist's version of "home" with pink hued blossoms and smoke out the chimney and a picket fence was baloney as far as I could tell.

Looking up as my brother and I came into the room, Mom combed her fingers through her chestnut hair as she turned to the nightstand for a Kleenex.

"Daniel. Jess. We have something we'd like to say to you," Robin Stanley said.

This was how he opened the first of our many "family" get-togethers. He needed to explain how we had ended up at a ruined raspberry farm on the road to nowhere. It was his first use of the pronoun *we* when referring to Mom and himself as a married couple. It offended me. The pronoun was reserved for my real family and for the exclusive use by my father. Robin Stanley tossed off *we* like propaganda.

"We want you to know, this is temporary." He told us that *we* would move into a brand-new tract house as soon as *our* financial situation improved.

My mother interrupted him. "Tell them when, Robin."

"Well, as soon as the bank clears my loan. Simple as that. What do you think, new house here in town, make a go of it?"

"Danny, are you listening?" my mother said.

She had been born and raised in Oklahoma. Despite years of learning to speak without betraying her roots, traces of her upbringing came out when she was stressed. I found her regional accent charming, although she said she hated her Southern drawl. "When you talk like an Okie, people think you're stupid," she told me more times than I can count. The way I saw it, her soft voice was spiritually Southern and full of color. She painted pictures with words. Through her voice you could see the relics of houses in a sea of prairie grass. To this day her voice plays in my mind like a Saturday matinee, in full Technicolor. I have adopted the rhythm of her speech in spite of my not having lived anywhere near Oklahoma, or outside California for that matter, until the year we moved to Oregon.

"Dr. Stanley's ex-wife filed some kind of lawsuit," my mother said. Her Baptist drawl was coming through, and she blinked at her new husband. There was a hint of disapproval on her lips. "She wants *us* to pay her credit card debt."

Robin Stanley squinted and swiped his hand through the air as though he was trying to erase the very idea from her mind. "No no no," he said. "I explained that to you."

I smiled at his uneasiness. Here was some ripe gossip that I would include in a letter to my father. I had been writing postcards to him since the day we left San Francisco, but because we had moved twice during our stay in Medford, I never received any replies. I called Dad on the phone once from Medford, but our conversation was brief. I was thinking about how much I missed my father when Robin Stanley raised his voice.

"I told you not to worry about that, Karin," he said. "She has no legal right. None. I'll take care of it."

My mother dropped her gaze to her fingers as she pinched the fabric, worrying the sides of the quilt.

Robin Stanley turned toward me. "Did you hear what I said?" he asked.

I shrugged because my feelings were still stinging from his remarks about beating off.

"Don't you like it here, Daniel? Isn't your room okay?"

I gave him what I thought he deserved, an incredulous look that said, "You've got to be kidding?"

The cords in my stepfather's neck tightened. "Answer me."

I turned to my mother, but she wouldn't look up. Feeling lost, I said, "It's alright, I guess."

Robin Stanley rubbed his hands together. "We have to make due. For the time being. We will move into our own house when time permits, Lord willing. But understand this." He raised a finger. "My practice comes *first*. It costs a small fortune for a doctor of optometry to open an office. We're all just going to have to learn to be patient...oh look, I made a pun."

He smiled to himself. I noticed he was the only one in the room smiling.

"This isn't so bad, is it?" Mom said, trying to come across as brave.

I looked for and hoped to see the person I thought I knew, the woman who had raised me, but she was no longer there.

"We can put up with this for a while. It'll be fun, living on a farm, right?" Robin Stanley said to my little brother. "Tell you what. We can get some chickens."

"I wanna dog," Jesse said.

"No. Look, I've explained this to you, Jess," Robin Stanley said. "We cannot afford a dog right now."

Jesse's open mouth leaked spittle onto his chin, and Mom got off the bed to wipe him with her Kleenex.

"Oh, Jesse," she said.

"Chickens. You'd like that, wouldn't you?" Robin Stanley said.

When my brother failed to answer, my stepfather again turned toward me. In that instant the charade fell away like a curtain being drawn, and I saw hostility in his eyes. I wondered if it had something to do with our visit to the barn. I wondered if I hadn't paid enough attention to his electrocution story.

"Teach *you* some responsibility, hey, Daniel? Taking care of chickens."

"Danny's responsible," my mother said, finally in my defense. She seemed to suck up the tension between Robin Stanley and me to make it her own.

Robin Stanley's mouth tightened. This was his way of showing disapproval. In the short time of our acquaintance, I had learned that my stepfather practiced a kind of self-deceptive vanity. Despite years of failure and indecision, he imagined himself as someone far greater than he was. His inadequacies caused him great frustration and disappointment, and his resulting discontent with life was like a wet blanket over all of us. Nothing seemed to be in his favor, or ours now that we accepted his bad luck by proxy. He had expected his new wife not to criticize or to show disapproval of our living situation when in the company of others, especially in front of the boys over whom he was just beginning to flex his authority.

My mother withdrew to the corner of the bed. "You can take care of chickens, can't you, Danny?" she said.

Rather than address my poor defeated mother, I faced Robin Stanley squarely and said, "Yeah, sure. No problem."

"Good. Then." He slapped his thighs. "All settled."

Finally, when I thought he might excuse us from this painful assembly, Robin Stanley patted the quilt for his bride to fall in line.

"Let's pray together, shall we?" He grasped his hands between his legs.

My mother gestured that I should shut my eyes as we listened to Robin Stanley's prayer. In it he asked for the Lord's forgiveness for our sins and for His protection in hopes that we, His people, should find our way to loving one another as we were loved. He prayed for "the boys" to grow up strong and true "in the Faith." Most of Robin Stanley's prayer wasn't a prayer at all but a kind of complaint against me, that I should "improve" myself in the eyes of his god.

In the end, scattering our Amen's, Jesse burped.

"Jesse!" Mom said.

I laughed and so did my kid brother in turn.

The humor was lost on Robin Stanley.

"Excuse yourself," he barked.

Jesse broke into tears, and Mom gobbled him up in her arms. She whispered as though into her own ear, "It's okay, Jesse, my love. It's okay. Come on, honey. Stop cryin' now. Stop cryin'."

C. Marcus Parr

Chapter 2

They enrolled Jesse in Bible School, which was run by the Valley Shepherd Community Church where my mother and Robin Stanley worshipped. They took Jesse every Sunday, but I refused to go. "You can't make a person be saved, Karin," my stepfather had said. I was grateful for his disregard. He considered me hopeless which saved my Sunday mornings to spend alone, lying on my bed and listening to music.

I was too old to attend Bible School; otherwise, whether I wanted to be saved or not, Robin Stanley would have forced me to go. Had we stayed in California, I would have finished out the ninth grade in junior high. But in the Strand school district, middle school students were promoted as freshman, and so I entered Union High School.

The kids had another name for it—the Onion. Built in 1962, the buildings were originally painted a rose hue that had faded over time to the color of onionskin. At the corners of the administration building were four turrets that displayed the school principles. Over the years, pranksters had so often defaced *Fidelity*, *Truth*, *Knowledge* and *Light* with graffiti that nobody could read them. It was an unwelcoming and depressing place, especially in the fall when the skies were dull gray.

Down the hill from the administration building, the sports field shone like a ray of hope with its vibrant grass and bleachers. Over the summer, someone had coated the bleachers in fresh paint. On the morning that I was enrolled, before the first bell, I stood alone to stare at the baseball diamond and football field where kids were gathering for first period. I hoped that I might earn some respect on those fields and take back part of what had been taken from me in the move to Oregon. I imagined a scenario in which my name would appear in the school newspaper for an outstanding catch in a Friday night football game. At my old school, the competition had been fierce, and I had never made it past second string in any sport—football, basketball, or baseball. With less competition at Union High, I figured, I might earn the chance to play varsity.

But my dreams of glory were never realized, and my first day at the new school proved disastrous. I got in a fistfight with a kid who would later become my best friend.

Hitch McDonough was the only sixteen-year-old I ever met who looked prematurely grown up. He shaved every day, I think. His shoulders reminded me of muscles on a bull, and he wore his black hair longer than the style of those days. He was always combing it back with his hands. He was quick to smile and quick to battle, which, in my way of thinking, is a dangerous combination in a sixteen-year-old.

My first class, period one, was Physical Education, eight o'clock in the morning. It wasn't bad enough that I had zits on my chin from the stress of the past few months, but I got assigned to first period PE. This completed the stretch of bad luck. The last thing I needed was to stand naked in a shower, on my *first* day, with a bunch of kids whose main order of business was to make me look the fool. Instead, to my relief, the coach told us to sit on the bleachers inside the basketball court, fully clothed. He called out names from a roster and assigned lockers and delivered a talk on personal hygiene. Coach Montgomery used the phrases "be that as it may" and "without further ado," which sounded like something you'd say at a Rotary Club meeting, not a bleacher full of high school boys.

He said, "You what brought your gym clothes can go and suit up. For you others, your combination locks'll get handed out, at the athletic office."

There I found myself in a line of boys that didn't know me or want to know me. As the new kid, I didn't say a word to anyone. I stuck out as weird, as different from the friends who paired up to tell stories about summer vacations. A few of them joked at my expense. I wasn't dressed like them, in flannel, Wranglers and worn out baseball caps. When I reached the office door, the coach stood nonchalantly tapping a pen against a clipboard.

"Name?" he asked.

"Dan Aiken."

Coach Montgomery's head was nearly the size of a pumpkin. He combed his hair forward in a bowl cut on account he was balding. He found my name on the roster and handed the lock to me along with a combination of three numbers printed on a strip of paper.

"Locker one twenty-one," he said and squinted at me like he smelled something offensive.

I made my way to the boy's showers where I searched the maze of metal lockers for mine. This was where the promise of the day ended badly.

After matching up the numbers, I inserted the lock through the latch and closed it shut. When I tested the combination, the lock didn't open. I tried it again but realized that Coach Montgomery had given me a lock that did not match the numbers on the piece of paper.

"Shit," I muttered.

"You kiss yer mother with that mouth?"

I looked up. A kid was standing there with a towel wrapped round his waist. Earlier, I'd heard the boys mixing it up in the showers, and I figured that he had been the loudest in the bunch. Their cries bounced off the tiles and echoed throughout the locker room.

I ignored him.

I again worked the combination and spun the dial once more, all the while quietly cursing Robin Stanley for his blame in the matter.

"Out of the way, dipshit," the kid said.

I looked up again. "What?" I said.

Two boys, seniors who knew the kid as a troublemaker, were returning just then from the showers. They knew the signs of a potential fight, and they gawked like spectators at a car accident. The taller of the two poked his buddy in the ribs and laughed.

"You deaf?" the kid said.

This was the last thing I needed, but I was not about to be bullied by him, no matter how scared he made me feel.

"I heard you," I said.

I faced my locker, and as I rubbed my chin with the palm of my hand, I glanced back at the seniors who snickered like donkeys. The gauntlet had been thrown. A pack of other boys were drawn by the scent of violence. Some in Jockey shorts, some wrapped in damp towels, all at various levels of immaturity, some with voices yet to crack, others with chest hair. They loitered to watch the new kid get his ass kicked.

My dad had always told me to stand up against adversity. "Otherwise," he said, "it'll never go away. Dog you forever."

"What're you lookin' at, idiot," the kid said.

Resigned to it, I faced my rival straight on.

"Not looking at fucking much," I said. I had tried to sound cocky and self-assured, but my voice cracked.

Swearing comes naturally to boys who try to assert themselves, but this was like drawing a line in quicksand. The kid cocked his head to get a better look at the poor fool he was about to beat up.

"What'd you say, faggot?" he said.

Then he dropped the towel and exposed himself, cupping and waggling his dick at me.

The other kids laughed.

Once the put-down was complete, he pulled on his Jockey shorts, turned and walked away.

Fool that I was, I said, "Fuck you, asshole. Fuck you big time."

I do not remember who threw the first punch, but I got the worst of it. After the coach broke it up, the big kid and I were sent to the principal. We sat outside the office, as far away from one another as possible, among half a dozen chairs along the wainscoting and frosted glass. He sat there picking his teeth, and I covered my face in a blood-soaked towel. He had a swollen lower lip from my pushing him into the lockers. I, on the other hand, had yet to stop a nosebleed, and my left ear still rang from a roundhouse punch.

His name was Hitch McDonough, and I learned that he was the meanest son of a bitch at school. He was not afraid of anything, not even adults or high school principals. Nothing mattered to Hitch McDonough. He was like a criminal in training or something. He was quicker to anger than anybody I ever met in life. But he could be generous, too, and at times empathetic, traits that I had yet to learn he had. In the world of Hitch McDonough, nothing was more valuable than loyalty to your friends.

"I never did anything to you," I told him, my voice sounding nasally and worn out. "Why'd you pick on me?"

Hitch worked the toothpick between his teeth in about as casual and defiant a pose as I have ever seen in front of a principal's office.

"Because you're new," he said matter-of-factly.

The towel the coach had given me was dyed red. I put my head back and anchored it firmly, hoping to staunch the flow before Principal Horvath found time in his schedule to discipline us for fighting on the first day of school.

Hitch laughed. "You fought back, though. Most of 'em just cry for their mommies."

Because it was my first day and my first offense, Principal Horvath cut me a break. He was a tightly wound, bald man in a black suit with an old-fashioned tie. He wore little round spectacles that he removed theatrically when he handed me a letter to be signed by my father. I tried to explain, Robin Stanley wasn't my *real* father but my stepdad. I realized halfway through just how irrelevant it all was, that my dad lived in California, eight hundred miles away. I accepted the letter resentfully.

Hitch McDonough got it worse. Principal Horvath issued him a three-day suspension.

The remainder of the day was uneventful by comparison. After each bell I handed my teachers a letter, informing them of my status as new student, and in each classroom, no matter where I sat, kids looked at me as though I was road kill. After the last bell, I boarded the bus for my long ride back to the Stanley farm. It was the worst day of my life.

After getting dropped off by the bus on the county road, I was making my way toward our cutoff when Hitch McDonough intercepted me. My nose was still swollen, and I had a headache. The heavy strap of the canvas book bag dug into my shoulders. I carried a letter of reprimand in my pocket, which was another excuse for Robin Stanley to mistreat me. Confronting Hitch McDonough once more, on this my first day, was the last thing I needed.

He smoked a cigarette, a Marlboro Red, and slouched against a fence post, his book bag discarded behind him. When he saw me, he snubbed out the smoke on the rusted barbwire and took up a position in the middle of the blacktop.

I stopped a good car-length away.

"I don't want any trouble," I said. I shook my head at the thought that I would have to walk past this asshole everyday on my way home from school.

He said nothing.

"Look, you can't blame me for your suspension, okay? You started it."

He took a step forward.

I held my ground and dropped the book bag. My fists clenched. I was thinking, two fights in one day was two too many.

We circled each other in an imaginary orbit before Hitch pulled up and laughed.

"You'd hit me again, wouldn't ya?" he said. "Tough little shit."

I stood at the ready.

"How's the nose?"

I said nothing. My heart was beating so hard, if I had opened my mouth I was afraid he would hear it.

He leaned forward as though to shake my hand. I looked at his open palm for the dirty trick it was.

"Hitch McDonough."

"I know your name. Remember? In the principal's office," I said, keeping my distance.

Hitch raised an eyebrow as if to say, no hard feelings. I could tell he wasn't mad at me. I shook his hand, relieved by our sudden truce.

"Dan," I said. "Dan Aiken."

"I know. *Remember?*" he said sarcastically.

He squeezed my hand once, just to inform me of the kind of brutal beating he could have given, and then he let go. He reached into his flannel shirt pocket and pulled out the half-crushed pack of Marlboros, shook out one and stuck it between his lips. Then he gestured with the pack. "Want one?" He squinted. Here was another of his gauntlets.

I shrugged and cautiously took a cigarette. It was the first cigarette I had ever smoked, but I didn't have the guts to refuse the offer. He snapped open an old-fashioned chrome Zippo lighter and palmed the flame. I leaned into it, took a drag and slowly exhaled. Not so bad, I thought, faking it.

He gave me an all-knowing nod of the head as though we were old buddies, long-lost pals or something. I peered at him through cigarette smoke, and coughed once, my eyes watering. I gathered saliva in my mouth and spat sideways. All of it—the significant nodding, spitting, blowing smoke rings—choreographed gestures in a ritual to prove how macho we were.

"Come on," he said. "Lemme show you something."

The Cascade foothills around Strand were home to leftover logging apparatus and railroad tracks from a boom now gone bust. Hitch took me through the undergrowth at the side of the road to a train trestle that spanned a deep gully. "Welcome to Alder Bridge," he said. We crossed a trestle constructed of rusted-out iron and creosote timbers, rough cut and worm eaten. The rails had long been removed for scrap, and as we leaped from one railroad tie to the next, I resisted the temptation to look down. Below, boulders looked the size of houses. Gusts of wind whipped my jacket. From far below came the growl of whitewater.

Halfway across, Hitch turned and said, "Watch the north side there. The planks're rotted out."

We made our way to a spot well above the trees, over the water. The river cascaded in a rush to get away from the high country, water showing like quartz on jade. I felt as though, if I shifted my weight, I would drop to my death. Hitch dangled his legs casually over the side. I managed to do the same without showing fear.

"What river is that?" I said.

"Deep Creek."

Hitch grimaced through Marlboro smoke.

Taking a drag, I said, "What're you gonna tell your folks? You know, 'bout the suspension."

I was trying to fit in by mimicking Hitch's speech, but the words sounded phony like a bad actor in a piss-poor play.

Hitch blew a smoke ring and flicked the butt, watching it fall. The embers separated from the filter, which made me worry a bit. A burning cigarette in all that fuel could spark a fire, but his aim was as sure as his good luck. The ember hit a crescent-shaped pool beside an alder.

"It's just Pop an' me. No *folks*. I won't tell if you don't."

I laughed to myself at the ballsy self-confidence of Hitch McDonough. I crushed the Marlboro on a railroad tie and roughed the filter along a streak of creosote until the fibers floated away on the wind.

"My stepdad...he'll be pissed," I said, finding my true voice again.

Hitch wrinkled his brow. "New people move here, you hear about it. How come I never heard a no Aiken's?"

"That's because it's the Stanley's. Just up the road. My kid brother and me. And my mom. She married Dr. Stanley."

"Not *Robin* Stanley?" Hitch grinned at my expense.

I cringed.

He pulled a toothpick from his shirt pocket and rolled it around his tongue.

"Robin Stanley could suck the daylight outta the sun and turn it dead black. He's your stepdad?" Hitch held a deadpan smirk.

I gave a nod, and he turned away. We were lost in our own thoughts for a time, listening to the rapids below.

"Still got that note or'd you throw it away?"

I took the letter out of my jeans pocket and unfolded it, handed it to him.

"My first day," I said with a shake of the head. "And I get in a fight."

"*Fight?* Hell, was no fight. Tussle maybe, but no fight."

I squinted at him. His attitude was beginning to piss me off. My nose ached, and a thick crust of dried blood had plugged my nostrils, forcing me to breathe through my mouth. Here was the guy who had ruined my first day at school telling me it was no fight.

"Whatever," I said. "My stepdad's going to, you know, make it hell to pay."

Hitch laughed. "Here. Gimme a pen or something."

"What for?"

Hitch grabbed my book bag, and when I reached for it, he yanked it away and searched the front pocket. He removed my geometry textbook and flattened the principal's letter, working the crease with his thumb and getting a kick out of reading it.

"What're you doing, man?" I said.

He poised my Bic pen above the paper and with a flourish, and to my horror, he signed the letter.

"Shit."

"Look. Horvath's a jerk, okay? You think he's, what, gonna call your stepdad? Check out the signature? Gimme a break. He'll never know."

He folded the letter and shoved it between the pages of the geometry book and returned it to me.

I didn't thank him. I didn't say anything. I just stared at Deep Creek rushing below the trestle. In the lengthening afternoon shadows, the creek gleamed like aluminum. A bird of prey rode an updraft.

"I got two fags left," Hitch said, rummaging through his pockets.

I reached out my hand.

"You want a brew with that?"

He pulled a can of Budweiser from his backpack.

We sat there talking about nothing in general and everything in particular, sharing the beer. It lubricated my vocal cords, and I ended up spewing some hateful harangue about Robin Stanley. I told Hitch about my brother, and I talked proudly about my Dad. I might have gone on too long, because Hitch said, "Sounds like he ain't your dad at all, but some kind of god you worship."

We laughed at that. It felt good to laugh. As the sun shone through the trees, we packed it in and went our separate ways.

When I got back to the farm I went directly to my room. I stank of cigarettes, and I could feel the effects of the beer. I did not want to get caught and suffer my stepfather's quotations from scripture on intemperance. Drinking was frowned upon in our household, or at least, in the *former* household of my real mom and dad. I took Robin Stanley, for all his talk of fundamental evangelism, for a teetotaler. Mom, of course, was dead set against drinking ever since she brought Jesse into the world. I was happy the day she quit. The last thing in the world I wanted was to return to the old days when she used to pass out on the couch. If caught with beer on my breath, she might disown me. My parents had already been culled out and winnowed down to one. The last thing I needed was for Mom to give up on me, too.

A knock came at the bedroom door, and my mother poked her head in.

I was listening to U2 through the earphones of my Sony Walkman. When I saw her at the door, I pulled off the headset.

"Have you seen Jesse?" she asked.

I shook my head, holding my breath. The door closed, and I shut off the player. I heard voices outside, my mother calling for Jesse. I could make out where Mom was by the sound of her shoes on the gravel. Eventually, she found my brother. He must have been playing near the barn.

"Jesse, you're all dirty," she said, her voice muted through the wall.

My brother protested in his tongue-tied manner. He did not reason with my mother but whined. This was his way.

"Come on. Pick up your play trucks. Come on," Mom said.

A few minutes later, she reentered the bedroom without knocking. I had yet to wash off the smell of tobacco or to swallow a jigger of mouthwash to cut the beer residue. I was lying on the bed, and when she sat next to me, she did what she always did—she placed the delicate palm of her hand on my forehead.

She pulled up.

"Danny!" she said, sniffing at the space between us. "You've been drinking."

"Not really."

She had a terrible look of disappointment.

"Don't lie to me."

"A beer. Not even that. Half a one."

Her hand was at her mouth, as if holding back tears. She wore a load of mascara and did not want it to run. In the years before she met Robin Stanley, my mother wore very little make-up. Maybe a little color to accent her blue eyes, or rouge on her high cheekbones. But from the day they got married, Robin Stanley insisted she wear foundation and powder, the works. He said, it made her look stylish, but in fact she was inexperienced at applying make-up, and she ended up looking like a Kabuki dancer.

"Why on earth would you do that? Where did you get it, Danny? You didn't steal it, did you? Oh my God."

"No, course not. Look," I said, sitting up. "I met a kid. Showed me this old train trestle, and we found a beer. Some bums must'a left it or somethin'. It's no big deal."

Again, I mimicked Hitch's way of talking. I don't know why exactly. Perhaps to assure my mother that I was fitting into my new surroundings.

"You know how I feel about that," she said.

"I know. Look, won't happen again, all right?"

Her hand gently touched my nose, and she became more concerned.

"Have you been in a fight?"

She stood up, was beside herself with worry.

Everything worried my mother. News reports of kidnappings, public television specials on infectious disease, rumors of war. Everything. Every article she read sent her into a tizzy. She worried about the ways the world could hurt, or heaven forbid, kill her boys. As such, she told us to beware of the danger outside the front door. The world was our enemy, and everything in it, as far as she was concerned. It conspired to either ruin our health or break a limb.

My mother was uncertain about most things in life, and at one time she was emotionally unstable, but of this I hold the deepest conviction—she loved her boys down to our marrow. We might disappoint, we might irritate, we might get in trouble on occasion, but nothing came between us or diminished her devotion. She loved us.

"Tell me you weren't in a fight," she said. "Not on your first day of school?"

I sighed. There was no sense in lying. She caught me with the goods. I had to fess up.

"It was nothing. Wasn't even a fight. More like a tussle."

She sat next to me on the bed and touched my face, tenderly examining for injuries. Her eyebrows narrowed as though this were a Greek tragedy or something, instead of just a schoolboy fight.

"Are you okay?"

"Yup. Got all my teeth." I smiled.

She shook her head. "I'm so worried about you, Danny. Look, I know this isn't fun right now, but it'll improve over time. You and Dr. Stanley, you hit it off okay, right?"

That our conversation had somehow segued to include my stepfather really irritated me. I hated hearing her say his name. But my mother's happiness meant the world to me, and so I lied by agreeing with her.

She smiled. And then a cloud fell across her face.

"It's just with Jesse," she said. "I don't know. Please, promise me you won't come home with beer on your breath. Ever again."

"Promise."

The lens of her eyes filled with tears that threatened to spill out.

"The smell of it. Brought back memories, Danny."

A single tear, like a precious gem, fell from her eyes and baptized my hand.

I reached out, and we hugged one another. Even to the undeveloped sensibilities of a fourteen-year-old boy, I could tell that she was troubled. It had less to do with my illegal activities on a train trestle than our situation at the Stanley farm.

"Please," she whispered. "Don't do that again. Promise me."

"Don't cry, Mom. It's gonna be okay."

She squeezed me as though she never wanted to let go.

Chapter 3

Over the weekend, after our first full week of school, I took Jesse wading in Deep Creek below the train trestle where Hitch McDonough and I had smoked.

On Saturday morning, after I helped Jesse to get dressed, I stowed a bottle of water, apple juice packets, and two peanut butter sandwiches in my book bag. In the kitchen I announced, "We're going wading below Alder Bridge." Eve and my stepfather said that I had to get Virgil Stanley's permission, should any chores be left untended. We had been assigned duties—something Robin Stanley said would teach us about the responsibly of living on a farm—but they were nothing more than make-work jobs. Stacking firewood. Sweeping the walkway. Picking weeds and watering the vegetable garden. It was not work a genuine farmer would engage in, as far as I knew, just something Robin Stanley could lord over us.

We had a stretch of warm weather for the week. The patchwork lawn bordering the doublewide trailer was brown from a dry summer, and two of Virgil Stanley's plum saplings needed watering every day, lest they die. On Saturday, the air was smoky from fires in the Cascades, and the east wind rose in coarse gusts in the morning, bringing higher temperatures from the basin east of the mountains. Virgil Stanley worried about wildfire as he watered his saplings. "We're in for it," he declared.

As we waited for the old man's approval to go, Jesse whined about wanting to run off, but I held firm his hand and kept him alongside me.

"Just where'n blazes you an' that kid think you going?" Virgil Stanley asked.

"Waiting!" Jesse shouted. "Gone waiting!"

"He means wading. Down the creek," I said.

When he removed his FFA cap, sunlight struck Virgil Stanley's eyes as though they were shards of black obsidian. Rank disapproval deepened the lines in his forehead. It was his way of saying I was completely ignorant of worldly matters, things that mattered. Running off to play in a creek didn't match up to his principles of what needed getting done.

"Something wrong?" I said.

"You just gonna waste the day?"

Jesse enthusiastically pulled at my hand. Sweat loosened my grip, and he broke free and ran wildly in circles around Virgil Stanley's plum saplings until I caught and wrestled him to the ground.

"Calm down, Jesse. Take a breath. It's okay."

Virgil Stanley drew back and set his jaw with scorn, passing judgment on my brother and on me.

I stood Jesse up to brush the powdery dust from his pants and T-shirt, and the old man turned away. I could tell, he wished that his son had married a childless woman who wouldn't bring a retarded boy and disobedient teenager into his home.

"Chores done?"

I said, "Yes," but it was a lie.

Rather than excuse us or wish us well, he directed the hose water to the drip line around the base of the sapling. The gesture said it was all well and good for do-nothings the likes of us to go off and waddle in a creek while he had work to do. As Jesse and I made our way down the gravel driveway to the county road, I glanced back. The old man was watching us, but quickly looked away. I had caught him at something. I had caught him in an idle moment of longing after youthful liberty.

"Know what, Jesse?" I said in a soft voice. "Virgil Stanley's a phony, just like his son."

"Virgal Sammy's a phony," Jesse repeated.

"No, no, Jesse. Don't say that."

Jesse sang *Virgal Sammy's a phony* long after we left the county blacktop on a cut along the hillside trail that took us to the creek beneath Alder Bridge. He often repeated phrases that either Mom or I spoke without thinking. The worst, of course, was my cursing, which Jesse learned to parrot. Thankfully, he lost interest in the repetition about Virgil Stanley. I hoped he wouldn't say it again at a badly timed moment, at the dinner table or while we sat watching evening television programs with our new grandparents snoozing in their recliners.

Our pediatrician in California had diagnosed the severity of my brother's retardation and had labeled it moderate to severe. My brother was often sick as a baby, and Mom worried incessantly about his health. A runny nose could mean nothing but galloping pneumonia. A moan about a headache was surely the sign of a tumor taking root in his brain. He survived the usual childhood bumps and scrapes, but I suppose my mother's over-protection came from a sense of guilt for having caused his infirmity in the first place.

Jesse was pudgy and short for his age, and pigeon-toed. On this day, he wore his favorite T-shirt—a picture of Disney's Winnie The Pooh—and he had on a new pair of Nike running shoes. On the previous day when we went shopping as a "family," Robin Stanley insisted that Jesse wear a size larger than the shoe salesman had recommended. "Don't worry," Robin Stanley told my mother, smirking at my brother's infirmity. "He'll grow into them. Besides, he won't wear them out. He can hardly walk let alone *run*." Jesse was unused to the Nike's, and on our hike down the embankment to Deep Creek, the shoes tripped him up more than once. He never did grow into them.

My little brother liked to wear a Giants baseball cap backwards, the way I wore mine, but it made him look even more dim-witted than he was. Mom was forever turning Jesse's cap forward. The cap made his ears stick out all the more, and I don't blame my mother for wanting to switch it around. Jesse had small eyes and epicanthic folds, physical defects characteristic of Fetal Alcohol Syndrome. In California, one Saturday after baseball practice, a teammate of mine pointed at my brother and said, "What's up with that kid? He looks like a Chinaman or something?" It was not the first time that I got in a fistfight to defend my kid brother.

Near the train trestle, we started down the embankment toward the creek with Jesse behind and me leading the way. After a few steps, he tripped and fell. We slid down the carpeting of damp leaves before I caught an exposed root and saved us. After that, we made our way more carefully with Jesse in front and me behind, gripping the fabric of his Winnie The Pooh shirt.

Deep Creek ran briskly, despite the drought, and the rush of water and crash of the falls gradually dominated all sound the deeper we went. As we cleared a stand of Doug fir, the trestle came into view above us like a leviathan of timber and rusted ironwork. We stopped in the clearing, and when I pointed out the trestle, Jesse clutched at my leg. "It's okay," I assured him. "Just an old thing." The roar of the whitewater drowned his reply.

The trestle vaulted above us in a crazy perspective of cantilevers, support posts, iron cabling. A perfect blue sky shone behind. Vetch and blackberry vines had consumed the lower footings along the bank, and over time they had inched their way across the span, cascading in great falls of greenery and twisted tendrils, dangling like snakes. We stood in the shadow of the trestle until Jesse whined about the cold and his fear, and we continued our descent into sunlight.

The steep angle of the hill flattened out near the bottom where seasonal flooding littered the ground with stones the size of bread loaves. We came out of the woods and into a patch of sunshine, and Jesse raised his arms in a broad smile. We whooped and hollered.

Raptors in the treetops took the air and cried out, which made Jesse whoop all the more in hopes of spooking the bunch.

"Do you like this?" I shouted.

"Dammy...yeah."

He was the happiest I had seen him since our arrival in Oregon.

Molecules of mist floated through the air from a bend of rapids above us. The mist dampened his face, and his cheeks glistened. He wiped away the water with both of his hands, giggling the whole time.

We sat on a boulder that sloped gently into a quiet crescent pool away from the rapids, and there we removed our shoes. I showed Jesse how to untie his Nike's and then how to roll his socks into a ball and stuff them inside the shoes. When we were done, I arranged our two pair of shoes out of harm's way, and then I rolled up the cuffs of his pants. I took his hand, and we approached the pool.

When our toes touched the water, Jesse squealed for how cold it was. Here the creek over time had gouged out a smooth bowl in the rock where fish hid in the shadows and where people came to bathe. The water was deep and the current strong enough to tug at our calves. I kept a tight grip on Jesse's hand. Rotting vegetation made the rocks slippery. He lost his footing and fell forward and splashed us both with creek water. I cheered him on by mistake, and he took it for a game and began to hurl himself down into the pool. I scowled and raised my voice that it wasn't funny, that the water was dangerous. Running creeks were not to be trifled with.

We ate our lunch on a boulder in the sun. Around us came the chattering and twitters of small yellow birds, American goldfinches, in the branches, at ease with our presence. Jesse shivered from the cold, and I wrapped my jacket over his shoulders and replaced his socks and shoes. He ate his sandwich and choked only once, gulping too quickly for all the excitement of our adventure.

I checked the time and rummaged the pocket of my book bag. In it I had carried Jesse's seizure medicine. He had to take small doses of Dilantin three times a day to keep from having epileptic fits, convulsions as they're called. My mother had issued an unnecessary reprimand. "You be sure to give him his pill at the allotted time," she said, but I knew more about my brother's medications than she did. I had taken on the responsibility from the beginning, and sometimes I had to remind her that it was time for Jesse to take his drugs.

I removed the childproof cap and shook out the small blue tablet. Jesse popped it into his mouth without objecting, as though it were sugar candy. Although I pulled another apple juice carton from the bag, he had already swallowed the pill. But he gladly took the juice anyway.

We loitered there beside Deep Creek for another half an hour. After I folded up the lunch bags and tossed our apple core far into the woods, I laid down on my back to gaze at the sky through the lattice of trees. Jesse did the same, and as we lay there, I could feel his body heat through my clothes, and I felt the even pulse of his breathing. It came in a rhythm like the beat of the river rapids.

I leaned back and daydreamed of building a hiding place, a fort in the woods. I saw myself notching poles cut from the surrounding trees and locating them evenly until I had constructed four walls, a sanctuary from Robin Stanley. I opened my eyes and saw the creek. The only sound in the world was its reckless run over the smooth rocks. What if the river flooded and swept me away from my hiding place? I doubted I could survive long, tumbling inside the thick gravity of black water, pulling me down as I paddled madly for the surface. I was imagining my funeral when I fell asleep after a while.

I awakened with a start when I could no longer feel Jesse beside me.

Sitting up, I saw my brother foundering in the wading pool, fighting to keep his head above water. He was drowning.

I bolted for him.

The more Jesse struggled against the weak current and flailed his arms to keep balance, the further away he slipped.

I ran into the creek at ankle depth and lost my footing on the slick surface of the submerged boulder. My legs went out from under me and sent me crashing sideways onto my hip.

Stunned, I scrambled on all fours toward Jesse just as his head went under.

I grabbed his wrists and pulled him to safety.

After carrying him up the boulder into the patch of sunlight, I set him down.

We shivered, our clothes heavy with creek water. Jesse was too bewildered to cry. He sat there holding his breath with his mouth open, his eyes fixed in a wild askance.

"It's okay, Jesse. Take a breath. Come on. Take a breath."

I was stripping off his T-shirt when he stiffened and his eyes showed only white.

"Don't do this, Jesse. Don't have a fit, okay? Come on. Relax, buddy."

At the age of two, Jesse had his first grand mal seizure. His pediatrician called it a tonic-clonic seizure, and it scared the living daylights out of my mother. She said Jesse could have died. Over the years of our caring for him, I became familiar with the warning signs and what to do when the Beast, as we called it, presented itself. Jesse would begin by opening his eyes and mouth, and then stiffen his arms and legs in a rigid fall to the ground. The most dangerous phase of the seizure was an involuntary constriction of the chest. And there was always concern that Jesse's tongue would obstruct his breathing. This phase usually lasted half a minute and launched the second phase, a violent rhythmic convulsion of the body.

Beside Deep Creek, Jesse and I fought the Beast for what seemed like fifteen minutes but in reality could not have been longer than a minute or two. In the end, when his breathing normalized and the convulsion subsided, my brother shut his eyes and fell asleep briefly in my arms. Within a few minutes, he was awake.

"Feelin' better, partner?" I said.

Jesse shook his head. "Dammy, I don't feel good."

I had been witness to more awful episodes than this relatively minor seizure at Deep Creek, and I was grateful it hadn't been worse. I felt responsible. All it would have taken to end my brother's life was for me to have slept undisturbed on the boulder, in the warm sun, for a minute longer. Had I not sat up when I did, Jesse would have drowned.

When we returned to the Stanley farm, my mother was the first to see our bedraggled wet bodies. Her scream brought Virgil Stanley out of the barn and Eve out of the trailer. They converged on us along the gravel driveway.

"What in blazes name...?" Virgil Stanley said.

Mom lifted Jesse into her arms, and she, with Eve clucking alongside her, carried him into the doublewide. The screen door slammed shut behind them with a rifle shot.

Virgil Stanley walked away, shaking his head, muttering, "You boys got no sense. None at all."

Robin Stanley walked up to me, huffing and shaking head as though this were the first time in recorded history that any boy anywhere had managed to do something stupid.

I stood there, shivering in the lengthening shadows, buffeted by the east wind, determined not to let my stepfather get the upper hand. Jesse's health was something he knew nothing about. He had never shown the least interest in my brother's medical condition or treatment. Who in hell was he to tell me what to do, to point out my failures?

"I can't tell you how disappointed I am," Robin Stanley said.

"It was an accident."

"There is no such thing as an *accident*."

Robin Stanley had reddish hair speckled gray from his childhood brush with electrocution. His barber in Strand kept it reasonably short except in front where a long wave was combed back to the side, parted on the right, and set with gel. The wind had tousled the lock of hair, and it curled across his forehead like rat's tail.

"You're grounded," he said.

I almost laughed. Here was this miserable excuse for a man, someone I had no respect for, disciplining me. He had no power over me. We were nearly the same height, and I had far more meat on my bones than he. Because of his slight build, I could best Robin Stanley on my worst day. If it came down to it, I could have flattened him. Busted his nose or blackened an eye. Who was he to tell me I was grounded?

"Wipe that smile off your face."

Robin Stanley shook with anger. It coursed through him like a jolt of hatred.

I despised him, and he knew it. He knew that I didn't care for him or his family farm.

He gripped my shoulder and tried to shake me, but I yanked free and took a step back, my fists clenched. Derision worked up a froth between us, until my emotions betrayed me, and a lump mounted in my throat.

The confrontation turned to his advantage, and he stepped away and put his hands on his hips. He clicked his tongue against the roof of his mouth.

"You are a very troubled young man. Just a big baby." He shook his head. "You can bluster like a rooster for all the good it'll do. But I'll have a talk with your mother...and then we shall see, won't we, see what we shall do with you."

He returned to the trailer, and I followed a minute later, silently cursing my faint courage.

There was no privacy in the doublewide, and so I retreated to my bedroom. There, Mom and Eve Stanley helped Jesse into flannel pajamas, threading arms as limp as boiled spaghetti-noodles. After a grand mal seizure, after a visit from the Beast, my kid brother was fatigued, and he usually slept for ten to twelve hours straight. When my mother saw me in the doorway, the animosity in her eyes brought me up short. Jesse's well-being was her crusade, and she took my simple negligence as a personal affront. Eve Stanley, on the other hand, merely attended the boy as though he were no more or less important than scouring the kitchen sink.

Robin Stanley entered the bedroom behind me and said, "Karin, may I speak with you in private, please."

"Yes, Robin."

Eve Stanley left the room quickly, but my mother paused with her hand on the doorknob and looked back at me.

"You did this," she said. "You did this on purpose. To hurt me. To get back for bringing you here. That's what this is all about, isn't it?"

I was about to say that the accident with Jesse had nothing to do with anything. It was just a mistake, something that had happened, but she shut me off by raising her hand. She took a quick breath and sighed. She was about to say something but words failed her, and she shook her head and left the bedroom. I sat on Jesse's bed and gently pressed my hand on his cheek, checking his temperature, and I leaned down to kiss him. He had a post-epileptic scent I was familiar with, a sour milk odor that coated his skin. "Sorry, buddy," I whispered. "You sleep well."

I was offered no dinner that night, something of a punishment of Robin Stanley's design. I lay on my bed in the glomming light and listened to Jesse breathe. His breathing came in the soft, pliant rhythms of a normal boy, and I was grateful for it. Beyond the walls, I heard adult voices. I distinguished each among the participants as they argued over what should be done with me. Eventually, after the dishes were washed, dried and put away, the television came on with a laugh track from a situation comedy. I could hear Robin Stanley's hateful laughter above the sound of the television.

In the dark, I got off the bed and went to the window. A full moon was setting behind a line of trees at the back of a neighbor's pasture. The rows of Virgil Stanley's raspberry canes marched toward the moon, in diminishing perspective, strangled by blackberry vines. The vines were coiled into something like razor wire that put the field off limits to any meaningful use. This was how it felt being imprisoned in Strand, in that doublewide trailer, cut off from my former life, my father, and California, surrounded by obstacles to freedom. There were few stars that came on at twilight, one or two,

Ceres the Dog Star and Mizar of the Big Dipper, barely visible in the dazzling wash of moonlight.

I lay back on the bed, despondent and angry, and as I shut my eyes, I tried to shut out the world. I fell asleep.

By midnight, hunger awakened me. All was quiet save for crickets singing to the peaceful laziness. The moon had set. I sat up and looked through the window. The sky was ablaze in starlight, more stars than I had ever seen before. From my bedroom window in San Francisco, when fog did not veil the night sky, there were few stars. But here, in Strand, I had some difficulty separating one from the other. The stars were like inexhaustible sparks fixed against the black perspective of night.

Through the dark house I made my way to the kitchen, taking each step cautiously so as not to creak the floorboards. I ate a chicken leg in the light of the opened refrigerator and drank a glass of orange juice, ever vigilant should Robin Stanley waken to confront me. Then, on my return to the bedroom, I paused by Robin Stanley's desk. It was a solid piece of oak furniture along the wall near the only bookshelf in the place, something I had not paid any attention until that moment. A curiosity amused me. I was curious about what the desk contained, should it be valuable to my stepfather. In revenge, I thought about either stealing or destroying something that he owned.

The biggest object on top of the desk was his personal Bible. A leather-bound book, it was thick as a cinder block and taped with colorful tabs marking favorite passages. I picked it up, and the book opened effortlessly to the approximate middle of the Old Testament, at a place where a small bronze key was hidden between the pages.

I held the key and pondered its significance. Sitting in the chair, and using my free right hand to substitute for sight, I touched the hole of a lock in a side drawer. There I fit the key and turned it soundlessly. The drawer opened.

At that hour, the starlight fell through the kitchen window with enough lasting glow to expose the contents—pornographic material, pictures of naked women clipped from dirty magazines. I leafed through these, elevating one or two of interest into the light. Here was a photograph of two women having sex, another taken from a newspaper advertisement for women's undergarments. A woman urinating, another exposed in an unnatural position.

"Robin's a porn freak."

A rush of self-righteousness suddenly puffed me up.

It was within my power to expose Robin Stanley by dumping the drawer for all to see, but I decided on a more subtle approach. After locking the desk as I had found it, I placed the picture of the two women having sex between pages of the Bible along with the key to the drawer. I replaced the book where I'd found it and left the room.

Back in bed, I took over an hour to fall back to sleep for the excitement of knowing that a time bomb ticked in the living room. My mind turned over the likely things Robin Stanley might say to my mother. The discovery would paralyze him. But what could he do? Nothing. He couldn't face up to me, not in front of his new bride. He might mumble something in private or threaten more chores to keep me in line. He might make my life more difficult, he might pour on more restrictions, but he would never confront me publicly over the matter. He would know that I knew his dirty little secret. That's all wanted. I had him dead to rights.

Chapter 4

After my mother filed for divorce in California, my father told me most lives were disorderly and that mine was no different. "This won't be the last mess you face in life," he said. The way he said it made me feel ashamed somehow, as though the divorce was my fault. Against his wishes, my mother took us out of state, and despite his political connections and skill as a lawyer, my father did nothing to stop her. I couldn't help but wonder why not.

I have no doubt that my father regretted the divorce, but I also knew him as a practical man who accepted loss and learned to move on with his life. As an attorney-at-law in the City of San Francisco, my dad was a corporate in-house counsel, a realist who defended accounting fraud and breach of contract. Some of his greatest victories were over the protection of intellectual property rights, and his corporate clients paid him handsomely, but the practice of law made a bitter man out of my father. "Always expect the worst in people," he told me. "Then, should they surprise you with integrity…well, nothing lost, nothing gained, you know?"

When Mom, Jesse and I were living in an apartment in Medford, before Robin Stanley crawled into our lives, I did not see my father for more than three months. He and I had little telephone contact during that time. Mom couldn't afford a cell phone. What little income she earned on a substitute-teaching wage was eaten up by rent and food. Throughout those early days, we received one letter from Dad. The fact of the matter is, the letter was not from him but from my dad's divorce lawyer. He refused to pay child support unless we relocated to San Francisco. In reply, I wrote a five-page letter, more or less begging him to reconcile with Mom. After we moved to Strand, Robin Stanley forbade me to call my father except once a month.

On a Sunday morning, one week after Jesse fell into Deep Creek, I stood in the kitchen to make a call using the Stanley's only telephone, a Harvest Gold wall model from the 1970s.

"Tell the operator to reverse charges," Robin Stanley said. "Costs too much."

"I can't reverse the charges." I gestured with the handset. "Operator won't let me."

"Then don't make the call."

My stepfather left the kitchen for the yard, letting the screen door punch loudly on its spring, and I dialed my father's number, a direct call. I figured, by the time the Stanley's got their telephone bill, I would be either long gone or living with my dad, beyond the reach of my stepfather's arbitrary discipline.

The phone rang in the house where we used to live, and I imagined the white phone on the walnut table near the staircase that led to my bedroom. In my mind I saw the phone in my parent's bedroom and the phone in the family room, the other one in the kitchen. I counted their number. Was it five or six? I remembered how good it felt to live in such a beautiful home among expensive furnishings and fine art paintings, and a profound sense of loss began to gnaw at me. Whatever hope I had of speaking to my father was gone by the third ring. The answering machine picked up.

"Hey. This is Ponce...leave a message. I'll get back to you. Ciao."

He sounded so happy.

Ponce had been my father's nickname since childhood, a name my grandmother had given him. My father's full name is Daniel Farrington Aiken, Sr., a name we share. We also share an Irish ancestry, his grandmother having left County Fermanagh for Scotland. Later, she immigrated through Ellis Island to South Carolina, of all places. When I think of the Old South, I cannot imagine it overrun by Irish Protestants, but nonetheless that was where my great grandmother came to live. She married a man named Augustus Scharphorn of Savannah. They had nine children—four of which died—and they moved the family to Chicago when the textile economy went sour after widespread banking failures. Back then, there were jobs to be had in the Illinois meatpacking industry. The Scharphorn's youngest child, Lenora, married my grandfather, Arch Daniel Aiken of the Waukegan Aikens, and gave birth to my father. After he grew up and attended Boalt Law School at the University of

California at Berkeley, my father never returned to live in Chicago or Waukegan, Illinois.

My dad was a man's man. He loved top-shelf liquor and top-shelf women, and not necessarily in that order. On my fourteenth birthday, soon after my parents had separated, Dad told me that most cultures around the world would have considered me an adult. To launch me properly on the road to manhood, he took me around to his San Francisco haunts. We visited a client of his in the Tenderloin who had rebuilt a pipe organ on the second floor of an old church. I don't remember the man's name, but he played a Bach fugue. The bass notes rattled my teeth. Next, Dad took me out to lunch at The Tadich Grill on California Street. The male waiters acted surly to the few women seated in the restaurant.

"All part of the floor show," Dad said in a whisper, leaning across our small table.

"Why're they so nasty to 'em?" I asked.

"Years ago, Tadich's was an all-male club. Lunch counter, sure, but people called it a club. Only men ate here. The waiters back then, they're long gone, but these new guys, I don't know, they sort of adopted the tradition, know what I mean?" He winked. "They treat women that way because, well, it's a tradition."

I nodded my head, although none of his Byzantine world made any sense.

We ended the day with a slow drive down Kennedy through Golden Gate Park, and later we watched the sunset framed in the picture windows at the Cliff House. He ordered a vodka martini, and I had a Virgin Mary with a stalk of celery in a skinny glass. Our waitress was a stunning blond in a tight miniskirt, and my dad couldn't keep his eyes off her. It shocked me that my father was attracted to other women. Over drinks he told me about his legal caseload, and he gave me some advice. "Danny," he said, "the spoils of this world are divided between winners and losers. You've heard the old saying—to the winners go the spoils?"

"Yes, sir."

"Good. Then I want you to do what I do."

I gave it a second before I responded. "You mean, become a lawyer?"

He shook his head and corrected me. "It's *attorney*, son. Lawyers do taxes. I'm a court attorney. There's a difference." He took a sip of his martini. "Yeah, sure, you want to go into law, great, but that's not what I'm talking about. Just make certain, when you're up against it, the other guy loses. You understand me? Always, *always* look out for Numero Uno." Then he called over the waitress, handed her a big tip and ordered another round.

All in all, it was an okay birthday, spending it with my father.

Less than nine months later, my mother married Robin Stanley, and I would celebrate my fifteenth birthday in Oregon. My birthday fell close to Christmas, which by default reduced the number of presents I could expect to receive. Jesse, whose birthday came in the spring, was always buried beneath piles of gaily-wrapped gifts. I was not above comparing the number on Christmas morning when my presents oftentimes were combined.

But my previous life in California—birthday presents and lunches at Tadich's Bar and Grill, living at our house in Pacific Heights, hanging out with my friends—was over. Living with a self-righteous stepfather on a farm overrun by weeds, I expected my new life in Strand to be deficient, depressing and lonely.

*   *   *

In early October, we attended a Sunday church picnic. The weather had turned foul during the previous week and made outdoor activities unpleasant and wet. Rather than dress for the picnic in traditional shorts and short-sleeved shirts, Robin Stanley told us to wear raingear and parkas. We looked like Eskimos. It was the first time I heard the term "raingear," but the longer I lived in Oregon, the more I understood the necessity for waterproof clothing.

Before we left the house for the picnic grounds, I asked Virgil Stanley to take a message should my father return my telephone call. The old man made no commitment either way. Eve patted me on the wrist and said, "Don't worry, dear. We'll take care of it."

Due to the incident at Deep Creek, Robin Stanley and my mother treated me as though I had shot the neighbor's dog or blasphemed the Baby Jesus. Day after day, they spoke in the command form of the English language by telling me what to do and when I was expected home. My punishment did not fit the crime. Jesse had not come down with so much as a head cold, and he had long since recovered from the grand mal. I expected their indifference toward me to soften, if not Robin Stanley's, then at least my mother's. But whenever her overriding will appeared to soften towards me, Robin Stanley gave a sidelong glance that sustained her resolve, and my punishment continued.

On our way to the picnic, the congregation gathered in the parking lot of Valley Shepherd Community Church before traveling by bus to Wildwood Park on the mountain. On the bus, Jesse sat next to me and played with a windup toy airplane that Robin Stanley had given him. It was a contemptible form of bribery, in my opinion. Our stepfather did not give me anything that day. He and my mother sat behind us, and I half-listened to his chitchat about the optometry practice. The grand opening had taken place that week, and he boasted about the numbers of patients he expected to see in his new office.

"Advertising in the paper was a stroke of genius," he said. "We can't go wrong. It cost a lot, I know, Karin, but look, even with the coupon discount, all those people needing frames and eye exams, we'll do just fine."

"If you say so, honey."

Honey? She used to call my dad that.

My stepfather said, "Two folks at church came up to me in the parking lot. Said they were going to drop by. Sometime this week. Isn't that great?" He acted like a child with a new toy.

"Dr. Robin Stanley, Optometrist" had opened in Strand to very few customers. At least, this had been my impression as I rode past it each day on the school bus. His office was on McGrath Avenue, the main street in Strand. In the past week, I saw my stepfather through the front window, passing the time of day alone, dressed in a white tunic and reading a *People* magazine. His grand opening was not grand by any stretch of the imagination. In point of fact, it had been pathetic and discouraging.

On the yellow church bus, my brother wore the only pair of Dr. Stanley's Special Frames sold that week. Jesse did not need glasses.

His eyes were fine, but Robin Stanley had insisted that "spectacles" would make him look smarter. "Think about it, darling," he told my mother. "Maybe it's all he needs, something to improve his esteem." My stepfather fitted Jesse with a sturdy pair of horned rims, a style I remembered seeing in pictures of the tragically dead rock star, Buddy Holly. They were entirely unsuitable to a five-year-old. He broke them within an hour, but rather than replace the pair, Robin Stanley wrapped masking tape through the nose bridge. "For the love of God, Karin, can't you watch that boy? Frames don't come cheap."

I could not help but wonder, after I had uncovered the porno in his desk drawer, was my stepfather feeling anxious; was he waiting for the next shoe to drop? Over the course of the week, he must have realized that his privacy had been violated. Surely he realized, it was I who had exposed his secret life. Who else could have rifled through his desk and slipped those ugly pictures into his Bible? But he made no accusation. Nothing in his behavior appeared out of the ordinary. Was he biding his time, waiting to confront me at the dinner table, name my *malfeasance* and *malicious intent* (words that my real dad would have used) and lay out the facts of the matter? Of course not. Admitting that he owned the pictures would have damned him. Still, it irritated my sense of fair play that he continued on as though nothing had happened, as though he held the keys to absolute moral authority. *Everything* had happened. *Everything* had changed. Like a fool, I had expected his world to collapse. I wanted to see his dishonesty laid bare in my mother's eyes. But nothing of the kind happened.

It disappointed me terribly.

Earlier that week, after brushing my teeth and making for the bedroom, I walked past his desk and noticed a glimmer of shame in his eye. He was reading from the Bible as he did every night, after my mother had gone to bed. He glanced up, and I could tell, doubt seized him as he contemplated the nature of sin. I knew that he knew that I knew about his stack of porno. I knew that he knew I'd been the one who violated the desk drawer, but I also knew the matter would remain unaddressed. No admission or confession would ever pass his lips.

Behind Robin Stanley's potential disgrace stood a threat. Should I make a mistake, should I lose in this struggle between us, he would remove me from my mother's sight. Already, brochures from an evangelical military academy had shown up, scattered like idle threats across the kitchen table, left there for me to *discover* on my own. After the accident at Deep Creek, my mother and he had many conversations about my future, and none of them were meant to insure my prosperity but rather to convert me to their brand of religion, something I resisted. But on that evening, as I walked past my stepfather, his eyes had the look of a cornered predator. I sensed his desperation, that ours would be a battle for survival. I was determined on the advice of my father to make sure he lost. And yet, whether he or I were victorious, both of us would lose in the end. I knew this to be the nature of the world.

*   *   *

They held the church picnic at Wildwood Park, in the barbecue shelters out of the rain. Pastor Sonny Vickers directed us in worship, singing praise songs and praying for the salvation of our community and for our embattled country. The pastor got agreement from almost everybody that we lived in a sinful nation, in a secular culture. He asked us to pray for the "holocaust of millions of dead babies," a horror that had resulted from the "abomination of abortion." We prayed for a man who was on trial for allegedly shooting a physician at an abortion clinic in South Carolina. We prayed that an evangelical believer would be elected President of the United States so that our country would be "born again and saved before the Rapture."

After limited exposure to it, by then I had had my fill of evangelism.

Robin Stanley was a deacon at the Valley Shepherd Community Church, a bragging point he mentioned at grace every night before supper. He prayed in hopes his good deeds were written down in the Lord's accounting book. We prayed for this or that person who had fallen sick or lost their job, never a stranger but always an influential member of the church. Yet, for all our supplication, nothing happened. People still died or went on unemployment insurance, and despite his ulterior motive to add customers from among the faithful, his optical store remained empty.

After prayers, Mom stood loyally at her husband's side as he introduced her around to a few of the church ladies. My mother was the prettiest woman there, in the same Laura Ashley dress she'd worn at her wedding.

"You must be a very proud mom," an overweight lady told her. "Your boys are so well groomed. You *will* be having more, you and Dr. Stanley, I mean?"

"And be a stay-at-home mom. Our bodies are a living sacrifice," another piped in.

"Well, actually, no," my mother said, answering both questions. "I'm a substitute teacher with the Union School District. We can't afford babies right now."

"Oh, so you'll be working *outside* the home?"

"The boys aren't in home school?"

My mother smiled her most benign smile, desperately trying to please everyone. By the time she mustered the nerve to explain to those small-minded women—"Substitute teaching does not interfere with my duties as a wife"—they turned away to speak to someone else and shunned my mother. I could tell, the encounter left her feeling hollow and degraded, but as she looked to me for support, I also turned away. I regret doing that, but how was I to behave toward this woman who was acting more like Robin Stanley's bride than my mother?

None of the men, it seemed to me, wanted anything to do with Robin Stanley. He did not fish, hunt, or own a four-wheel drive with a gun rack. These were keen points of manhood that separated him from their culture. Conversations between the men and him ended abruptly or were never begun. They were outdoorsmen and veterans of foreign wars. They celebrated Veteran's Day with vigor and they showed the colors on the Fourth of July. They had USA flag decals on the rear windows of their trucks that read, "These colors don't run." Robin Stanley did not fit the round hole of their square world. He was an odd fellow, an abnormally shaped man with white hands and narrow shoulders and absurdly reddish hair, someone marginalized and ill at ease. He was unacceptable in their society.

Robin Stanley was not alone in feeling out of his element. I, too, was friendless, but that afternoon gave me a chance to observe the testing of his moral fiber. The church leadership, all of them men—no women were allowed in positions of authority—gave my mother a hug upon introduction. Their affection sparked jealousy in Robin Stanley, but it had the opposite effect on her. She cooed in her Oklahoma drawl for all that masculine attention while fears of infidelity ate away at her husband's self-confidence. At the picnic he had expected a more reserved affair. He had prepared his wife for a coming out party, a second wedding reception from among church friends and fellow believers. But when nothing of the kind materialized, Robin Stanley shrank away to brood alone at an empty table while my mother engaged in lively conversation with her new friends.

There was one man in the congregation who was not physically effusive to my mother—Ned Horvath, the Principal of Union High School. He saved Robin Stanley from insecurity but at my expense. After he and my stepfather spoke for a few minutes, Robin Stanley waved me over.

"This is my son," he said, a hand resting on my shoulder, all for show.

Principal Horvath shook his head. "Oh, Daniel and I know each other, Dr. Stanley. As you well know."

My stepfather was nonplused. He jabbered on about how he met my mother at a church function, pointing her out and describing their traditional wedding ceremony. "We've relocated here to bring the boys up right, although Daniel's not saved yet," he said. On and on he went, until eventually his mind like a blind squirrel stumbled across Principal Horvath's meaning. "What did you say?"

"Well, I mean, the letter," the principal replied.

Robin Stanley glanced at me. I was a portrait of stoicism.

"I know nothing about a letter," he told Principal Horvath.

"Oh? Then we have a problem, don't we?"

Both adult men reminded me of a firing squad, their eyes getting a bead on the condemned. The execution was about to begin.

"Would you explain to me what's going on?" Robin Stanley said.

I confessed to the details of my crimes, the fight with Hitch McDonough and the forged signature. I owned up to signing the note (keeping Hitch out of it) on an abandoned railroad trestle. I left out details about smoking and drinking beer. Leave it to say, Robin Stanley shook the principal's hand, apologized on my behalf, and upheld a code of behavior suitable to a church picnic. He wore a mask of contrition. He expressed regret for my "sins" while I was stood up before Principal Horvath like a five-year-old. He began nervously to quote from scripture; great bilious reams of it, as though trying to restore his piety, but as soon as we were alone Robin Stanley let loose with a barrage of threats.

"For this," he said, "you will pay dearly. Getting into a fight on your first day. Falsifying my signature. This will *not* stand, I can tell you that."

He shook from anger and fought to regain control over his emotions. I am convinced an evil person lived inside my stepfather, just below the surface. On more than one occasion, he revealed a symbiotic evil twin, but at the picnic there was a kind of giddy exhaustion in his anger. I think he realized that he had enough evidence now to persecute me for the crime of sticking pornography in his Bible. His sudden good fortune at my expense was almost more than he could bear.

I was humiliated when he pulled me through the picnicking throng of churchgoers in a flight to locate my mother. We found her in the company of Pastor Sonny Vickers, delighting him with her Southern charm. Robin Stanley was more than happy to put an end to that. He argued with my mother while I stood a little ways off, outside the shelter, while they considered the moral depravity of my character. In the beginning, Mom put up a good defense in my honor until she connected the dots. Hadn't I come home stinking of beer and cigarettes after my first day at the new school? When my demerits lined up in a kind of harmonic convergence, she joined Robin Stanley in reciting a list of my faults. After that, their only difference of opinion was how severely I should be punished.

The exact nature of my punishment was to be saved for our ride home, in the car.

They began to walk off together to rejoin the picnic, Robin Stanley taking up my mother's hand. They were allied against the prodigal son. My mother stopped and turned on me. Through a hint of Oklahoma belle, she said, "Let's try as best we can to enjoy ourselves for the rest of the afternoon, shall we?" Her eyes were full of disappointment.

There were other kids my age at the picnic, but they seemed brainwashed. They looked like the children of cultists who pasted on a smiley face. One of them repeated, "The Lord wants you to have a nice day" and "Let's witness together." They were overly polite; said *please, sir* and *thank you, ma'am*. They were of a fashion suitable to the previous decade with big hair and plaid pants. None of the girls showed skin or wore tight skirts with their midriff hanging out, and the guys looked like poster boys in a hick magazine. The friends I'd left behind in San Francisco were into girls and alternative music. They defied their parents' wishes as a matter of course. To the church kids in Strand, the outside world did not exist. They sang praise songs, and worst of all, they obeyed their parents. How should I be expected to get along with them?

Jesse, on the other hand, was getting along well enough, fitting in with the younger kids. I ended up sitting by myself to eat a spare picnic lunch, wishing lightning would strike Robin Stanley dead.

My saving grace was Hitch McDonough.

Across the way, beneath the canopy of a cedar grove, the silhouettes of three boys gathered around a barbecue pit, smoking cigarettes. Even from a distance, as they stood in tree shadow, I could tell they were drinking beer from cans, probably illegally. When I recognized Hitch McDonough among them, the dull day seemed to brighten.

I tossed the remains of a rubbery hotdog into the trash and went briskly across the lawn in the rain. When I was halfway to the cedar grove, Hitch McDonough looked up.

"That you, Danny Boy?" he called out.

I entered the grove, grateful to be out of the drizzle and hidden in the shadows below the trees. "Hey. What's up?"

"More'n you got."

Even in the poor light, I could see marks on Hitch's face. He had a cut below one eye and a bruise on his chin. Hitch turned to his friends and said, "Dan Aiken, Troy and Larry."

I recognized Troy from school. He stood out, was a lanky kid with bad acne and spiked hair the color of pumpkin. Without removing the cigarette between his teeth, he grimaced and nodded coolly at me.

I knew Larry from his reputation. He was defensive tackle on the senior varsity football squad, made All Conference in his junior year, about as tough a son of a bitch as you could find. He weighed half again what I weighed in my wet clothes and stood a good two inches over me.

"Smoke?" Larry said.

"Thanks."

I took the Marlboro, and Hitch McDonough flipped open his Zippo and put flame to it.

Quietly, I said, "What happened to you?"

"Me'n my old man got into it, is all," Hitch said.

I glanced toward the shelter, trying to look cool and apathetic. To my chagrin, both Robin Stanley and my mother were intently searching for me, hands cupped over their brows as if to shade out a nonexistent sun.

"Shit," I said, palming the cigarette.

Hitch lifted a Budweiser and took a sip. "Your stepdad's here, huh? What, you go to church now?"

"I hate the fucking church."

"What's it like?" Larry asked.

"Like the kids've been lobotomized," I said.

Troy squinted at Hitch. "What the fuck's that?"

Hitch playfully slapped him on the back of the head, hard enough to make his point. "Dumb fuck."

Over my shoulder I glanced toward the church picnic. My mother stood outside the shelter, hands on her hips. She'd seen me. I could see the defeated slope to her shoulders, the downward cast of her face for the loss of her reckless son. Robin Stanley had long since given up on me. He moped near the outdoor sinks, shaking his head and pressing the tension from his eyes between an index finger and thumb.

I crushed the Marlboro on the stone barbecue pit and tossed it among the flames.

"Gotta go," I told Hitch.

"Right."

I heard empathy in his voice as if to say he knew what I was going through, that we each had our cross to bear where our parents were concerned.

I jogged unenthusiastically toward the picnic shelter.

As I was about to walk past, my mother caught my arm and said, "Who is that boy?"

"Nobody."

On the church bus, neither Mom nor Robin Stanley spoke to me. They sat like Easter Island statues, mute and stone cold. But in the Buick on the drive home, Robin Stanley recited the litany of penalties I would pay. He was not so much grounding as he was imprisoning me in the doublewide trailer. I was expected to be home no later than thirty minutes after the last school bell. No sports, no after-school activities, nothing. And under no circumstances was I ever to "congregate with that awful McDonough boy." I was told he was nothing but trouble, which I knew. It was my reason for hanging around him.

"If you violate this, Daniel, if you break the rules," Robin Stanley said, "your punishment will only get worse. Do you understand?"

I said nothing.

"You unnerstan," Jesse shouted. "You unnerstan!"

"Jesse, sweetheart," Mom said, a gentle shake to her head. There was love in her eyes for her youngest, but not for me.

To my mother Robin Stanley said, "I think we need to seriously consider military school." And then to me he said, "I cannot understand how someone can get in so much trouble so quickly. This is a small town, Mister. You'd better think about your reputation. Are you listening to me?"

I said nothing. I was too angry to say anything to the unreasonable bastard.

C. Marcus Parr

Chapter 5

High school was a meat grinder where raw material went in and something like sausage came out. Hardly any of the students at the Onion took pleasure in it. Most saw the compulsion to attend class as either a waste of time or a bump in the road to adult freedom. Overcrowded classrooms, low pay, and little respect from the community burned out our teachers fairly quickly. Many had the thousand-yard stare of battle fatigue. You can't fault them when you consider, they had to teach kids like Hitch McDonough, kids who saw education as meaningless. For me, the experience would have ended badly as well had it not been for a teacher named Mr. Phelan.

I met him on a cold bright October day, before the opening bell. I had delayed going to Gym class for as long as possible, hanging around Hitch McDonough, Troy and Larry. The temperature dove into the thirties that day, and Larry and I were bundled in parkas. Hitch wore a red Filson. Troy wore a Miller Lite T-shirt, and said we were "pussies" for wearing jackets. We idled near a bench at the front of the administration building. A brass plaque dedicated the bench to two teen-aged girls who had died in an automobile accident a few years earlier, in the eighties.

"Hey," Larry said, poking Troy in the ribs. "Here he come."

Troy palmed the bill of his baseball cap and looked askance. "Who?"

"There, you idiot. Mr. Phelan."

As Mr. Phelan limped toward us, Larry crushed out a cigarette and leaned sideways to exhale the last of it. His gut bulged between his parka and pants. He did not take a high school career in football seriously. Size was his talent. A two hundred and thirty pound frame compensated for what he lacked in discipline.

Troy snickered and pointed out Mr. Phelan's limp.

Relying on a cane and dragging what looked like a tool chest on wheels, Mr. Phelan threaded his way through the parking lot. He stopped across from us on the sidewalk and waved his cane. I had no idea who he was.

"Good morning, Hitch," he called.

Hitch spoke to me in a low voice. "He's a cripple but cut him a break. He's a good guy."

Mr. Phelan was unlike the other teachers at the Onion. He was the youngest faculty member, had an earnest face and the slender body of a distance runner. The wind tousled his non-regulation ponytail. He wore jeans, a crisp white shirt and sports coat, no tie.

"How you doin', Mr. Phelan?" Hitch said brightly.

"You boys playing hooky today?"

Over the course of our friendship, I learned that during times of stress Mr. Phelan's stump would undergo a kind of spasm when his leg muscles revolted inside his prosthesis. On that morning, he maintained control and managed a cheerful shrug. He advanced painstakingly up the stairs toward us, testing the stability of the fake leg.

"This happens once in a while," he said as a kind of off-handed apology. He looked directly at me while brushing back his hair. "Morning."

Larry said, "How's tricks, Mr. Phelan?"

Overhead, a commercial airliner made its final approach, jet engines drowning out our voices. The Portland International Airport was thirty miles away, but Strand stood directly in the flight path of approaching aircraft. I looked up. The fuselage of an Alaska Airlines flight was close enough to read the logo. It descended behind the administration building.

Troy nodded at the sky and said, "DC Nine."

Larry shook his head. "Seven Twenty-Seven."

"Looks bigger, 'pacifically."

Larry mouthed the words *fuck you.*

Mr. Phelan shook his head. "If either of you spent half the time studying as you do arguing about airplanes, no telling where you'd end up."

He turned to me and offered his hand.

"Don't think we've been introduced. Audley Phelan."

I gladly shook his hand.

"It isn't spelled O-D-D-L-Y. But A-U-D and so on. My mother was a Brit, Father American. My brother's named Evelyn…"

Troy laughed.

"Which is not unusual in *Mother's country*." He said this with a faked English accent. Both Hitch and I smiled at Mr. Phelan. "What boy in his right mind would want to be saddled with a name like that?"

"Mr. Phelan's got a bum leg," Troy declared, as if I hadn't noticed.

The teacher widened his eyes, astonished but not surprised at Troy's thick-headedness.

"That's right. I lost it years ago to an International Harvester. It's a fitting name." He slapped the fittings where flesh joined plastic at the groin. "Happened in Iowa. Where I was born." Another jet made its approach, loud as a howitzer. We didn't speak again until it passed.

Finding my voice, I asked, "What's in the case?"

"A telescope. I promised my students a sky show. Fieldtrip for the astronomy club." As an afterthought, he addressed Troy. "Astronomy? You know, stargazers?"

Larry poked Troy in the ribs. He scowled but was uncertain if Mr. Phelan had put him down.

The first period bell rang.

"Well, you better get to class."

We lumbered up the steps and separated in the foyer. I looked back. Mr. Phelan was having some difficulty pushing the black case up the wheelchair access. I turned away and jogged down the steps to the gym.

As luck would have it, my second period English teacher, Mrs. Dick, was ill and the substitute failed to show after the bell sounded. Two kids said they saw the substitute teacher leave campus, weeping into a handkerchief. "First period killed her," they told me. Until one of the school counselors showed up to fill in, the class was thrown over to chaos. Everybody chatted. Two boys shared a cigarette, blowing smoke out an opened window at the back of the room. When I asked the girl seated next to me what she thought of Mr. Phelan, she became excited. "He's a genius! Everybody tries to get into his Physical Science class. He's fun. Takes kids on fieldtrips to the planetarium at Mt. Hood."

How, I asked, could I get into his class, and the girl shook her head as though I would be the last person ever to get into Mr. Phelan's class.

"Only smart kids get in," she said. "Gotta waiting list a mile long."

*   *   *

After school, while I waited at the top of the bleachers before the last bus, I watched a varsity football scrimmage. The offense played the defense, wearing identical uniforms. The only difference was, the defense wore white bibs over the royal blue Union High jerseys. Larry worked his position as defensive tackle against the varsity offensive line. On the first snap, he broke through the two men assigned to block him and knocked the quarterback to the ground. Coach Montgomery blew the whistle, and even from as far away as the bleachers, I heard cussing. Larry looked up laughing, and I returned a subtle wave of the hand. The coach clenched his fists and yelled at the defeated lineman. Spittle flew from his mouth, and he exhausted great billows of steamed breath.

"So," someone behind me said. "Why aren't you out there?"

It was Mr. Phelan leaning on his cane, his free hand tucked in the pocket of his sports coat. An east wind blew that day, and temperatures had dropped since morning. He wore an Irish tweed cap askew, *jauntily* as the English would say, and I noticed for the first time a pair of wire-rim eyeglasses.

"Hey, Mr. Phelan. Where's your telescope?"

He smiled and glanced up at the diamond bright sky. "No sense dragging it home. We have a fieldtrip tonight."

The football scrimmage continued with a second snap of the ball, and the two of us watched the action. Coach Montgomery had assigned three linemen to block the All-Conference defensive tackle. When the two lines smashed into one another, their grunting and howls echoed across the sports field. Three linemen managed to stop Larry's forward motion while a linebacker, seizing the opportunity, rushed the quarterback and flattened him. Once again, Coach

Montgomery tooted his whistle. "Dammit boys," he yelled. Larry and the linebacker slapped high-fives.

"Do you play?"

I nodded.

"What position?"

"Wide receiver," I said. "Mainly Pop Warner in California, for two years. I was first string though." I wanted to brag about my trophies and sports medals, but what value did they have collecting dust in our old house in California?

"So, I repeat," he said. "Why aren't you down there?"

I picked up my book bag. "It's a long story."

My answer was unsatisfactory, and Mr. Phelan's open expression closed like a vise. You could not lie to the man or even offer the hint of a lie. He had a straight-ahead style that said, *Hey, life's short. No time for bull.* I did not want him to think I was snubbing him, so I slung the book bag over my shoulder and made him my father confessor. "My stepfather won't let me go out for sports. I'm on probation." I shrugged as if to say it was my fault, trying to appear contrite or noble despite the resentment I had for Robin Stanley.

"That your bus?" he said.

The last school bus was pulling away at the turnout in front of the administration building.

I winced. "Dammit!" And then. "Sorry, Mr. Phelan."

"No need to apologize. I swear, too, when words fail me."

There would be hell to pay for getting home late. Virgil Stanley would pile on more chores, and his son would chalk up another reason to pack me off to a military academy. Over the past week, I had managed to keep a spotless record. I was rarely late, returning home directly from school in the short time allotted. Life for me had become something lived within windows of time, taking advantage when opportunity arose. My stepfather's rules were constrictive, but I had eked out a marginal social life with Hitch, Larry, and Troy, even as an outsider and a couple of years their junior. But the opportunities were few. After Robin Stanley lowered the boom, I had no time to meet Hitch at Alder Bridge for a smoke and can of beer.

"Don't worry about it. I'll give you a lift."

Mr. Phelan drove the smallest car I had ever seen. It looked like a yellow shoe with cartoon tires. In the teachers' section of the parking lot, the car was lost between an SUV and a pickup truck.

The upholstery of the passenger seat was repaired with duct tape, and the suspension wheezed when I sat down.

"What kinda car is this?"

"Nineteen seventy-two Honda Coupe, two-cylinder air-cooled transverse motorcycle engine. Basically, a junker."

"Amazed it runs," I said.

Mr. Phelan laughed. "Don't underestimate it. Gets about fifty-five miles to the gallon." He inserted the ignition key. "Bought it used for three hundred bucks. Learned to work on it myself. The reverse is faulty. Broke years ago, and haven't bothered to fix it. So…would you mind getting out and pushing us back at bit?"

He fired up the engine, and I opened the door and pushed with my right foot. The car was so small that I easily managed to push us out of the parking space.

"Who needs reverse?" Mr. Phelan said. As we drove out of the school parking lot, he asked, "So, where to?"

I gave general directions to the Stanley farm, and we rattled along the county road out of town, toward the National Forest.

I tried to come up with something to talk about but my mind was dumb that day.

Finally, I asked, "So, you're an astronomer?"

"Strictly amateur."

He explained in detail the differences between amateur and professional astronomy. I don't remember most of what he said. He spoke in paragraphs while other citizens of Strand grunted in single syllables. Even a few of our teachers, Coach Montgomery in particular, butchered grammar, but Mr. Phelan was articulate. Unfortunately, I was anxious, and when I'm nervous, I tend to listen more to my own thoughts than to the other person.

"Tell you what. Why not join us tonight, at the school? Eight o'clock. Maybe it will spark an interest in astronomy."

I sighed. "Yeah, sounds great. Thanks, but I don't think my stepdad would let me. Probation and all."

Mr. Phelan took the corner from the county road to our street.

"Want me to talk to him?"

I shook my head, knowing there was no talking to Robin Stanley. "This is it, up here on the left."

The Honda came to a stop, and Mr. Phelan pulled the emergency brake.

"Hey," I said, unfolding myself out of the small car. "Thanks for the lift, Mr. Phelan. Appreciate it."

He leaned across the seat. "Listen. Think about it. Try to convince that stepdad of yours, okay? Tell him it's an academic activity. I'm sure he'll reconsider. Eight o'clock at the school."

I took a breath, and my mouth tightened in grim acceptance. I slapped the top of the yellow Honda and thanked him again for the ride, turning to climb the gravel driveway toward the Stanley farm.

*   *   *

Later that afternoon, I did not hear the phone ring or overhear Mr. Phelan's conversation with Robin Stanley. And so, after five o'clock supper when a car bleated its horn in front of the doublewide, I did not remove my Walkman earphones. I remained inclined on my bed, in the dark, marinating in teenaged angst.

Robin Stanley flipped on the bedroom light, and stood in the doorway with reading glasses in hand, the monstrous Bible under his arm. An expression of impatience shadowed his face. "Someone's here to see you." When I shuffled off the bed and slipped on my shoes, he grabbed my arm. We locked stares before I pulled away. "I want you to know I'm against this," he said in a low voice. "I'm letting you go against my better judgment. Don't let your mother down."

I had no idea what he was talking about. I was about to leave the bedroom when I stopped in the doorway and glanced at his Bible

"That's not the *illustrated* version, is it, Robin?"

Arrogance mixed with a sense of dread returned to his face.

A swarm of moths orbited the porch light, and as I stepped through the door, I swatted them and looked towards the gravel yard. There my mother stood in her apron next to a yellow Honda, arms crossed against the cold. She spoke with Mr. Phelan, who remained seated in the driver's seat, his presence at the farm for the moment still a mystery.

I trotted over to them and said, "Hey, Mr. Phelan. What're you doing here?"

My mother turned. "Didn't Dad tell you, Danny?" I shook my head, and she glanced at Mr. Phelan. "Your teacher called—"

"To remind you about tonight's fieldtrip," Mr. Phelan said, completing my mother's sentence. "Hop in. We don't want to be late." A look of disobedient mischief was in his eyes.

I asked my mom for approval, and she nodded. "Go get your coat."

When I returned to the yard, they were talking about Union High. I overheard my mother say something about teaching credentials. "I'll call Alice Rowland. She's on the Board. I'll put in a good word. I'm sure she'll…well, there he is." Mr. Phelan nodded when he saw me. "Let's get going."

I kissed my mom on the cheek, and she asked about what time we would return.

As I sat in the passenger seat, Mr. Phelan put the Honda in gear. "It won't be late, Karin. Some time, say, before ten thirty…?" The engine backfired as we lunged forward.

"Don't worry. Your son's in good hands."

In the side mirror, I saw my mother's reflection wave uncertainly.

*　　　*　　　*

Union High at night was an entirely different school. Floodlights cast a high prosperity to the rundown walls and threw ovals on the lawn like emerald stepping-stones. I carried Mr. Phelan's briefcase as we descended to the sports field. He leaned heavily on his cane and sounded out of breath with each step. "Soon as we set up…everyone's accounted for…I'll send you off. I need you to shut down these lights. You okay with that?"

"Sure, but how do I do that?"

Mr. Phelan said he'd explain everything about how to access the main switchboard once we'd set up the telescope.

"Okay," I replied happily. I would have picked up the litter had he asked, just to be out from under Robin Stanley's thumb.

Amateur astronomy proved a tedious pastime. Even with my help, it took Mr. Phelan nearly an hour to set up the equipment. A group of students and their parents stood around as he aligned the Condé optical axis of the twelve-inch reflector telescope. He consulted his *Index Catalogue* using a penlight and told us that Jupiter rose shortly before nine when he would align the optical axis of his reflector toward the Eastern sky. "Once the sun drops eighteen degrees below the horizon," he told us, "that's when night officially 'falls'." Mr. Phelan resented city lights. He said that Edison's invention had been a defeat for astronomy. "Incandescence reflects in atmospheric dust and masks the stars. But we're lucky. The moon rises much later tonight."

On the fieldtrip I met a girl named Marie Kaysen. Even in the dark, I could tell she was nicely put together, dark-haired, and shy enough to make me feel comfortable. We talked casually, and I learned that she had just turned sixteen, and so, of course, I kept my age to myself and let assumptions fall where they may. After all, I was the teacher's assistant, and the role made me seem more important than I was.

We stood in the night air, chatting, while Mr. Phelan periodically looked through the viewfinder. The atmosphere quavered as solar heat on the earth's surface evaporated, wreaking havoc with focal points. After taking the time to explain details of what we were about to see, he pointed behind us. Jupiter was rising above a line of cedar. The only sound was that of the reflector's ticking clock, matching the revolution of the Earth. Mr. Phelan reached down and pressed the "on" button of a portable tape player and invited each of us to look through the eyepiece. Johann Sebastian Bach accompanied my introduction to astronomy.

Mr. Phelan stood behind the telescope and rubbed his leg as he told students what to look for. "At least four moons should be visible. Can anyone name them?" When it was my turn, Mr. Phelan showed me how to adjust the focus, and I peered through the lens to see Jupiter in a wash of black. "Tomorrow, I'll show you all a chart, showing just how many earths would fit into Jupiter. It's made up entirely of condensed gases."

While Marie Kaysen questioned how it could be possibly made out of gas, I looked through the telescope at the celestial body, this remote object, this indifferent thing that gave no heed to whether or not I took my next breath. I stood transfixed. *I exist, Jupiter*, I thought to myself. *I exist*. When I pulled back, I caught Marie Kaysen looking at me. Most girls would have turned away, but she smiled with a sense of promise.

As Mr. Phelan adjusted the scope for our next viewing, I watched an airliner descend through clouds of starlight. The plane's running lights were awash against the Milky Way.

"Nature abhors chaos," Mr. Phelan said, "as much as it abhors a vacuum. Take the evening sky, for instance. The ancients, Greeks and the like, saw mythological figures in these same stars...."

While he spoke, I wondered if nature had arranged the constellations to spell phrases in an unreadable language. Had the stars been blown randomly about the sky or was there an intelligible pattern there? Were the cities of the world at night, with our neon signs and streetlights, perceived through telescopes by beings on another planet? Were the glittering amoebas of our city lights a kind of cuneiform that raised questions in the alien mind? Later, on the drive home when I shared my thoughts with Mr. Phelan, he said, "I love your idea, Danny. What a wonderful thought. Now, don't laugh. Creative thought is the basis of the scientific method. Without someone coming up with a hypothesis, where would we be?"

He told me that astronomers were sometimes guilty of shoddy thinking. "How often have you looked for something that's lost, and it turned out the thing was right in front of you all along, in plain sight? Isn't that the way things work sometimes?" he said. "The secrets of nature are concealed by the obvious. Even scientists mistake what they *want* to see for what is the truth."

I wasn't sure exactly, until years later, what he meant.

He said, "When biologists train their electron microscopes at the infinitesimal, the very small, how different is that from astronomers observing galaxies at unimaginable distances? I think they're observing one side of the same circle." His smile caught the Honda's instrument lights and gleamed in the dark. "So, your question about aliens maybe reading patterns or symbols in our city lights, yes, that's possible. Very possible indeed."

"I've never thought of science as something I'd be interested in," I confessed.

"Well, there's pretty much a science for everything, Danny. Take those rocks there." The lights from the Honda illuminated an excavated hillside beside the road. "Now you wouldn't think those rocks could talk, but they can. Don't laugh. Rocks can talk. The problem is, people who don't know their language can't hear them or understand what they're saying. To discover what rocks are saying you have to study geology. Geology is the language of rocks, simple as that."

"And astronomy is the language of the stars?" I said.

"Absolutely, Galileo."

He laughed, and so did I for what seemed the first in a long time.

C. Marcus Parr

Chapter 6

The town of Strand sat against the western slope of the Cascades and was made up of slapdash houses mostly, that and a few Quonset huts. A '60s-modern two-story building combined city hall, the library, and police station at the center of town. This style of architecture marked Strand as having had promise at one time, a promise broken and long forgotten.

The town came into being as a bodega along the Barlow Trail in the late 1800s. It swelled in population during the logging boom through the 1950s, only to collapse after the trees ran out. Strand was a quiet place because nothing happened there, nothing of any importance to a fourteen-year-old boy. During the months of my residence, I heard no rumors of robbery or assault. The citizens of Strand were conservative people, church going, suspicious of strangers, suspicious of anything that brought change to the community. Hitch McDonough told the story of a family that had lived in Strand for ten years until their house burned down, tragically killing them. The local paper wrote that the luckless family was "new to Strand, and largely unknown to the community." After *ten years*.

Signs of decay were everywhere. The whitewashed windows of Wink's Saloon, long empty, were like mortician's powder on a corpse. Strand lacked a cinema and shopping mall, sidewalks and adequate storm drains to handle the spring runoff. It was deficient in color and vitality. For tourists passing through, Strand had the look of a dying small town trying to save itself through contrived slogans—*Strand: Gateway to the Heavenly Cascades*. Faded banners hung from utility poles announcing "Pioneering Days," a weeklong celebration of Strand's imaginary past. Strand was an obstacle on the way to somewhere else, and it was my penitence to live here.

For the first few weeks of its existence, my stepfather's optometry office fared poorly. In spite of competition from a franchise optician in town, he established his office in the center of the shopping district, off the main street. He financed it on a line of credit through the bank, using the farm as collateral. Years earlier, to avoid an inheritance tax that would have lost the farm, the Stanley's deeded it to their son in hopes that he would pay the property taxes and allow them to live out their final days there. Without Virgil's signature or knowledge, Robin Stanley had staked his success by betting the farm. There was a large outlay of funds just to furnish the reception room. More money was spent on an inventory of eyeglass frames and an Ophthalmoscope and field screener for eye exams, equipment used to measure glaucoma and near-sightedness. Still, as the weeks passed, he saw few customers. It wasn't that people didn't know Dr. Stanley. His family had lived in Strand for over thirty years. What may have interfered with his success was, the citizens of Strand knew him all too well.

His business was often mentioned in our supper prayers. When he said grace for what seemed to last at least five minutes, he praised the Lord for our health and asked that my brother's "weakness of mind" improve, but mostly he asked that his new business be successful. "If that is your will, Lord," Robin Stanley prayed. On and on he went about the Lord "leading" myopic customers to the store. He indirectly wished for God's intercession to bring harm to the eyesight of the citizens of Strand for his financial gain. With his eyes squeezed tight, he would pray about meager cash receipts at the end of the day, about diminishing returns and mounting capital losses. I often peeked at him and marveled at his naiveté. Such an artless man, unformed and inadequate to the task of living, beseeching the Almighty to do something he should have done himself. It was pathetic. Once, there were tears in his eyes after he went on a little longer than usual, until finally he blessed the food, but by then Eve Stanley's dinner was cold. It was never very good anyway.

*   *   *

By mid-October, on a Saturday morning full of cold sunlight, Robin Stanley scheduled an appointment for my mother and me to be fitted with eyeglasses, whether we needed them or not. He complained that we had not shown enough support. He saw us as potential walking advertisements for the optometry office, and he encouraged me to tell friends at school where to shop for a new pair of eyeglasses. I told no one. I maintained a healthy distance from any association with the "Doctor," often denying that I knew him.

On the afternoon of our appointment, while Dr. Stanley tended to a customer, my mother and I were forced to wait. The reception area reflected Robin Stanley's personality. It was plain looking and without adornment save the two-dozen frames in a mirrored display case. The rented office furniture stood in contrast to the bare walls. He could not afford a receptionist, and so Mom had handled the phones and appointment book for the first week or so, before her substitute teaching position became permanent, thanks to Mr. Phelan. While we sat and waited, I flipped through the pages of a *Boy's Life* magazine.

My mother dropped the *Us* magazine in her lap and turned to me. "I forgot to tell you the news."

I glanced up.

"Dr. Stanley's ex-wife?" she said in a hush. "She might not…do you remember our telling you about, you know, the credit card thing? Well, anyway, Dr. Stanley said she's considering not pushing it. The lawsuit, I mean. Isn't that great?"

I could not have cared less if his ex-wife had declared a moratorium on all future demands over credit card debt. I didn't care. None of their concerns were my concerns. They'd been treating me like the Bad Seed all week, so what did I care about Robin Stanley's situation with his ex-wife? None of it mattered to me. The town of Strand and state of Oregon were not my home, not my birthplace. Oregon was nothing like California, as far as I could see, where my genetics had been framed and nurtured, where I knew the geography better than the whorls of my fingerprints, and where the landscape itself seemed a part of me. Why should I give a gnat's ass about Robin Stanley's financial difficulties with an ex-wife that we only recently learned of?

"Does that mean we get to move back?" I said.

My mom shook her head.

"Danny, we're just going to have to…we're just going to have to be patient with this whole deal, okay?"

To show my mother how little patience I had over "this whole deal," I flipped angrily through the pages of *Boy's Life,* not pausing over the articles or pictures but whipping through the magazine in short order. When she registered disapproval with a click of the tongue, I dumped the *Boy's Life* onto the pile next to my chair and searched for other reading material to avoid her stare.

There were few choices, *Field & Stream* and *Ladies Home Journal,* all of them boring. Robin Stanley had paid for a subscription to *Boy's Life* through a Valley Shepherd Community Church fundraiser. The tattered and outdated *People* and *Us* magazines, *Field & Stream* and the others were discards from the town's sole dental office. There was nothing in Dr. Stanley's reception area that spoke of prosperity. It reminded me of what a social welfare clinic must be like in a poor county.

"Danny, I need to ask a favor of you."

I looked into my mother's downcast eyes.

"Are you listening to me?"

"Yes, ma'am."

"I want you to consider getting baptized with me."

"No, I can't. I *can't.* Don't ask me that."

"Don't say *no* right away."

How could I tell her that my faith lacked all conviction? How could I even begin to explain to her the hypocrisy I saw at Valley Shepherd Community Church? What words could express my hatred for their pride and public claim to absolute moral authority?

"If you did, it would be supportive of everything your father is trying to do here."

"*Step*father," I corrected.

My mother drew a breath. "Do this for me, Danny."

Dr. Stanley stepped into the doorway leading to the examination room. For my mother's benefit, he struck a professional pose, grinning through gapped, yellow teeth.

"Think about it," my mother said quietly, patting my knee.

Dr. Stanley buttoned the top button of his tunic. "You should be looking out for your future, young man."

He meant that I should look out for my future after I'm dead, and prepare for where I was to spend eternity.

"Jesus was baptized, Daniel."

"I know He was baptized, Robin."

"Don't you think you belong with your mother and me in Heaven?" Robin Stanley sounded so kindhearted in my mother's company. He had assumed a manner that was nothing like the harsh tone he took with me in private.

My mother stood and pressed the wrinkles out of her pleated dress. "Are you ready for us, Honey?"

"While Miss Mobley's eyes are dilating, we have time."

I huffed. *Of course, Miss Mobley, whoever she was.* His sympathetic tone of voice was for the benefit of the customer, not for my mother and certainly not for me. It was Robin Stanley masquerading as a "family man," the consummate Christian, the doting father, meant to raise his esteem in Miss Mobley's eyes should she be eavesdropping. It made me despise him all the more.

He invited my mother into the exam room, but before shutting the door, he gave me a disapproving look. Poker-faced, I continued my search for a readable magazine.

When it was my turn for the eye exam, I dreaded the thought of sitting anywhere near Robin Stanley. He told me to sit in front of a machine that measured my field of vision by using drop lenses. He shut off the overhead light and sat on the stool in front of me. I could smell his hand lotion and Old Spice aftershave. He explained every step of the procedure as though it was my first eye examination. I told him I wasn't nervous, but that didn't deter him. It was as though he play-acted at being a professional. He chatted endlessly about where he had attended Optometry College and that optometry was his second career. His first had been as a pharmaceutical sales representative, a detail man. He talked about the burden of tens of thousands of dollars in school-loan debt, in addition to child-support payments to the children of his previous marriage. I learned that he had been separated from his first wife for eighteen months and that his divorce was final just two months before the wedding in Medford.

And I learned something else about my stepfather.

When Dr. Stanley leaned forward to adjust the dials on a piece of equipment called an Optoscan, I could smell the odor of cigarettes on his breath. I had suspected him of sneaking off for a smoke when he volunteered to pick up something at the grocery store and came back chewing two sticks of Juicy Fruit gum, his Tweed jacket stinking of cigarettes. His teeth had a nicotine patina. Robin Stanley was a closet smoker, and I wondered if my mother was aware of it. I suspected he kept his tobacco addiction secret from his parents as well. Here was something to include on the list of lies, another deception to add to his stack of pornography.

When Dr. Stanley examined my eyes and tested the acuity of vision, he stated that I didn't really need glasses but that I should be fitted for them anyway.

"We want to insure your eyes stay well, Daniel."

He picked out a pair of frames, not unlike Jesse's pair, and fitted my mother with equally ugly tortoise shell frames. Since my lenses required minimal grinding, I left the office wearing my new glasses, to please my mother, but I planned to conveniently lose them at the first opportunity.

Afterwards, Mom picked up Jesse from Valley Shepherd Community Church School and dropped us hastily in front of the Dairy Queen in town. "I'm running late," she declared. "I've got a hair appointment and grocery shopping to do."

Jesse and I stood at the curb, holding hands. I felt self-conscious in the ugly eyeglass frames. "How long are we going to have to wait for you? Jesse'll be crazy with all the chocolate and sugar."

"Danny, look. Just be here—" She checked her wristwatch. "Around three o'clock, okay? We can agree on that, can't we?"

She said it in a way that sounded as though we had never agreed on anything, at any time.

"Okay," I said, "but what are we supposed to do until then, just hang out in *Strand?*"

She put the Buick in gear and said, "I'm sure you'll figure something out." As she merged with traffic, she said as an afterthought. "Don't get into any…."

I think she said *trouble*, but by then she was accelerating down the street. I removed the ugly eyeglasses and crammed them into my pants pocket before we entered the DQ. As my brother and I waited in line, I saw Marie Kaysen working the counter. When she looked up, she recognized me and waved. She looked good in the Dairy Queen uniform.

"That your kid brother?" she said loudly, above the racket of customers ordering fast food. She smirked through a wad of chewing gum.

"This is Jesse."

My brother bellyached about wanting to run off to the children's play area, but it was off limits. The last time we'd been there, he got his head stuck between the legs of a plastic unicorn in the fairyland display. The manager had to bend the legs to release Jesse and to stop his screams from driving away the customers.

Jesse howled. "Lemme go, Dammy. *Lemme go!*"

I kneeled down to his level and told him quietly, unless he behaved, we would have to leave just like the last time. No ice cream, no treats, nothing.

Marie showed surprise at his wild behavior. When he got like this, it was like trying to handle a squealing piglet.

Without offering details, I said, "He's a bit different." With the last five bucks I had in my wallet, I bought Jesse a sugar cone dip. Vanilla was his favorite with a hard chocolate coating.

"Nuts, Dammy. Please, nuts?" he whined.

"Marie, could we have nuts on that, thanks."

She returned with the cone and my change. "I dipped it in sprinkles, too. On the house," she said in a friendly smile as she leaned over the counter to hand Jesse the cone. She looked up at me. I could see the rumor of cleavage where her top button was missing. "Nothing for you?"

I shook my head.

"See you round then?"

I nodded and thanked her, feeling suddenly foolish and shy. We sat at a booth that was sticky from something spilled on the floor, and Jesse ate the ice cream. Watching my brother eat was not my favorite pastime but it was necessary. He gulped food that he liked, and he often choked. I'd never given him the Heimlich maneuver but had interrupted many meals to slap him on the back for reassurance.

Jesse managed to get most of the cone smeared on his face, hands and the tabletop. He looked like a chocolate mining accident when finished, holding out his hands to be cleaned and buzzing wordlessly about the uncomfortable stickiness.

The restaurant became more crowded with a busload of preschoolers on their return from a Mt. Hood fieldtrip. With all the kids and their chaperones mobbing the counter, I no longer had an unobstructed view of Marie Kaysen. I finished wiping the chocolate from Jesse's cheeks and towed him outside when he started up about the play area again.

In the parking lot I asked more or less rhetorically, "Where do you think we should go now?" There was nothing for teenagers to do in town, no cinema, arcade, or recreation center. I decided that we should take a walk.

We walked hand in hand away from the business district, along side streets lined with mature maple trees. The residential houses were small, bordered by picket fences. Beneath the canopy of tree shade, the traffic noise ebbed away until we heard only the crunch of our shoes in the leaves.

"Hey, Danny!"

A man called to us from across the street. He wore a pair of sunglasses and a floppy hat, Big Ben overalls. I did not recognize him right away. I stood there, wondering how anyone in that small town, other than a fellow high school student, could have known me.

The man removed his glasses but kept his hat on. "It's Audley...Phelan."

"Oh, hey, Mr. Phelan." It was then that I saw his cane leaning against a tree trunk.

"Who's that with you?"

We crossed the street to his picket fence. "My brother, Jesse."

Mr. Phelan leaned a rake against the fence and reached out. "Nice to meet you, Jesse."

Among my brother's more awkward traits was his morbid shyness. He hid behind my pants leg. "It's all right, Jesse. Mr. Phelan's a friend."

Sensing that he would get nowhere with Jesse by being pushy, Mr. Phelan rubbed his hand on his overalls and reached for his cane. "Just as well. My hands are filthy. Say, you guys got time for a drink or something? I need an excuse to quit. Come on. Can I interest you in a Coke or an orange juice?"

Once inside the house, Jesse went immediately for a small brass refractory telescope that was set on a tripod before the front room window. I restrained my brother from messing with it, but Mr. Phelan said, "It's okay. Can't damage it any more than it already is." And in a lower tone, he added, "Doesn't work all that well anyway."

He lifted Jesse onto a stool and patiently instructed him on how to look through the eyepiece and how to focus by using the two knobs. Jesse warmed to Mr. Phelan. "Want some orange juice?" he said and turned toward the kitchen while I stood within striking distance of my brother. It wasn't that Jesse was naturally destructive, but common gadgets frustrated him. At the Stanley farm, after answering the phone a few days before, Jesse could not figure out which part to speak into and ended up throwing the handset against the wall. A week earlier by mistake he stepped on one of his plastic airplanes. When he realized the wing was broken, out of frustration he smashed the toy to pieces, beyond repair. At Mr. Phelan's house I made sure that Jesse behaved.

"A Coke for you and juice for Jesse." Mr. Phelan limped back to the kitchen and returned with a can of beer that he rolled across his forehead. He popped the tab and slurped the foam. "There's nothing more refreshing than a cold one after yard work, even on a fall day. Hey, let me show you round the place."

We talked as we toured Mr. Phelan's property, which had been one of the first homesteads in Strand, now greatly diminished from its original size. "How many acres do you have?" I asked.

"They call this a junior acre. But I just maintain what you see here inside the picket fence." He slapped his artificial limb and smiled. "Bit difficult to garden on one leg."

There were three buildings on the property. All had cedar siding, painted white, and the window sashes edged in black enamel. Mr. Phelan explained that the Amish painted their farmhouses in this fashion. "I like the style," he said. "I converted that old silage tower into my astronomical observatory. I have a thirty-inch reflector up there."

I did not understand what he'd meant.

"Like the telescope we used at school, only bigger," he explained.

I pointed to a cottage in the back of the lot, set beneath a mature gum maple. "What's that?"

"That's the Chalet. The guest house, although it isn't much of a house per se. And no guests have ever spent the night in it. But it's perfectly nice. Small kitchenette. Two bedrooms. Little parlor in front."

"Look, Dammy," Jesse said, straining to pull me toward the cottage. "Dollhouse. Dollhouse."

"Calm down, Jesse."

With some difficulty, Mr. Phelan kneeled before my brother and got his attention by looking right into his eyes. This was so off putting to Jesse that he immediately gave up his demands to see the cottage.

"Jesse, would you like to come visit me some day? If your mom and dad'll allow it, I'd let you gaze through the big telescope. You can get so close to the Moon, it's like you're walking among the craters. And the *stars!* They feel as though you could touch them. Would you like that?"

Jesse looked up at me, too confused to speak. Most adults paid him very little attention. At the Stanley farm he was largely ignored.

"It's okay, Jesse," I assured him.

Jesse pulled away and pointed at Mr. Phelan. "Somepun's wrong with him, Dammy. He walks funny."

"Well," I explained, "Mr. Phelan hurt his leg a long time ago."

Mr. Phelan stood up, having to push against his cane and steady himself on the trunk of a fruit tree. He combed back strands of hair that had come loose from his ponytail. He asked what Jesse's age was and where he went to school. When I told him Valley Shepherd School, he almost choked.

"What's wrong with that?" I said.

"Well, he needs special instruction. Teachers trained to work with him, help Jesse attain his full potential. I don't think he'll get that at a church-run school." Mr. Phelan spoke as we made our way across the lawn toward the back porch of his house.

Inside the house, in the hallway leading from the porch to the kitchen, the walls were lined with framed black and white photographs from the American Civil War. When I commented on how many there were, Mr. Phelan explained that he was a "bit of a Civil War buff."

"Love to collect memorabilia. The least expensive and most enjoyable for me are these reproductions," he said. "I couldn't afford numbered prints, mind you. Not on a teacher's salary."

Jesse showed interest in a picture of a stream of soldiers marching on a road. The split-rail fence along the roadside, stones and trees, farmhouses and barns in the background were shown clearly in focus, but the soldiers appeared as a blur, because they were in motion. They appeared to be transparent.

"Ghosts, Dammy," Jesse said in awe. "Look. Ghosts."

Mr. Phelan knelt next to my brother, and together they stared at the photo. For my benefit he said, "It's the hour before the worst one-day battle of the war. You can't make it out clearly, but that's Antietam Creek. Sharpsburg, Maryland, there. See the church steeple? These are Union soldiers. Over twenty-three thousand casualties that day. So, Jesse, you're absolutely right. *Ghosts.* Ghosts marching to their destiny."

It was closing in on three o'clock, and I gave our excuses, that my mom was picking us up in front of the Dairy Queen. After thanking him and shaking his hand, I walked back to the center of town with Jesse in tow, whining about not wanting to leave Mr. Phelan's place. On the drive to the Stanley farm, Jesse couldn't stop telling Mom about the teacher who walked funny, about his brass telescope and his ponytail, about the orange juice, and about walking on the Moon and touching the stars.

Glancing toward the backseat, my mother said with an edge of annoyance, "What's he going on about, Danny?"

"Don't worry about it, Mom." I hugged Jesse. "We walked on over to Mr. Phelan's place. He has an astronomical observatory, that's what he calls it. Big telescope, the whole works. Anyway, Jesse's just a little excited, is all. Aren't you, Jesse?"

"Stars, Dammy. *Stars,*" my brother said. He pointed at a billboard of cartoon stars in a field of black, advertising a local men's club.

"That's right," I said, and kissed him on the top of the head. "Stars."

Chapter 7

Few solicitors visited the out-of-the-way Stanley farm. And so, when two men in business suits called to share the Gospel, my brother ran to tell me about it.

"They wearin' tuxedos," Jesse said excitedly.

On a late Saturday morning, I was stacking firewood in the barn under Virgil Stanley's orders and had noticed what I suspected were Jehovah's Witnesses drive up our road in a white Cadillac. With Bibles and pamphlets in their hands, they knocked on our front door.

"An' they asked if Mom knowed God's secret word."

"*Secret word?*" I said. I removed my Giants cap and wiped the sweat off my brow.

Jesse bobbed his head up and down earnestly.

"Mom told 'em we gotta book an' she can look up the secret word any time she wants."

He'd meant the Sacred Word, which was becoming something of an issue in our new lives. Ever since our mother joined the Valley Shepherd Community Church, Robin Stanley urged her to be baptized. When he pestered her the first time, she explained that she had already been baptized in Oklahoma, at her parents' Baptist church. "Right on the Arkansas River," she said, near Osage where she spent her childhood.

"But you're born *again* in Christ, Karin," Robin Stanley said. "Do it as a declaration of your renewed faith in Jesus."

He started in on it again when we were seated at the kitchen table after supper for one of our "family" meetings. In an endless lecture he praised the virtues of baptism and criticized my enthusiasm for astronomy by twisting it into something unholy. "Mark my words, the antichrist will be a scientist." He told my mother that none of us knew how many years we had left before God called us "home." There was only so much time to find our place in the ranks of God's faithful, before the Final Judgment. It was all made clear, he said, in *Revelations,* the assurance of Christ's return and of God's sovereignty over Satan.

Robin Stanley usually got heated during these discussions about religious matters, but on this night he was especially animated. He preached to us on the four living creatures who give honor and thanks to the Lord God Almighty, all the while the twenty-four elders fall down before the throne. There are lions and lambs in the *Revelations* story, which Jesse liked very much because, when they were mentioned, he clapped. When my stepfather mentioned the opening of the seven seals, Jesse barked like a sea lion.

"No, no," Robin Stanley said. "You don't understand."

He embellished scripture by giving a detailed account that led up to the opening of the Abyss. He said that smoke from the Abyss will darken the sun and sky, and all manner of demons will crawl across the Earth.

"Nonbelievers," Robin Stanley said, turning to me, "will be tortured for five months by locusts."

"What's a locus, Mommy?" Jesse asked.

"It's like a cockroach," I told him, locking stares with my stepfather.

Of course, Jesse whimpered after his mind imagined billions of cockroaches the size of horses swarming out of the ground and torturing him for five months.

"Okay, okay." My mother comforted my brother. "I think we've had enough for one night."

"But Karin," Robin Stanley exclaimed. "I haven't talked about the Rapture yet."

"Not tonight, Robin," she said, rocking Jesse gently in her lap. "Some other time."

*   *   *

A few days before Halloween, it snowed. We had endured an east wind all night, and in the morning, snowdrifts against the back of the doublewide bound us inside. I prayed—actually *prayed*—that school was canceled.

Over the previous week, Robin Stanley subjected me to his spiteful rules composed in perfect penmanship and stuck under a magnet on the refrigerator. After school each day, I fell under the tutelage of Virgil Stanley. The old man was a taskmaster. He ordered me to clean out the aluminum cans that he had tossed over the years under the trailer. He told me to sweep the straw on the second floor of the barn and tend the few rows of raspberry canes that the Stanley's kept for personal use. He expected me to know how to change the oil in the old truck. It was a rusty Ford F-100 on bald tires, parked next to the barn. For fifteen minutes I searched for the oil pan and plug, not knowing a carburetor from the radiator, before Virgil lost patience. He pushed me aside, peevish about having to complete the chore himself. He said, "I don't have time for this. What do you people learn down there in sunny California?" He did not so much teach me how to change the oil as make clear my worthlessness. I suspected Virgil Stanley spent most days thinking up complicated chores to confirm my level of incompetence.

But on the day it snowed, all bets were off.

For weeks Robin Stanley had promised to buy studded snow tires for Mom's Buick, but he'd neglected to do so. The Stanley farm was down a quarter mile of gravel driveway off a four-mile stretch of poorly maintained county road that led to the state highway. On this morning my stepfather realized that the state-operated snowplows and cinder spreaders would not reach the county roads until well past noon. This left him no choice but to put chains on the tires.

Jesse and I listened to the radio for news of school closures but the announcer failed to mention Strand, just the Portland metro area schools. My mother rushed into the kitchen to declare, "School is on. This is not a snow day." This put my brother and me in a scramble to prepare for the day. Every member of the household ran around as though to make up for lost time. Mom was into her second week of substitute teaching, after the regular teacher developed complications from outpatient surgery. As she got dressed and hurriedly put on make-up, she told me to wash Jesse's face and dress him in extra layers for his day at church school. Later, sitting at the kitchen table and reading my biology textbook, I completed my homework from the night before when Virgil Stanley's list of chores had taken priority. My stepfather, always the Boy Scout but never prepared, walked into the kitchen wearing an orange jumpsuit. "Why're you dressed like a convict?" I asked. To put chains on the tires, he replied.

Virgil Stanley poured himself a cup of coffee and headed out to the barn, but not before he complained to his wife. "You spend too much time on the phone." Eve was sitting on a kitchen stool with the handset pressed to her ear. She'd been on hold with a mail-order company. She collected Regal Limited Christmas tree ornaments in a series. She also collected hand painted plates of border collies, although the Stanley's did not own a dog. She registered a complaint with the mail-order company for discontinuing the series before she had saved enough money and found the time to complete the collection. Also, she wanted to know why she had not received her complementary tennis bracelet with her last order.

By the time we left the farm, it began to snow again. With Robin Stanley at the wheel and still in chain-gang attire, we fishtailed down the driveway and onto the county road. The snow on the road was virginal. Nobody had ventured out before us. But this did not stop my stepfather from doing his Presbyterian best to keep his appointments and to make sure that his family kept theirs.

I had an agenda to keep, as well. "Mom?" I said. "Mr. Phelan says Jesse could improve if he gets special attention. If he went to a special school, I mean."

"Where?" my mother asked.

"Well, he said there's a school in Boring that specializes in learning disabilities. Mr. Phelan says—"

"Oh, Mr. Phelan says this, Mr. Phelan says that," Robin Stanley whined.

"Honey, maybe we should check into it."

"What does Mr. Phelan know?"

"He knows a lot," I said.

"He's just a *teacher*, Daniel. Nothing but a teacher."

I don't think it dawned on Robin Stanley that he had insulted Mr. Phelan *and* my mother's profession in a single statement.

"What the hell do you know, Robin? You're just worried it'll cost too much," I said.

"Don't you talk to me in that tone." He craned his skinny neck to shoot me a nasty look.

"Please, both of you, not this morning, please," my mother begged.

"Well, just a minute, Karin. How much am I supposed to take from him? He sticks his nose where it doesn't belong. He lies to me. And now, in my house—"

"*Your* house?" I said.

"Under my roof he says Jess should go to a—"

"It isn't *your* house," I said. "This car doesn't even belong to you."

Robin Stanley stiffened and gripped the wheel. He pulled slowly to the side of the road and came to a stop. In a sudden arc, he reached back and slapped my face. The crack sounded worse than it felt. I've had worse slaps from Hitch McDonough when we horsed around, but it shocked my mother, a woman who had never laid a hand on us, even when she had been drinking.

"*Robin!*" she shouted.

"Asshole," I muttered.

"I can't believe it," he said.

"You're a goddamned phony, Robin," I said, pressing back against the seat, reaching for the door handle.

"Goddamn phony…" Jesse repeated.

"Jesse, don't say that," my mother chimed.

Looking to Karin, Robin Stanley said, "Will you listen to the language he subjects me to?" He was shaking. Obviously, the slap hurt him more than it hurt me.

I opened the door and jumped out of the car.

My mother lowered the window. "Danny, get back in the car. Danny, please."

"I'll take the bus," I said. "Leave me alone." I pointed to the shelter at the side of the road and I high stepped through the powdery snow.

His voice muffled through the steel of the Buick, Robin Stanley said, "Leave him be. Karin, leave him be."

They drove on, and the Buick cautiously rounded the corner, the chained tires spitting a cloud of dry snow, leaving me alone by the roadside. I realized what my stepfather should have known—there would be no buses this day. No one was going anywhere.

Considering the weather, it would have been wise to stay home. But not for Robin Stanley. No, he had to prove that nothing, not foul weather or even a foul-mouthed stepson, would prevent him from achieving what he had set out to do.

The air was deathly cold but the snow had stopped falling. The world seemed blanketed in stillness, in grays and soft shadows, the only sounds coming from clumps of snow settling to the ground from the branches of fir. The snowfall had made everything new again. The landscape was pristine and unsullied by the handiwork of human beings.

I figured, mulling over my options in the bus shelter, I had about ten to fifteen minutes before Robin Stanley realized that the rest of Strand had stayed in bed an extra hour rather than put their families at risk on the road. He would eventually turn the Buick around and head back to the farm, but not for at least a quarter hour, long enough to pay Hitch McDonough a visit.

The McDonough mailbox was not far from the bus shelter. I headed in that direction, book bag over my shoulder, trudging through the snow. The road rose up and curved in a dogleg to the left for about fifty yards. Off to the right, seated on a scavenged piece of wood, was a black mailbox with the name *McDonough* miserably lettered in white paint.

I had never before visited Hitch's house, although we were neighbors. He was not the sort of kid who wanted friends to drop by. Hitch had a reputation at school for being feral, more man than boy, and a loner for the most part. I, on the other hand, had no reputation. I was the new kid, plain and simple. I was the Californian. I had no idea how Hitch felt about California. It never came up in conversation. Other than those few occasions when we smoked on Alder Bridge, Hitch pretty much kept to himself. It wasn't that he was secretive. Rather, he was cagey, always working a scheme in his mind, planning a heist or a mean practical joke to play on some unsuspecting sucker. That was the Hitch Way. He did things but he didn't talk about it before hand. And afterwards, he didn't brag much about it either.

I had become a dues-paying member of the Hitch admiration society. It wasn't hero-worship but respect that I felt. Hanging around someone where spectacular disasters took place, most of which he orchestrated, was fun. Larry and Troy were also members of this exclusive club. Whereas Larry was pretty much a freestanding spirit, a high school football star, who had a life outside of Hitch, Troy was the ultimate toady. Had I known the word *sycophant* when I was fourteen, I would have used it to describe him.

The only reason Troy dyed his hair orange was because Hitch told him to. The kid had no imagination. He was as dense as mud. Hitch made fun of Troy behind his back and sometimes included me in on the hoax. Hitch would crack a joke meant to be bogus and he'd give a sly wink. Troy would howl hysterically while the rest of us sat straight-faced. "What? I thought it was funny," he'd say. It was pathetic really. Because of the things Hitch told him to do, Troy got into more trouble at school than the rest of us combined. He was on a first-name basis with Principal Horvath and his telephone number was at the top of a list to call when trouble brewed. All of Troy's pranks and pratfalls were done to impress Hitch McDonough, his hero. I suppose, Hitch was hero to all of us. He was a minor god in our pantheon of bad apples.

Through snow high enough to fill my shoes, I made my way down a hairpin driveway to the McDonough homestead.

Their place was worse off than the Stanley's. The house was a hodge-podge of small buildings cobbled together out of unpainted trash wood. The siding had rotted with age and turned brown. The roof was nothing more than tarpaper. Sections were covered in a blue plastic tarp held down with 2 x 4's. Thick wild berry vines had found their way through most of the windows, tacked as they were with cloudy plastic sheeting. As I approached, a scrawny dog barked and strained against a chain.

Someone rushed out onto the screened porch and yelled. "Shut up, goddamn it!"

It was Hitch's old man, Wallace McDonough.

He stood on ivory blue feet. He had on a "wife-beating shirt." The tank top was riddled with holes and stains under the armpits. He wore a pair of boxer shorts, and his gut drooped over the elastic band. When he yelled at the dog, his stomach muscles tensed up and sucked the belly inward.

Unashamed and bald-faced, not unlike his son, Wallace McDonough took a few steps forward when he saw the intruder on his property.

"Who the hell're you?"

"Good morning," I said. "I'm a friend of Hitch's."

"Ya mean *Greg?* He ain't here."

For a second or two my plans for the day fell apart. My heart sank. It was a long walk back to the Stanley farm.

Having heard my voice, Hitch pushed open the screen door and strolled past his father to greet me. "Hey, Danny. How's it hangin'?"

Wallace McDonough shook his head and returned indoors but not before once more yelling at the dog to shut up.

I stood at the bottom of the porch steps, grinning. "No school today."

"No shit, Sherlock? Hey, stick around, alright? I gotta take care of something. Only be a minute."

I waited for what seemed like half an hour. Inside the McDonough house, I heard the occasional shout as father and son got into it a little. A door was slammed. Another door opened and shut. I heard water running and the muffled arguing of Wallace McDonough deep within the medley of decay. And then, in the quiet minute that followed, I listened to the melting snow as it fell in clumps from the branches of Douglas fir trees. From behind the house, the engine of an old automobile roared to life. Crunching across the snow, a metallic green Plymouth Duster with primer on all four fenders rolled into view. Behind the wheel was Hitch McDonough, laughing like he was going to run me over.

The car came to a stop next to me, skidding a few feet on the ice. Hitch leaned out the driver's window and said, "Get in."

"You're not old enough to drive, are you?"

He stuck a Marlboro in the corner of his mouth and said, "Get the fuck in."

We drove to town at our peril. Near the highway we passed my mother's Buick, but only Robin Stanley was in the car. I ducked below the dashboard, and Hitch teased me mercilessly.

"Man, you're a chickenshit."

I said, "Look, do you even have a license? I'm in enough trouble as it is."

"I ain't under age."

I gave him a sidelong glance. "You're a sophomore, right?"

My statement made him mad, and for a moment, I thought he was going to hit me.

"Listen, asshole. I got held back. Twice! I'm a lot older'n you."

I swallowed. "Okay, okay. But…do you have a license?"

He shook his head.

"Well, that sucks. We get caught, I'm gonna get killed by Robin Stanley."

"Fuck Robin Stanley," he said.

Our first stop was the state-run liquor store. Hitch left me in the Duster with the motor running. Alone, my doubts began to rack up and I thought of ditching my friend right then and there, making a run for the Dairy Queen. I rapped a palm against my forehead at the sheer stupidity for agreeing to come along. What was Hitch doing inside the store—stealing beer or robbing the place? My heart raced with worry. He came running outside empty-handed with the proprietress waddling after him and shaking her fist. We nearly slammed into another car in our escape out of the parking lot.

"Smooth," I said. "Real smooth."

"Relax, dickhead. I know another place."

We took the highway up the mountain. The Oregon Department of Transportation had plowed and cindered the roadway. The road was clear, and the traffic ran with commuters to Portland, catching up on time lost due to the snowstorm. About five miles out of town, Hitch pulled into a convenience store. I knew the store. An Asian couple ran it. They were frail-looking people whose son attended Union High. Hitch stepped out of the Duster and leaned through the window. "I'll be back in a minute. These folks're pushovers."

While waiting, I fiddled with the radio but found it broken. It didn't even pick up static.

Hitch returned with a small brown paper sack. He stuck the keys in the ignition, laughing at his ballsy success.

"What's in the bag?" I asked.

"See for yourself."

Two packs of red Marlboros, and a sleeve of matches.

"Can I have one?"

Hitch was having trouble turning over the engine, but when it caught, he grinned through crooked teeth. "Take a pack. I filched 'em."

"You a thief now?"

He nodded. "What, you gone Christian on me?"

"No." I ripped open the pack and pushed in the cigarette lighter.

We reentered the highway and headed back to Strand. He told me to light him one. After a couple of drags, he fished around in his jacket pockets and pulled out two twelve-ounce cans of Budweiser. He laughed outrageously when he handed one to me.

The can was ice cold, and beer on that snowy day was not the first drink that came to my mind. Hitch popped open the other and sucked the foam off the lid, all the while keeping his hand on the steering wheel. I followed suit with the cigarette dangling between my lips. I took a drag, removed the Marlboro, and before exhaling, gulped down a mouthful of beer. I coughed, and beer dribbled out of my nose.

"Smooth, Aiken. Real smooth."

We drove to the Strand Cemetery on the flank of a remote hill overlooking the Willamette Valley. This was where Deep Creek ran in the open before meeting up with the Clackamas River farther below. The vista was a patchwork of nursery stock farms where shades of green, ochre and autumn rust shone through the melting snowfields. The world was quiet while Canada geese beat the air in an arrow southward. Stands of conifers on the edge of the cemetery seemed powdered in sugar, and patches of snow held the ground in places safe from the sun. I felt peaceful sitting in the Plymouth among the dead, feeling more alive than I had in months.

"Say," Hitch said, "Larry says he seen you at practice. You didn't tell me you were gonna try out for football?"

I shook my head. "I can't. No after-school activities. Robin Stanley's orders."

I knew what Hitch was thinking. We both said in harmony, "Fuck Robin Stanley."

In the distance we heard the mournful song of a freight train rolling down the mountain, returning from Hood River, loaded with apples and pears. As it made its way in and out of the forest curtain, we saw glimpses of it on the switchbacks. The click of its wheels tapped rhythmically against the rails. Within the hour, almost all of the morning snow had melted and a few columns of cloud rose like mountains over the distance. When we heard the train whistle blow again, much farther away, Hitch pointed westward to a break in the forest where the tracks gleamed in sunlight and the train was silhouetted against the last snow bank.

"Hey, bet I can count the cars and you can't," Hitch said.

We lost count at thirty-five.

I was thinking about Robin Stanley's talk about *Revelations* when I asked Hitch, "Do you believe in heaven and hell?"

He thought for a while before answering. "No such thing."

"Then what happens, you know, after you're dead?"

"You go to the same place you got fixed up with a conscience the first time. After you see a rerun of your life, all the crap you did, all the good stuff, you either feel good about what you did or you feel bad."

"I saw this in a movie somewhere."

"No, you didn't. Listen. For the rest of eternity you're made to see what you did when you were alive." Hitch grinned when he said this. "For some assholes, like your stepdad, it would be hell. For others...?"

Hitch took a drag.

"Well, then what *do* you believe in?" I asked. "If there's no heaven to look forward to."

He blew a smoke ring.

"I know what I don't believe. All the crap they preach in that church of yours. Eternal life and make-believe. Sin and guilt. Just somethin' made up 'cause they're afraid of death."

I laughed. "So, it's more about what you *don't* believe."

Hitch regarded me momentarily before turning away. "I believe in that." He gestured at the blue distance. "Nothing nicer than that. Makes most of the shit in life worthwhile."

We were quiet for a time. Then he said, "There's evil in the world. I seen it. And good people, I 'spose. But I can't stomach all their crap about demons, the Holy Roller types." He crushed out the cigarette. "I ever tell you, they drove a friend of mine nuts, ended up in the state hospital?"

"Really?" I said, sitting up, paying attention.

Hitch nodded. "Thing is, he wasn't nuts. His mother was. And his goddamn pansy-ass father. They were missionaries, off the fucking wall. They ran his life by the book and drove him crazy." He shook out another Marlboro. "His mom caught him whacking off, you know, with pictures a naked chicks."

"Jesus." I thought about Robin Stanley's hidden stash of pornography.

"His dad beat him and locked him in the closet."

"You kidding me?"

Hitch shook his head. "He started hearing voices, and I thought, shit, it was just, I don't know, what *they* did to him. After I heard about it, I told his old man to leave him alone, it'll clear up. But he got worse, and they put him in the nuthouse. Said he was possessed by demons. His mother counted 'em. Says she saw eighteen demons come outta him. Can you believe that? It's what your Robin Stanley believes in. Demons."

"That's crazy," I said, leaning back.

"Yeah. Poor old Jon, knew him since first grade. The only demons in his life was his mother and dad."

We smoked Marlboros and drank Budweiser and joked and cared about nothing and nobody on the face of the earth, just the two of us, and the friendship we formed that day felt like it would last a lifetime. Then, as the sun touched the rim of the world, we drove home.

Chapter 8

"Where are your spectacles?" Robin Stanley said.

The three of us, Robin Stanley, my mother and I, sat in the kitchen after supper. I looked up from reading a school library book on astronomy.

"*Where* are your spectacles?"

The word *spectacles* amused me. "My what?" I smirked.

"Eyeglasses."

I swallowed, knowing there'd be hell to pay. "I lost 'em."

"You lost them? How could you *lose* them?"

I shrugged. "I don't know." I looked to my mother for support but found none. "Fell out of my backpack. At school, I guess."

"Did you check lost and found?" my mother asked, trying to be helpful.

"Yeah," I lied to my mother.

"How do you lose a perfectly good pair of glasses in what, two weeks? I can't believe it," Robin Stanley said.

"People lose things all the time. They're gone, Robin, okay?"

"No," he said, "it's *not* okay. You have no sense of responsibility. None. You're a shiftless loser."

"Robin!" my mother said.

Robin Stanley bridled his rage when he looked at her. "How else…what else do you call it, Karin? He's the most irresponsible boy…I can't stand it." He returned his attention to me. "You're *impossible*. Losing your glasses. Nobody loses their glasses."

Calmly, my mother repeated the words in a shaky voice. "My son is not a loser."

The three of us stared at one another for a moment, caught in the eye of the storm.

"What do you call it then?" Robin Stanley said finally, getting up from the table.

"Danny is no loser," she said, her eyes downcast.

Without another word, Robin Stanley stomped out of the kitchen and out the front door of the doublewide.

*   *   *

By early November, Hitch McDonough fell into a depression. He was down and nearly crippled by it. He had had an argument with Larry in which a shoving match progressed to blows. The high school all-conference defensive tackle was out for the season with a broken middle finger of the right hand, an injury suffered after flipping off Hitch McDonough. Neither of the boys was suspended because Principal Horvath knew nothing about the fight, and Troy was sworn to secrecy under threat of a beating. Larry explained his injury as an accident, something that had happened when he slipped on black ice in the parking lot. The upshot was the dissolution of their friendship. Troy no longer worshipped at the Hitch altar, and Larry said he wanted nothing more to do with the "prick." And so our posse of four was reduced to a pair. I didn't so much miss Troy and Larry, but their absence seemed to eat away at Hitch's self-confidence.

He and I began to meet regularly between classes, and we ate lunch together. After school we had our customary smokes on the county road, but Hitch acted sullen and moody most of the time. It felt as though I had befriended something as unstable as nitroglycerin. At that time, Hitch was about as much fun as a tick on a dog.

One Friday during our lunch period, he told me to meet him after school, at the usual place.

Of all the time I hung out with Hitch, I never knew exactly how he got to and from school every day, to and from the county road that his father's property and the Stanley's bordered. I rode a yellow school bus most days, unless my mother was substitute teaching at Strand Middle School, in which case I rode with her. I never saw Hitch on the bus, not in the back with the loud kids or in the front with the kiss-asses. And I never saw him drive the Duster to school. That afternoon, after the bus deposited me at the side of the road, I ran into him at the usual spot, smoking a Marlboro.

"Hey," I said.

He shook out a cigarette and offered it to me. I wanted to decline but thought better for it.

With our cigarettes burning, we hiked across Alder Bridge over Deep Creek. As we stopped in the middle of the trestle, it crossed my mind that Hitch might commit suicide. I cannot say why the thought crossed my mind. It just did. It may have been because Hitch didn't say much. He stared down at the raging waters of Deep Creek. I knew that the fight with Larry had definitely bothered him, but there was something more.

With our legs dangling above the abyss, I told Hitch about finding the pornography in Robin Stanley's desk drawer. He didn't even smile. I think the story made him feel better, but he showed no change in emotion. I gave titillating details of the photograph of two women in the throes of sex along with the ridiculous underwear advertisements clipped from newspapers.

Hitch said, "So, you showed 'em to your mom?"

I shook my head. "She doesn't know."

"Chickenshit."

I conceded his point and told him how I had replaced the pornography in the desk drawer and stuffed the lurid photograph of the lesbians in the Bible, for Robin Stanley to discover at his next reading. I had exposed him, I told Hitch, but in the most subtle way imaginable.

"Was the porno any good?" Hitch asked.

I shrugged.

"Porn's one thing," he said, "but not the real thing."

Hitch pulled a fresh pack from his shirt pocket and lit a cigarette off the butt of the old one, exhaled and leaned back.

"My old man and me," he said. "He's been hittin' the sauce, a lot lately. And anyway, last week he told me, said I had to move out."

"Move out?"

Hitch nodded slowly and took a drag, not looking me in the eye.

"My granddad lives in Arkansas. I'm thinkin' about going down there'n live with him."

Here it was—more bad news, another disappointment to add to my inventory of regret. The only true friend I had in town was leaving. After little more than two months of friendship, Hitch McDonough would depart for Arkansas, a destination that might as well have been Jupiter.

I looked away because I didn't want to show him the defeat in my eyes.

"You wanna come with me?" he asked.

"To Arkansas?" I stubbed out my smoke.

"Yeah. What's wrong with that? It's a nice place. Not much different'n Strand really."

Why not? I thought. What was holding me to Oregon? The farther away I got from Robin Stanley the better. Why not take off and leave a note, like a suicide note, stating that I could no longer stand to live with the bastard? It would serve him right. Then I thought about Jesse and my mother. My running away would expose my kid brother to our stepfather's tyranny, but it would destroy Mom. Inasmuch as I wanted to, no, I couldn't run away and leave them in Strand. The solution to my problem was to convince Mom to divorce Robin Stanley, but to do that I would have to drive a wedge between them. I knew it was my duty to save my mother and Jesse from our captivity on the Stanley farm.

"Naw, I can't go with you, Hitch. But I might meet up with you later, down there. I got some business to take care of before, you know?"

Hitch made no immediate reply. He looked at me briefly but turned away. I could tell, he respected my decision, and in some way I think he knew the nature of the "business" I had to take care of.

"I ever tell you 'bout the Kaysen sisters?"

I shook my head. "I know a girl named Marie Kaysen."

He winked. "Lives in Dover. Annette and Marie. The Kaysen sisters."

Dover did not quite qualify as a proper town. It was a district outside Strand with a city limits sign that posted a population of twenty-eight. The Strand Post Office served Dover, although the local police department had no jurisdiction there. The Strand cops left crime fighting in Dover to the Clackamas County Sheriff's Office.

"Annette Kaysen? She go to our school?" I asked. "I don't think I ever..."

Hitch shook his head.

Annette Kaysen did not attend Union High because, as Hitch put it, "She's been home-schooled since Horvath expelled her." The expulsion had something to do with her getting caught with another student "doing it" in the back of a car, between classes.

The Kaysen sisters lived with their mother, Jaye-Ann Osthoff, and her boyfriend, a man named Nicky Jim, in a rented farmhouse up the road from nowhere. I knew that Marie Kaysen had just turned sixteen. Annette was seventeen. Hitch said, "She rocks."

Since the girls' mother worked two part-time jobs and the boyfriend was useless, Annette was home alone most days, and Marie often cut classes to be with her.

"Marie's dumber'n shit," Hitch said.

I shook my head. "She seems pretty nice. The night Mr. Phelan held that astronomy thing? She was there. She's not dumb. Works at the DQ."

"Yeah, like you gotta be Einstein to work at the Dairy Queen."

Hitch stared at the half-distance, at the world of his making where he was boss and captain of fate, where everything should have made sense except for the gravity of adults beyond his control. His volatility of mood changed. It left me guessing if it was for the better or worse. He seemed to be mulling over two opposing arguments, not unlike a cartoon angel of his better nature arguing with the devil about what to do.

"That Arkansas thing bothering you?" I asked cautiously so as not to tip the balance of our friendship.

He stood and flicked the cigarette away in an implicit answer. "What do you say we visit the Kaysen sisters?"

It took us nearly a quarter of an hour to backtrack from the trestle to the McDonough place where Hitch "borrowed" the Plymouth Duster against his father's wishes. The district of Dover was not much to look at, just two abandoned logging warehouses and a cone incinerator that was used to burn tree slash. All industry had been ripped out after the National Forest Service limited logging in the region. Dover might have had potential ten to twenty years ago, but I saw it as an inconsequential blight in a treeless landscape. There appeared nothing of value. Aggressive old-growth logging had denuded the hills, and since the harvest took place before the state law obliged loggers to replant, only opportunistic trees had taken root; *junk trees* the locals called them.

The Kaysen sister's lived on the northern slope of the mountain, on a failed nursery stock farm ruined by erosion that ran a gully through the main field. It was no place any rational person should care to own. At one time, someone had tried to make a go of it only to fail or give up when the land itself turned against them. Ferns seemed the primary crop, that and stump moss on the north side of the junk trees.

A weather-beaten two-story farmhouse, the Kaysen home was copied after the saltbox style. On the east-facing wall, wind had stripped the cedar siding leaving mere scabs of paint at the nail sets. The windows were unadorned, black eye sockets. The only life in the house came from a second-floor window where rock music played through a cheap stereo.

There had once been a barn on the property, but the spine of its roof sagged and threatened to collapse. This was where Hitch parked the Duster, beside the ruin.

When he stepped out of the car, he cupped his mouth and yelled.

"Hey, Kaysen!"

Almost immediately Marie came to the window, her head wrapped in a bath towel. She spoke to someone inside, and the rock music was shut off.

"Go get your sister," Hitch said.

Annette leaned out the window and shouted. "Come on up!"

Hitch seemed familiar with the habit of making himself at home, entering through the bare front door without knocking and by taking the rough-wood stairs two at once. I followed cautiously. By the time I entered the Kaysen sisters' bedroom, Hitch was sitting comfortably on a twin bed, grinning, his hands cupped behind his head.

"Aiken, Annette Kaysen." Hitch acted like he owned the place. "You already met Marie. Where's your sis? Thought I saw her."

I looked around, but Marie was not in the bedroom.

Annette shrugged and laid down on the bed next to Hitch.

Annette was skinny but at an age when rampaging breast development defied her neglect of good nutrition. She had long blond hair tied up in pigtails with rubber bands, and she wore a short skirt and pink halter-top. Annette's most striking facial feature was a bump on the ridge of her nose, a souvenir from a childhood injury. Of the two, Annette was the more feminine, less tomboy than Marie. She preferred dressing up and playing princess in a make-believe duchy. She loved the movies but could rarely afford to go. She kept a stack of out-dated movie magazines next to her bed along with posters of stars Scotch-Taped to the walls. She had studied all the Hollywood celebrities and knew details of their tenuous relationships. Annette could recite who was hot and who was not.

She leaned into and kissed Hitch on the mouth.

When Marie entered the bedroom, hairbrush in hand, Hitch and Annette had advanced from the making out stage to preliminary petting. Marie saw my petrified gape at Hitch's advancements beneath Annette's top and said, "Take a picture, why don't ya?"

Annette pulled away from Hitch and scowled at her sister. "That's my brush."

"No way. Anyways, be quiet. You'll wake Nicky Jim up, they'll be hell to pay."

The brief quarrel ended with Annette saying, "Then get out."

Marie threw the hairbrush on the floor and stared angrily at her sister. She gripped my hand and pulled me out of the room, slamming the door behind us. I followed her hasty retreat downstairs to the front porch where she slammed the screen door for further emphasis.

"Fucking bitch," she muttered and plopped herself down on the steps. I sat sheepishly next to her, close enough in hopes that we might do what I had seen in the bedroom. She wore a pair of cut-offs and a white T-shirt with the Rolling Stones sticky fingers logo. She tossed back the feathers of her brunette hair that had stuck to her face.

"So," she said. "What brings you out?" She combed her hair with the fingers of her right hand.

My mind went blank as I watched her simple feminine movement that may or may not have come naturally. For all I knew, Marie had practiced for hours in front of the mirror the many ways to drive boys nuts. How was I supposed to answer her? Should I tell her that Hitch had suggested the visit and that I had come along for the ride? Girls like Marie expected boys to act cool, to have the snappy comeback to leading questions. I knew nothing about how to play the game, which was a defect in my development that *acting cool* had been invented to hide. And so I said nothing, acting cool.

From my shirt pocket I pulled the pack of Marlboros and offered her one.

She hesitated, shook her head. "Nicky Jim. He sees me smoking, the prick'll tell my ma."

"We can sit in the Duster? Hitch's car," I suggested.

As we sat in the backseat of the car, blowing smoke through the open windows, our shoulders touched, and I gained a measure of confidence through the familiarity.

I asked, "Tell me, who's Nicky Jim?"

She sat up, her mouth open in mock astonishment. "*You* don't know Nick James Gunderson?"

"No. I don't. I'm new to town."

She leaned closer to me, and said, "I'm just messin' with you. Nicky Jim thinks he's a famous outlaw. He's nothing but a drunk and a mooch. Lives off a us and my mom."

I took a drag like a cowboy. "Famous outlaw?"

"Got out a prison, I don't know, six months ago. Mom picked him up at where she worked at the time. Tollhouse Saloon, in Strand? Anyways," Marie continued, "he's been here ever since."

"What was he in for? In prison, I mean."

Marie scratched her eyelid with the fingernail of her little finger. "Armed robbery. Drugs. He's a felon. That's his truck over there."

A battered Dodge truck, rusted out with a cracked windshield, sat parked at the side of the house.

I wanted to say, *And your mom lets him live with you?* But I didn't want to upset our equilibrium in the back of the Plymouth Duster. Marie stubbed out the cigarette and fit an arm around my waist. She looked up at me expectantly. Instead of responding with words, I kissed Marie Kaysen on the lips.

It was as though I'd thrown a mysterious switch. Marie opened her mouth and thrust her tongue into mine. She tugged on the buttons of my 501 jeans and lifted my T-shirt out of the waistband. After thirty seconds, after my delayed response, as I tried to recover from the surprise of her enthusiasm, she pulled away and gave me a puzzling look.

"What's wrong?" she said. She might as well have asked why I had not peeled off her shorts by now.

"Nothing."

I tried to kiss her more convincingly to return us to that sexual landscape we had momentarily abandoned, and it worked. With her chest heaving with quickened breath, she pulled off the sticky fingers T-shirt and in a single maneuver unsnapped her bra, keeping it on but letting the straps tumble off her shoulders. As we kissed again, my hand naturally found its way to one of her breasts.

Once again, she stopped.

"What're you doin'?"

I felt clueless, up the proverbial creek. This was a first-time event for me. Protocol must have been broken. Sitting there breathing through my mouth, I awaited further instruction.

"Kiss 'em. Don't just handle 'em," she said as she removed the bra.

Our foreplay pretty much progressed in this manner, in fits and starts, until the two of us were down to our underpants, lying side by side in the back seat of the Duster. The city of Strand and the planet disappeared from my mind along with Robin Stanley and my responsibilities back at the farm. Virgil Stanley's pointless chores and Eve's dinners served on cracked plates vanished from my mind. It felt as though I had crawled into a velvety cocoon, a secret place hidden away, where this soft, responsive creature introduced me to the most exciting thing in the world.

It was within this moment of ecstasy that we heard a man shouting.

"Get the fuck outta here!"

Seconds later, as Marie and I sat up and disentangled, Hitch opened the driver's side door and jumped in.

"Out, Marie!" Hitch said as he turned over the engine.

Somewhere in there I heard the deafening blast from a shotgun as Nicky Jim fired his weapon into the air, an exclamation point full of steel shot.

Marie grabbed her clothes and jumped out the back door. The Duster fishtailed down the gravel driveway toward the county road.

I looked back, but could not see where Marie had gone.

A skinny shirtless man with long hair, his arms covered in blue tattoos, shook a shotgun at the retreating car and swore gutturally at the top of his voice.

When we reached the road, Hitch glanced back at me. "You may wanna pull up them pants," he said, half smiling as he combed a free hand through his greasy hair.

Chapter 9

In every corner of Robin Stanley's life, my mother found deception but she had yet to put things right. Instead, she submitted to living in her in-laws' doublewide and to changing the way she did her hair to please her husband and to tolerating his outward disapproval of her eldest son. Eventually, I came to realize, for things to get better, I was going to have to take matters into my own hands. I had to take responsibility for shining light in the corners of my stepfather's lies. And so I vowed to do just that.

An opportunity arose to test my commitment a few days after Hitch and I had visited the Kaysen sisters. In the late evening, I overheard Robin Stanley and my mom arguing in the kitchen.

Our day had passed as most days on the farm passed, in peaceful tedium. I was still on restriction, which kept my movements to and from school to a minimum of social contact. Mom taught at the middle school, as a substitute, more or less on a permanent basis, and Dr. Robin Stanley's optometry business continued its descent toward bankruptcy. As though coming in relief to our dismal lives, in early December, Strand enjoyed what the locals called a Chinook. Prevailing westerlies blew warm tropical air off the Pacific. The wind held the fragrance of gardenias. As applied to this December wind, "Chinook" was a misnomer. Traditional Chinooks were named in Canada. They are warm, dry southwest winds off the Rocky Mountains. In the advent of our Christmas season, before temperatures iced up the standing water or built snowdrifts like cold hatred against the doublewide, our Chinook was like a warm kiss on a block of ice. Or a brief respite before serious winter set in.

On this night as I was returning from brushing my teeth, on my way to Jesse's and my bedroom, I overheard my mother say, "…what on Earth do you expect me to do, Robin?"

I sensed an argument in the air for the forced whisper of their voices. They had intended to keep the dispute to themselves, but the anger in my mother's voice did away with all sense of privacy in that small house. I saw the fight as raw material for gossip to include in a letter to my dad, as maybe a way to encourage him to save my mother—and to save me—from Robin Stanley.

"Karin, it's just for a little while longer. Yes, I know. I should've told them. But we needed the collateral. How else was I going to open my business?"

"But to use the farm, I don't know. I just don't think that's right. You've got to tell them."

"Look," Robin Stanley said. "In six months—"

"*Six months?*"

"In six months or less...*six months or less*, I'll have the loan paid off. My folks'll be none the wiser. They won't even know about it, okay? Just be patient."

"Be patient!"

"Please, Karin, keep your voice down."

"Don't tell me to keep my voice down. I have been *more* than patient. I have put up with living in this, this motor home for as long as I can stand it. Don't tell me to be patient. *Don't you dare.*" Her Oklahoma accent was showing through in frustration.

I stood in the shadows near my stepfather's desk, hidden from the flood of light pouring through the open kitchen door. For a few seconds, as they lowered their voices even further, I could not make out what was said until Robin Stanley mentioned something that further provoked my mother.

"You can*not* expect me to live here another six months. Having to walk between your folks' chairs to go to bed? Do you even know what kind of shame I feel every night?"

Her words came just short of shouting, and I half expected Virgil and Eve Stanley to stir from their bedroom to investigate the ruckus. Nothing of the kind happened. Their argument would remain secret, except from me.

"Then tell me something, Karin. Tell me something." Robin Stanley's voice was edged by a brittle whine. "This one-legged teacher of yours, this Mr. Phelan—"

"Mr. Phelan got me my job. And I need that job."

"Well, I think people at church are beginning to talk."

"It's the only steady income…what on Earth are you saying? What people at church?"

"That's right, that's right," Robin said, his voice rising. "Look, it's not your fault. You have no idea. Small towns are notorious for this kind of thing. You can't break wind without everyone talking about it. I'm just saying, for your own reputation, you're spending far too much time with this *Mr. Phelan.*"

"I am not spending time…who would say such a thing?"

"Please, keep your voice down."

"Who would say such a thing? Who told you this?"

I stepped cautiously through the dark to improve my position near the kitchen door.

"Oja Palmquist."

"The pharmacist?" my mother said.

"He saw you and that man having coffee, over at the Tollhouse."

"It was a cup of coffee, Robin. Not some kind of liaison. Are you accusing me of having an affair, because if you—"

"*No!* No, of course not."

Robin's voice sounded like the voice of reason. I could tell he was afraid of provoking my mother any further.

"This has nothing to do with me," Robin Stanley said.

I knew it had everything to do with Robin Stanley, and I hoped my mother's skills of perception recognized her husband's deceit as easily as my ears had.

"You simply cannot go traipsing around town on the arm of another man, Karin."

"I am not…how can you say such a thing?"

"People get the wrong idea."

"Traipsing around town? Do not insult me."

"I'm saying this for your own good."

"Do *not* insult me!"

The legs on the wooden chair ached against the linoleum floor as my mother stood abruptly. She walked angrily across the living room but stopped when she noticed something moving in the dark. If Robin Stanley's own rampant jealousy were not enough, my eavesdropping proved the ultimate betrayal of her privacy. As I was about to explain how sorry I was, she seemed to come to a decision in her mind, and she continued across the room to their bedroom. As the door shut, I wondered if she had taken into account my devotion when gauged against her husband's dishonesty and petty manipulations.

When Robin Stanley walked through the door, he saw me cast like a half moon in the kitchen light. "What is this? More of your sneaking around behind my back?"

I said nothing. I ought to have threatened the bastard with recrimination and exposure of his drawer full of pornography should he ever upset my mother again. But I said nothing. I drew back to the shadows in a cowardly retreat to my room.

*   *   *

The next morning, when I mentioned at breakfast that I would be assisting my teacher that evening at the Amateur Astronomy Club fieldtrip, Robin Stanley said, "What? With that Mr. Phelan?"

"It's an academic activity, Robin."

"I forbid you to go."

"I have to go."

My stepfather shook his head while he slurped up his scrambled eggs.

In the morning, the kitchen was a beehive of activity. Eve Stanley stood at the stove to work a rasher of bacon in a skillet, oblivious as usual to our family dynamic. Virgil sat behind a newspaper, raised like a rampart to the battlefield at the table. Whether they chose to ignore the root cause of our bickering or were too simpleminded to get a handle on it, I cannot say. The Stanley's were the sort of people who had given up on life long before reaching middle age. Only the shells of their former lives remained. They were like holograms that went through the routine of daily living, completing chores by rote. They would continue to go through the motions until one day at breakfast we would look up and discover them gone. This could hardly be considered a great loss of two people who were never really *there* in the first place.

"I'll flunk the class if I don't go." I said this, knowing full well that Robin Stanley had no clue whether or not I was a member of Mr. Phelan's physical science class.

My stepfather shook his head. Worry engraved the underside of his eyes.

"I have to go," I said in quiet defiance, glancing up at my mother as she entered the kitchen for the first time that morning. A heavy use of eyeliner failed to conceal that she had been crying at her vanity table.

Jesse sat in his highchair and nibbled at a square of toast while splashing his free hand in a "bowl a stupid," his reference to *cereal*, a word his tongue had trouble forming. The highchair was too small for his frame, but it confined him to a corner of the kitchen where Eve Stanley could more easily sweep up his breakfast debris.

Taking a seat at the table, my mother said in a soft Oklahoma drawl, "What's this all about, Danny?" A chilly distance seemed established between her and my stepfather.

"You're not going," Robin said. "If I have to, I'll call your *teacher* myself and give him a piece of my mind."

"You can't do that, Robin." I could hardly keep from grinning at the absurdity of Robin Stanley standing up to anyone, even a one-legged science teacher.

"Danny, would you tell me, please, what is going on?"

"Stargazing…" I began to tell my mother.

"Stars, Dammy," Jesse exclaimed.

"That's right, Jesse. Stars." I explained the circumstances to my mother and stretched the truth to my advantage. I said that I was required to attend Mr. Phelan's astronomy excursion to Mt. Hood. I went so far as to say where we would rendezvous, how many students and parents had signed up for the event, and what my duties were. "I basically help carry the equipment. I have to go."

"Are parents invited as well?" she asked.

I looked at Robin Stanley. "Sure."

"Well, then, I'll be joining you."

Here was a schism, a break in the allegiance between my mother and Robin Stanley in the course of our civil war, the one fought against my willfulness. My mother had more or less affirmed her realignment to my side of the conflict by defying her husband's wishes. Robin Stanley's sense of shock was palpable. The loose skin of his pocked cheek trembled as he tried to cover the disappointment in his wife's decision to join me—and Mr. Phelan—at our Amateur Astronomy Club outing. Neither my mother nor her husband argued this point, but any observer worth half their salt could feel the tension in the air. Not even my brother's burping broke the spell of uneasiness that was descending on our household like the Four Horsemen of the Apocalypse.

Finally, my mother said, "It is all right if I come along? Tonight, I mean?"

"Sure. Of course. It'll be great, Mom."

*   *   *

At five o'clock, sixteen of us took a yellow bus from the school parking lot to Wildwood Park on the mountain. My mother sat next to Mr. Phelan in the seat behind the driver. I sat alone with the equipment in the back while the other kids paired up. I could not keep from staring at Mr. Phelan and my mom. Although I sat too far back in the bus to hear what they were saying, I imagined that they liked one another. Once, when my mother laughed at something Mr. Phelan had said, I wished that the church gossip were true, that my mother and my teacher were in the grips of an affair. At our rendezvous point in the park, where we met up with people who had driven their own cars, I conscientiously helped set up the equipment to impress my mother. She swelled with pride. I could sense it. Eventually, after tapping the coordinates into the hand controller, Mr. Phelan explained what we were about to see. I was too distracted to listen. Instead, I scanned the faces of huddled students and parents for Marie Kaysen. She didn't show up this night, to my disappointment.

Later in the evening, when I grew bored by the routine of kids and their parents taking turns at the telescope, I walked off by myself. Mr. Phelan must have noticed that I wandered off. He soon followed to make sure I didn't get lost in the woods.

In a clearing, he called out to me. "Danny, you all right?"

I glanced back. He was plainly having difficulty walking through the brush with his cane. Beyond him, I saw silhouettes of the amateur astronomers. "No, I'm fine," I said.

Mr. Phelan limped up to me. "Hold up."

We walked off, away from the voices in the dark, closer to the towering perspective of trees whose black branches reached upwards. Between the supplicating fir and the specter of the galaxy, I felt insignificantly small. A burst of starlight soared over us like frozen fireworks. The night is framed as a transcendent moment in my life.

"Amazing, isn't it?" he said.

I shook my head the way people do when overwhelmed by the profound. "You don't see the night sky like this. In the city, I mean."

"Again, Edison's invention washes out most of what you see here."

Neither of us spoke for a while. I tried to make sense of it, the vast richness of space, giving birth to all those "suns." And the unimaginable distances! What did the wretched plight of Daniel Farrington Aiken, Jr., matter when compared to cosmic indifference? How should my troubles measure up against the likes of Jupiter?

"Mr. Phelan? Can I ask you something? Why'd you pick me, you know, for your astronomy assistant?"

He seemed taken aback by my question. "Well...honestly? You were new to Strand. I figured you'd fallen in with a bad crowd. Thought I might try to, I don't know, save you, I guess." He laughed.

"Hitch isn't such a bad kid," I said.

"Don't get me wrong. Hitch McDonough isn't a bad guy, you're right. But Larry Edwards and Troy Weber?" Even in the dark, I could see Mr. Phelan's exaggerated gesture. "No, you're better off spending your time here than getting into trouble, don't you think?"

"Sure," I said.

We fell into an uncomfortable silence for a time. A cold breeze blew strands of Mr. Phelan's hair, and he combed them back with the palm of his hand.

"At my alma mater," he said, "your intellectual sophistication was measured by how well you accepted the Earth's irrelevance in the universe. Do you know what I mean by that? Good. You can see why. On the surface of it, I mean." He gestured casually at the sky.

When I didn't respond, he continued in a different vein. "Do you know the story of Copernicus?"

I had read something about Copernicus in a library book on astronomy. "He…I think, he changed everyone's thinking about astronomy?"

"Cosmology, actually. Copernicus broke the rules. He went against the Church at the time, saying the Earth was not the center of the universe, but a planet among a brotherhood of planets. He was the first to say that we orbited the Sun. They nearly killed him for it. Ultimately, his view was accepted but not until long after he was dead. It changed our orientation, how we see the universe. How we see ourselves in it.

"But now science has shriveled us to the size of a pea, I'm afraid. They've made the Earth a speck of dust in all this. Before Copernicus, we were the center of everything. Now, our solar system is one of billions." He chuckled. "To make matters worse, we're in a backwater, near the edge of an outward spiral arm of an average-sized galaxy among *billions and billions* of galaxies."

I laughed at Mr. Phelan's impersonation of Carl Sagan, the host of the television show on PBS.

"Like that Monty Python song," I said.

Knowing it, he sang a verse.

Just remember that you're standing on a planet that's evolving
And revolving at 900 miles an hour
It's orbiting at 19 miles a second
So it's reckoned
A sun that is the source of all our power….

We laughed.

"It makes me feel, I don't know," I said. "Makes everything seem stupid or something."

"Meaningless?"

I nodded in the dark.

"Well, there are two perspectives of this, I suppose. We can view life as just a flash of consciousness in an uncaring world. Or we can see life as meaningful, with a purpose. Knowledge will help you sort out which perspective to choose. Education, Danny. That's the key."

One of the students called Mr. Phelan's name, asking for help.

"Be there in a minute," he called back. Turning to me, he said, "In any of your math classes, have they taught you about logarithms yet?"

"Next year."

"Well, humans come out somewhere in the middle on a logarithmic scale. This scale measures the smallest things imaginable. Now compare that to the distance from where we're standing (he pointed) to the edge of the universe. Do you understand what I'm saying? Humans fit somewhere in the middle of these two measurements, between the nearly infinite and the infinitesimal."

"Really?"

I found what he had said difficult to understand and hard to believe. I wondered if Mr. Phelan were making things up to make me feel better, to feel less disheartened.

"I don't think it's a fluke that human beings evolved as they have. Earth, it's exactly in the right place, the perfect distance and attitude in space to support life. Venus is too hot, Mars too cold. And the solar system itself, if it were any closer, say, to the center of the Milky Way, the Earth would have been bombarded by deadly gamma rays. This would make the likelihood for life well impossible. And don't get me started on Jupiter. Without it, comets and meteorites would have bombarded Earth long ago. Without Jupiter, you wouldn't be standing here. Earth would be nothing but rubble."

I had heard enough of Robin Stanley's illogical take on "intelligent design." To hear more about it from Mr. Phelan would overturn my confidence. I wondered if he and my stepfather were cut from the same pious cloth. Had I completely misread the teacher? Was Mr. Phelan an evangelical?

"You're saying God did this and put Jupiter where it is. On what day was that in Genesis?" I asked.

"No. No. Don't take me the wrong way. I'm not saying that." Mr. Phelan sounded a little irritated that I had misunderstood. "How you see yourself in relation to the universe is a matter of personal choice. Your religious view, if you will, is different from what I'm talking about."

"I don't have a religious view," I said close to a whisper, but loud enough for him to hear me.

"I'm saying," he continued, "that on some level, the data suggest the existence of human beings isn't a fluke. It is as though we were *made* for the universe, and it for us."

The thought crossed my mind that, had any of Mr. Phelan's coincidences been different, he and I—and the rest of humanity— would not be standing in the dark, mulling over the miraculous accident of life.

"Copernicus was more right than he knew. The Earth is not the center of anything, let alone the universe. But also, when you look at science, really *look* at it, it teaches us that the sheer fact of our lives, on this planet, at this time and place, is a miracle." He put a hand on my shoulder. "Life is not something to waste, Danny. It's mystical and poetic. All it takes to go beyond one's assumptions...or narrow mindedness...is to seek answers for yourself. None of the answers are simple, but they are elemental." As he turned away, he said as an afterthought, "I have found no deeper meaning in my own life than reflecting on the nature of existence in the presence of starlight."

Mr. Phelan returned to the hobby astronomers and to my mother who smiled broadly at his approach.

Chapter 10

During Christmas break a savior came into my life in the shape of a letter from my dad. The letter threatened a child custody lawsuit should my mother not return Jesse and me to California. The U.S. Postal Service delivered the certified mail on my birthday. It was by far the best present I have ever received.

At the kitchen table, while I opened gifts and while Eve Stanley put the final touches to a homemade angel food cake, Robin Stanley leaned against the wall. He looked like he wanted to be somewhere else. He had separated himself from the celebration as an indifferent observer, as a spectator to the festivities. He sipped black coffee and peered at me over the rim of the mug, planning for, as I imagined, my departure to a military academy come January, anything to divide me from my mother.

My mother snapped pictures with a disposable camera of me opening my presents and of Jesse eating Cheerios. Virgil Stanley chose not to attend the tradition of counting birthday candles and presenting gifts. Instead, after dinner, he retreated outside to string Christmas lights on the eaves of the doublewide. To my way of thinking, this was not unlike dressing up a corpse.

While Eve frosted the cake, my mother handed a letter to me with the envelope torn open. It was from my father. Of all the promises inside the envelope, which my mother and stepfather had already opened and read, I expected a check made out to me. Perhaps a brief note from San Francisco wishing a happy birthday. The last thing I expected was a legal document.

I read it and could barely hide from Robin Stanley my sense of surprise. I turned to Mom. "What's this mean, that we get to go home?"

"No," Robin Stanley snapped. It was his first word spoken to me all night.

"But Dad says he'll sue," I said to my mother. "We *have* to go, right?" I scanned the letter for the specific language. I found it awkward to read the legalese, wondering why lawyers just couldn't write Standard English. "Something about the offending second party...?"

Robin Stanley shouted. "Don't you even *think* I'm going let that *shyster* take you boys!"

My ears rang, and just as suddenly, the kitchen was thrown over to a charged stillness. Eve Stanley mumbled her son's name, and I glanced at my mother.

Robin Stanley regained his composure and said in a more controlled tone of voice, "Your mother...your mother and I have discussed it. You're not going anywhere."

"Robin..." my mother began.

He shut her up with a wave of the hand. His eyes darkened as he set his teeth and worked his jaw muscles. His mouth tightened as it usually did when he disapproved of something.

"Not on your life. He doesn't know who he's *dealing* with."

Doesn't know who he's dealing with? I was tempted to remind him point-blank that my dad was a high-powered attorney with political connections. What was a failed small-town optometrist when measured against the weight of Daniel Farrington Aiken, Esq., attorney-at-law?

"Robin, we don't have the money to pay for a lawyer."

Eve Stanley, generally oblivious to our family arguments, was serving us helpings of cake and doling out flatware. She registered surprise when her son slammed his coffee cup against the kitchen counter.

Black coffee erupted from the mug, splashing Jesse in the highchair.

I looked from my mother to Jesse and back to my mother, shocked by this outburst. Eve Stanley, unused to her son's display of emotion, returned to the counter with the plates and picked up a dishrag to wipe up the spilled coffee. She acted as though what mattered was not the resolution of a quarrel but the tidying up an unclean kitchen.

"Robin—"

"Don't start with me, Karin." Robin Stanley's voice quavered and his eye twitched. "Don't you *dare* imply I can't provide for my family. Don't you *dare!*"

"I'm not—"

He raised an index finger and waggled it, his lips pressed tightly, quivering as though he was about to burst with tears. The rise of tension in his body seemed to exhaust Robin Stanley and drain him of any further things to say. Instead, he lowered his arm and took a breath of defeat. And then he walked out of the kitchen, for the bedroom. We sat in stunned silence when we heard the close of the door latch.

The lenses of my mother's eyes blurred with tears as she struggled to regain control over her emotions. She was determined not to let her husband's blunt pride get the best of her.

Jesse whimpered softly. I folded my father's letter and replaced it carefully in the envelope.

Eve Stanley put a piece of cake before me on the table and said, "Happy birthday, Danny. Many happy returns."

*   *   *

My father's letter plunged Robin Stanley's relationship with my mother into crisis. Before this, had my stepfather not felt as though he were drowning under the weight of financial difficulties, my father's challenge to his authority now threatened to sink him. Fear of losing control of his world changed my stepfather's behavior. He foreswore all pretense of hiding an addiction to cigarettes, and ended up smoking openly on the back porch, at least during the few hours he was at home. On most mornings, he was up and out of the house before any of us stirred, wishing, I would imagine, to retreat to the relative peace of his optometry office. On a few occasions around suppertime, he would call to say that he had to work late. When he eventually returned home, he sat at his desk to study the Bible well into the night to avoid my mother. When she asked, "What's wrong, Robin? Can we please talk about this?" he replied that nothing was wrong, everything was fine. He spoke in monosyllables, but his gestures toward me spoke volumes. Although nothing was said out in the open, clearly he blamed me for the letter from my father. Surely, he must have kept an account of my father's and my correspondence. To Robin Stanley's way of thinking, had I not written the letters to Dad, perhaps my father would not have been provoked into threatening a lawsuit. But no more threats were made by Robin Stanley to send me to an Idaho military school. There was no more probation. The endless lists of chores disappeared from beneath the magnet on the refrigerator. In fact, the letter had the effect of liberating me from his totalitarian authority. He seemed afraid to confront me, uneasy with the idea of upsetting the fragile stability we had established. He acted as though the material world were against him. He was reluctant to act for fear that his house of cards would collapse.

With my stepfather disabled and out of the way, I was free to live life on my own terms. Over the Christmas break, Marie Kaysen and I often saw each other after she got off work at the DQ. Without access to a car or cash to go out on a bona fide date, we walked for hours hand in hand, crisscrossing town, pausing to kiss near the play structure in Strand's only park near the reservoir. On most evenings we restricted our ventures to the downtown area, sometimes hanging out at the library until her mom picked her up at ten o'clock.

At one time Hitch joined us, and we three ended up at the park reservoir to smoke Marlboros and share a pint of filched Wild Turkey. Hitch built a trash fire in a picnic shelter barbecue pit, and as we huddled around, snow flurries drifted into the firelight. After a few weeks of depression, my friend's mood had improved. He bragged about how often he was seeing Marie's sister, Annette. Hitch rarely admitted to having feelings for anyone, but that night, between taking long draws of the Wild Turkey, he spoke freely. He seemed as enlivened by the liquor as he was by confessing his affection for Annette. "She's great," he said. "Can't believe she's been right under my nose this whole time."

"You hated her in middle school," Marie reminded him.

Wiping his lips, he laughed. "I gotta say, even back then, I kinda liked her. She, I don't know…I was shy round her. She intimated me, what do you call it?"

"Intimidated you?" I spoke too quickly, wincing at the idea of saying out loud that Hitch was afraid of girls, afraid of *anything*. I held my breath.

He squinted at me through cigarette smoke as if to say that I had overstated the obvious and was trespassing a boundary. *Intimidated* was clearly the right word said at the wrong time. To watch my friend's mood swings was like riding a roller coaster blind, never knowing how to predict or anticipate a steep decline. Finally, he handed the pint to Marie, but she refused.

From the shirt pocket of her Dairy Queen uniform she pulled out a joint.

"Now you talkin'," Hitch said, his mania once again brightening suddenly. Balancing the liquor bottle on the edge of the barbecue pit, he dug into his pants for the Zippo.

I had smoked weed before with my San Francisco friends, at parties, on the loose in Golden Gate Park, but I was not prepared for the muscle of this particular variety. Marijuana usually left me dry-mouthed, giggly, and momentarily disoriented but never so impaired that I couldn't speak. I had never been so stoned that paranoia crept into every thought.

After passing it back and forth with the common utterance of "'ere," we whittled it down to a roach. In the end, I staggered backwards and flopped down on the concrete edge of the pit.

"You okay, Danny Boy?" Hitch said, laughing so hard he coughed.

"Shit."

Marie reached out her hand. "I'll take that swig now."

Her inhibitions melted away under the influence, whereas I felt crippled by self-consciousness. Marie hugged the pint of Wild Turkey between her breasts and swayed to music playing in her mind. Hitch stared at her, fascinated by her sensuality in the firelight. Snowflakes tumbled out of the black sky and into the fire, vanishing in the heat. Marie opened her eyes and smiled modestly when Hitch caught her in a more or less private moment. She reached out and placed her palm against his cheek, and the bile of jealousy rose inside me. Hitch took her hand and pulled the girl to him. I thought that he might have expected Marie to kiss him or perform sexual favors as they embraced and danced closer to the flames, the pint of Wild Turkey dangling from Marie's hand, glinting in the firelight. All manner of resentful thoughts and fears passed through me in that instant. My stomach churned from the liquor, and blood pressure built up behind my eyeballs. Over the past two weeks, I had come to trust in the exclusivity of my relationship with Marie. She was my girlfriend and off limits to other guys. Hitch was taking undo advantage, taking advantage of vulnerability as he always did, stealing what was not his. It wasn't fair. Something had to be done to stop him.

I was on my feet, waiting for the dizziness to pass before I confronted him, when Marie awoke from her reverie and struggled against Hitch.

She managed to pull away.

"What gives?" Hitch said.

Marie shook her head. "I don't want to end up like my sis."

She said it so offhandedly that neither Hitch nor I took her meaning right away.

Hitch turned to me. "What you suppose she means by that?"

Visions of their shameless affection, real or imagined, still burned in my mind, and I was just beginning to resolve the paranoia that had pushed me to confront them. I had imagined the whole thing. Their release seemed to disarm any bad feelings that I had had. I must have looked pale and moonstruck in the firelight, motivated by the failed inertia of my jealousy.

Marie unscrewed the pint, and brought it to her lips. She swallowed. "You don't even know what's going on, do you?"

"Guess not. You gonna tell me?" Hitch said, hands outstretched, smiling broadly.

"My sister," Marie said, her head cocked to the side. "She's pregnant."

The word *pregnant* sucked the party mood right out of us. This was not a word easily spoken by any sexually active teenager, not without regret and anxiety. I watched Hitch as he leaned against the fire pit. The word itself was like a pile of bricks weighing down on him.

"She's pregnant with your kid."

"What're you saying, Marie?" I said. My tongue felt two sizes too big for my mouth and my voice sounded spoken by someone else.

"What you think she's saying, dickhead." Hitch shot me a look. His eyes were lost under a profound brow. The dark side of his nature had returned. "How do you know it's mine?" He took a step toward Marie. It was a posture he took when confronting people he meant to hurt, and it disturbed me that he took this attitude with my girlfriend. "Where's the proof?"

"You fucked her, didn't you?" she said.

"Yeah. A bunch a times. So what? I use protection, asswipe."

"That's not what she says. Says it was your *first time*. Says you were a virgin."

"Bullshit. I don't care what Annette says." Hitch blew off a lungful of tension. "Look, your sister sleeps with tons of guys. For all I know, she fucks your mother's boyfriend—"

"Nicky Jim knows all about it. And he's gunning for you. He's gonna kill you, he catches you."

"Whatever," Hitch said. The snowfall had lessened but still a few renegade flakes floated between us. "How does she know it's mine?"

Marie shook her head. "Are you gonna do the right thing?"

"The right thing? What, and marry her? That what you mean?" When Marie did not reply, Hitch said, "You're stupid, you know that? You're fucking stupid, both a you girls."

Marie's sense of betrayal and anger rose up inside her and she hurled the pint of Wild Turkey into the fire. The bottle shattered and the flames brightened briefly, consuming the last of the liquor.

She turned to leave. "Fuck you, Hitch," she said and walked away into the dark.

"Same to you, asswipe."

"Marie...?" I said hesitantly, taking a step forward, too stoned to decide how to respond exactly.

"Go fuck yourself, Danny," she said, her voice coming to me from out of the night.

*   *   *

If Hitch McDonough was my only friend in all of Oregon, Marie Kaysen was the only girl I knew in Strand. They were my life at the moment, the only people I could trust and confide in. I couldn't lose their friendship, not now, not when Robin Stanley was in retreat and I was left in a state of perfect freedom. I had made such plans. I figured, at some point, Marie would be my first one. We had nearly done it several times already but we had held back. Marie wasn't "saving" herself, she told me, but she wanted the first time to be in a bed, not on a park bench or in the back of a Plymouth Duster. I honored her wish and did so because of the promise it held. Being that close to something you dreamed about consummating but were denied was like seeing the largest trout in the brook forever beyond the hook of your fishing line.

On Saturday morning, still feeling some of the effects from Friday night in the park, I decided to pay a visit to Marie at the Dairy Queen. I wanted to patch things up. "Maybe if I tell her I love her," I thought out loud to myself as I walked from the Stanley farm into town. Marie worked on Saturdays. When I walked in, I saw her standing behind the counter, taking orders. Her face was a study in stoicism until she recognized me. She cocked her head to one side and pursed her lips. It was a gesture meant to tell me where to stick it.

I waited in line behind a family from out of state. I knew they were from out of state because they talked like film actors in movies filmed in New York City. All of their "r's" were softened into "ahs." I waited patiently for my turn, watching Marie work efficiently to fill their trays with burgers and shakes.

When it was my turn, Marie didn't say hello or even acknowledge that we were boyfriend and girlfriend. She just said, "What do you want?"

I wanted to reach out and touch her hand. I wanted to tell her that I was awfully sorry about last night. I wanted to ask her to forgive me for whatever it was she was so mad about. But she took a step backwards and crossed her arms in a defiant pose.

"Can you forgive me?" I said.

When she didn't respond, I leaned forward on the counter. "Look, can't we just start over," I said. "You know, go back to hanging out and stuff?"

It was at this exact moment that I was struck down by a searing pain radiating in my ear and through my head.

The pain drove me to the floor. Somebody was screaming. It was me.

"Your name Aiken?"

The voice of a man came filtered through the pain.

I heard Marie say, "Don't hurt him, Nicky Jim."

I managed to squint up at the man who was twisting my ear as though determined to twist it completely off. Nicky Jim towered over me in a kind of excruciating haze. The only thing I saw clearly was the filth that crusted the heel of his motorcycle boots.

"You come near Marie again and I'll cut your throat," he said. "You understand me, boy?"

I nodded yes. I just wanted the pain to stop.

"I didn't hear you," said the voice.

"Okay. Okay," I pleaded.

The pain stopped, leaving a residue of tender tissue and the sound of blood thrashing in my ear.

I looked up to see Nicky Jim push through the door for the parking lot. The store manager had come out from behind the counter to stop the abuse, to stop the man from hurting the customer, but he hesitated when Nicky Jim turned halfway around and shot him a look. "You don't wanna mess with me," he said. The manager threatened to call the cops, but by then Nicky Jim was in his truck. The tires squealed as he raced through the parking lot.

Marie was crying on the shoulders of some kid, a senior that I recognized from high school. Her eyes were puffy but they spoke volumes when we looked at each other. It was over between us. It was over not because Nicky Jim had threatened me, but just because it was over between us. The opportunity had passed me by, and like a lot of things in my life back then, I was forced to accept defeat. I was the California boy who didn't belong, who didn't fit in. It was about time, I thought to myself as I nursed my ear, that I accept my fate.

*   *   *

Three days later, my life took an entirely new direction.

When I look back on those days, as I evaluate what happened, the night Eve Stanley called me into the kitchen to answer the phone was a dividing line in my life. It strikes me as odd that so innocuous a thing as a telephone call can herald a reversal of fortune.

The promise of the call had initially given me grand hopes for reconciliation with my girlfriend, perhaps a liaison in her bedroom as I had so often fantasized. I ran to the kitchen and picked up the phone.

"Marie?" I answered.

"Danny Boy," a male said. "It's Hitch."

I fought to conceal the disappointment in my voice by pumping up my enthusiasm, but it came across as phony. "Hey, what's up?"

"You got a cold or something? You sound stupid."

"Surprised is all."

"Why?"

"Because you never call."

"I hate the phone," he said flatly. "I need you to get over here. Somethin' we gotta discuss."

"It's past eight." I shaped my hand in a cone over the mouthpiece to keep what I had to say from Eve Stanley. "They won't let me come over, not now. I can't."

"Fuck you, man." For the first time in our brief friendship, he sounded weak, desperate. "I'd do it for *you* in a heartbeat. I ain't asking much. Jesus! You gotta help me out here."

"What's wrong, dear? Everything all right?" Eve Stanley asked, keeping busy at the kitchen sink.

I covered the handset and faced her. "Sure, yeah, everything's fine. It's a friend. Calling about some homework." I smiled at her, and Eve Stanley returned to her task.

"Hitch?" I said.

"I'm still here, dude."

"I'd like to help you out, but…you know how they are."

"I don't wanna hear your chickenshit. I'll pick you up. The bottom of your driveway. Be there in thirty minutes."

There was no dissuading him. After he hung up, I listened to the dial tone before replacing the handset. It had the sound of finality.

*   *   *

The dilemma I faced was to meet up with Hitch by deceiving Robin Stanley and my mother. It was one of those rare times when my stepfather was home. Why had he picked this, of all nights, to come home for supper? Earlier in the evening, the tension between my stepfather and mother had undergone a change. I caught them in the kitchen, hugging one another. He was apologizing in their embrace with kind soft words that were shed like scales from the monster of their dispute.

Now, after hanging up the phone, as I stood in the kitchen, frenzied thoughts nagged me. I could hear Pat Robertson praying for donations with his customary number to call at the bottom of the screen while Robin Stanley and my mother sat in the recliners in front of the television. They were obstacles to my escape that night. My situation demanded a level of dishonesty that I had yet to pull off. Back in my bedroom, I slipped on work gloves, a Levi jacket, and a baseball cap. It was a costume as a cover for farm duties. As I passed through the living room, Robin Stanley glanced up from the *700 Club* and said, "Where do you think you're going?"

"I have some things I forgot to do. Out in the barn."

"Daniel?" My mother checked the time on her wristwatch to allow for the lateness of the hour. My brother slept in her lap, his arms and legs hanging like a rag doll over the recliner. Jesse was at that stage in life when he wished to prolong the special relationship between mother and child, and not give up his infancy. "Who was that on the phone?" she asked.

"A kid from school. Stayed home sick today." When my mother said nothing, I continued. "He broke his leg mountain climbing."

"*Mountain climbing?*" Robin Stanley said incredulously. "Where? In winter?"

I swallowed. When I resorted to lies, I usually gave too much information. It was like the condemned who tied their own noose on the gallows. "I don't know, but his leg's broken. Anyway, he needed the geometry homework assignment."

"So, where are you going?"

"Out in the barn," I said.

Suspecting a ruse, Robin Stanley asked, "To do what, exactly?"

I was not hard pressed to name a chore that I had not completed to his satisfaction. "I got the time—"

"*Have* the time," my mother corrected. She worried that Oregon had corrupted my grammar.

"I have the time. Thought I'd get to those raspberry crates. Clean 'em up for sale. My homework's done." I shrugged as though to imply, if they didn't want me to finish my chores I could always go back to my room and listen to music and sulk.

Robin Stanley's expression changed from distrust to pleasant surprise. I could tell what he was thinking, that all the discipline and "tough love" were paying off in a positive change in my behavior.

"Hey, Dammy," Jesse whispered, raising his head off my mother's breast.

"Like we talked about, Robin," I said, feigning a sincere look with eyes as clear as creek water.

"Good. That's good," he said.

He returned his attention to the religious program. He reached over to pat my mother's knee. As I stepped through the front door, I heard him say, "Well, looks like he's coming around. Just like you said he would."

After receiving my father's letter, after arguing in the kitchen, it had only taken them ten days to bridge the gap. It meant my freedom was under threat by this new realignment, by my mother's restored faith in her husband. The life that I had briefly lived on my own terms seemed like a Chinook in winter. As I walked past the glow of the Christmas lights strung across the doublewide, my mind worried at the edges of this change of circumstances. The truce between my mother and Robin Stanley threatened to return me to a world of hurt. How would I explain my absence should either of them come looking for me in the barn?

Chapter 11

The Plymouth Duster waited in the dark with the headlights off. The motor was running, exhaling exhaust like something mythic at the bottom of the driveway. When Hitch saw me, he flashed the lights twice. I opened the passenger door and slipped in.

"You're late," he said.

From the passenger seat I stared straight ahead. For the moment neither of us spoke. Hitch had yet to explain why it was so urgent that we meet and why I had to sneak out of the house. He feathered the accelerator in a nervous tick, and the dashboard lights brightened and the Duster convulsed from the torque. His toe tapped out an uneasy rhythm, something to do to fill the time as we delayed whatever it was we were about to do.

"What happened to your ear?" he asked.

I shook my head, not wanting to talk about it.

"Why you wearin' gloves?"

I glanced at him. His eyes appeared red like pig's eyes in the dashboard glow. I removed the gloves. "They're my disguise. Why am I here?"

"You'll see." Hitch banged the Duster into gear, and we fishtailed down the road. I worried that Robin Stanley would have heard the squealing tires and put two and two together.

"Where're we headed?" I said, shouting above the whine of the engine.

"Annette…" he began. His voice didn't crack necessarily, not as a lesser mortal's would have under the circumstances, but there were hints that suggested he was worried about his girlfriend. "She's been—"

"Yeah, I know," I said brusquely. "She's pregnant."

"No, you dumb fuck." Hitch wore a white T-shirt, a size too small for his muscular frame, and when he swore at me, I saw the cuts in his forearms flex like block and tackle. "It's that asshole, Nicky Jim."

Without even slowing down at the stop sign where the county road joined the highway, Hitch screeched around the corner on the Plymouth's bad tires. Terrified by the sway of the car on worn-out shocks, I clutched the dashboard. In the side mirror, I saw a plume of sparks where the old chassis scraped the asphalt.

"You wanna slow down?" I howled.

My caution only served to push Hitch to go even faster. At a rise in the road, the Duster and pavement parted company for a fraction of a second. An approaching car whipped past, the horn sounding a warning in a Doppler curve.

"Jesus, Hitch. Slow down!"

We came to a stop at an intersection where my breathing matched the panting motor of the Plymouth. I let go of the dashboard and leaned back against the bench, afraid of what my friend would do next.

"You gonna tell me what's going on?" I asked.

He turned to face me. "Nicky Jim's been doin' stuff to Annette."

"Stuff?" I squinted through uncertainty, hesitant to say what I thought he'd meant for fear he might hit me or crash the automobile into the trees at the side of the road. "You mean, like, molesting her?"

He slammed his foot on the accelerator, and we shot into a line of traffic behind three cars and a pickup truck, forcing us, thank God, to go more slowly.

"So," I said, the moisture in my mouth having dried up. "We're headed to Dover. To Annette and Marie Kaysen's?"

"Pay a little visit to Nicky Jim."

"Hitch," I said. "Remember what Marie said? He's gunning for you."

"Yeah. So what?"

He tipped back to pull something from the waistband of his jeans. It was a blue-black revolver, glistening with gun oil.

The sight of it robbed me of hope.

"I don't want any part in this."

His posture turned from coolness to a sudden rage. He pulled the Duster to the shoulder and slammed on the brakes, grinding the gravel beneath the tires. Dust clouded through his open window and settled on the bench between us. Hitch reached across and pushed open the passenger door. "Why don't you get the fuck out, you chickenshit?"

I winced when I thought he might hit me.

"Get the fuck out!"

"Look." I swallowed. "Don't do this, okay? You can't do this. You're not thinking straight."

"What, you think I'm gonna off the dude?" Hitch laughed in that mean way he had. "You think I'm *that* stupid? Spend my life in some prison 'cuz a that motherfucker?"

I shook my head. "No, I don't."

"Good."

He roughly reached across and gripped the door handle, yanked it shut. We sat staring at one another momentarily. My eyes and his were like opposing magnets in a dangerous polarity.

"I ain't gonna shoot Nicky Jim, okay?" he said at last, a calm coming over him like the eye of a hurricane. He put the car in gear and drove onto the pavement. "Just wanna put the fear of God in him, is all."

*   *   *

We idled the Plymouth through Dover, past desiccated raspberry fields and blighted homesteads, with the night closing around us like a hand. I said nothing more to Hitch for fear of provoking him. Along a stretch of highway, a gibbous moon rose in isolation above a line of trees where it shone through breaks in the clouds. From the bottom of their gravel driveway, the Kaysen place looked built of worn loneliness, and when suddenly the clouds parted and the world became saturated in moonlight, the two-story house and barn stood out like the ruins of a stage set. Yellow light filled one window on the lower floor of the house, the other windows like the dead eyes of a skull.

"You sure you wanna do this?" was all I asked.

Hitch shut the lights as he pulled up the driveway and parked behind a bramble of wild blackberry vines, concealed from Nicky Jim's line of sight. Before the moonlight waned once more, Hitch lifted the revolver and cracked the breach. The copper sleeves of live rounds gleamed inside, set within the metallic precision of the barrel.

"What kinda gun is that?"

Hitch slapped the revolver shut as clouds worked to close over the moon. "My old man calls it a Russian, Smith and Wesson forty-four. Says it saw action in the Indian Wars."

I said the obvious. "You stole it."

"*Borrowed.* The old man, he collects guns. Deals 'em. Spends more time at gun shows than at the shooting range. He won't miss it. He's got a million of 'em."

Climbing the incline toward the house, I found myself winded from the dread of knowing we could be shot dead at any moment. The least of my fears was whether Robin Stanley should hear about my shenanigans and ground me for life. Being shipped off to a military school sounded far better than scrambling up a muddy hill behind a friend who, I was slow to accept, had worked himself into a rage.

Hitch took cover between the barn and Nicky Jim's Dodge pickup. I sat on an upturned cinderblock, hands on my knees, sucking in great draughts of the night air, steaming like a locomotive.

My friend did not give me time to recover, and when he crouched around the corner, I called after him, "What're we doin', man?"

In an unexpected rush, he turned and was upon me, pressing the cold grip of the revolver against my face. His eyes flashed yellow in the dim light, and he whispered gutturally that I not speak, that I shut up forever. I smelled Wild Turkey on his breath, and whatever courage I'd managed to find crumbled inside me. His sudden anger silenced the inner voices that had encouraged me in the first place, all except one voice that scolded—*This is the biggest mistake of your life.*

Through an open door at the side of the barn, Hitch entered and I followed. I had not thought it possible for any place to be darker than the outside, but the interior was blind dark. We were forced to feel our way forward, shuffling our shoes across the broken concrete slab.

Hitch bumped into something, and the clunk of an overturned glass jar brought me upright. I held my breath. I followed the agonizing roll of it across the floor until it came mercifully to a halt against something else.

Through the weather-eaten slates of siding, we could see the house and its solitary illuminated window. We waited in anticipation, but no other lights came on.

I heard Hitch rustle in the pocket of his jeans. This was followed by a sharp snap of his Zippo lighter, and its wavering flame briefly revealed us standing in the midst of what looked like a failed chemistry experiment. He closed the lighter, and once again I stood blinking at imagery burned like a ghost on my retina.

Leaning toward Hitch, I said, "What is this stuff?"

I felt his hot stinking breath against my ear. "Crystal meth. Nicky Jim's a tweaker."

It was a small methamphetamine lab hidden inside the spine-cracked barn. Its exposure had the effect of multiplying my sense of danger. I wanted nothing more than to make a hasty retreat back to the Plymouth and to find myself safely returned to the Stanley Farm. This was a discovery that would lead to nothing less than personal harm. Perhaps even dismemberment and death. Ours was an enterprise without hope. We had found ourselves up against an impenetrable wall neither of us had anticipated nor had the wherewithal to breach.

We backtracked out the side door and into the moonlit landscape.

Kneeling next to Hitch in the mud, I whispered. "We go now. Call the cops. Tell 'em about the meth. We can let them take it from here." I believed my logic sound.

He shook his head. "Not leavin' without Annette."

"Don't do this, man." I gripped his arm, the one that held the revolver.

He snatched it away with a look that accused me of betrayal.

"Don't fuck with me," was all he said as he worked his way along the side of the barn, toward the house.

I trailed behind at a gap that widened with each step. My faith in our friendship had reached no mere stumble of doubt but plain distrust. Here I was, in the company of an armed sixteen-year-old bent on teaching a drug addict a "lesson" in respect for his pregnant girlfriend. Four months out of California, expatriated to this wet miserable countryside, here I was caught beneath the overwhelming Juggernaut of fate. I had arrived at this moment by the failed virtue of my own blind arrogance and poor judgment.

At the corner, where nothing but open ground stood between the barn and the house, Hitch stopped and gave me time to catch up.

I was about to beg him to reconsider when we heard the distinct mechanical slide of someone behind us, cocking a shotgun.

"If you got a weapon, drop it now," came a woman's voice. "Get your arms up where I can see 'em,"

"Shit." Hitch placed the Russian .44 on the dead muddy straw.

I raised my hands almost instinctually, and I felt oddly relieved that it had been a woman's voice I heard and not Nicky Jim's.

"Turn round," came the command.

As we turned, a flashlight shined in our faces, casting us as bit players in this, my second thoughtless act at the Kaysen farm.

"Walk this way, towards me. Leave the gun."

Hitch protested. "I can't—"

"Leave it!"

We went into the beam behind which in silhouette stood a large woman. The exclamation of the shotgun barrel was clearly delineated in the halo of the flashlight. It was Marie Kaysen's mother, Jaye-Ann Osthoff, a plain looking woman with a nest of teased hair. She wore what my mother would have called a housecoat, and she had on a pair of muck boots. In the light I could just make out her index finger threaded through the shotgun trigger. Her fake nails were painted with tiny crescent moons.

"Ain't you the McDonough boy?"

"Yes, ma'am."

I had never heard Hitch defer to or address an adult in so polite a fashion.

Mrs. Osthoff gestured the shotgun in my direction. "Don't think I know you. What's your name, what family you come from?"

I paused before saying, "The Stanley's, ma'am. I'm Robin Stanley's son." It pained me to say it, but if she were going to bring trespassing charges, then why not drag the reputation of my hateful stepfather into the mess?

"That your vehicle?" she asked. "Bottom a my road?"

"It's mine," Hitch said, defiance edging back into his voice.

"Well, boys, I'm gonna cut you a break. You promise to get off my property, go back home, I'll forget all about tonight."

"Yes, ma'am," I said, taking my first step toward freedom.

"Wait on a minute. You and McDonough here, you don't want me to wake up Nicky Jim, give you boys what's coming to you? Make you forget you saw anything up here."

"No, ma'am."

She leveled the shotgun. "Now get the fuck off my land before I change my mind."

Once we were in the Duster and Hitch fit the keys into the ignition, I took a breath and scratched the nerves that crawled up the back of my neck. I looked toward the house. Only the solitary light burned, a deceptive reminder of the menace that had met us in the dark.

Hitch turned the engine over and shoved it in reverse, the transmission clanging like a cathedral bell. As we drove down the county road for the highway, he said, "I'm gonna catch hell for losing that gun."

We had only gone about a mile when I noticed Hitch glance nervously at the rear view mirror.

"What?" I said. "What's going on?"

"Check it out. Someone's tailing us."

I looked through the back window.

"And coming on fast," Hitch said, as he accelerated into the curve.

I screamed above the whine of the engine. "It's Nicky Jim, isn't it?"

Hitch gave me a look, and I saw fear in his eyes for the first time in the few months of our acquaintance.

We were running for our lives through darkened country. Our headlights flashed against the trunks of trees along the roadside, trees that raced past like fence posts. I switched back and forth from looking out the windshield to checking on Nicky Jim's Dodge truck that was gaining on us.

"He's gaining, Hitch!"

"No he ain't."

The Plymouth squealed around a curve and one of the hubcaps came off. It flew across the road into the dark, only to be illuminated like a flying saucer in the approaching lights of the pickup.

Hitch screamed that I hang on as he took a hard right on what proved to be a gravel road. We bounced twice off deep ruts that I thought might stop us cold, but the car plowed ahead, throwing up a tornado of red dust in the taillights. Through this I could just make out the dim pair of lights of our pursuer.

We drove up an incline and found ourselves on blacktop once more. Hitch made the mistake of glancing behind to see Nicky Jim negotiating the corner. It was then that one of the front tires hit something in the road and exploded like a bomb beneath the car.

Hitch lost control, and we went into the ditch. Had the flat tire not slowed us down, the impact against the rise of a gully could have killed the two of us. As it was, we sat stunned momentarily before the headlights of Nicky Jim came up slowly from behind. We heard the crunch of truck tires on gravel as he came to a stop about ten yards away.

I was out of the car first, I'm not ashamed to say, and into the trees in a hard dash for safety. Hitch was soon beside me when we cleared the trees and found ourselves crossing a fallow farm field.

"He'll see us in the moonlight for sure," Hitch said breathlessly.

The report of the shotgun ripped overhead like the claws of something deadly shredding the night.

"Christ!"

I threw myself onto the ground, but Hitch gripped my arm and lifted me up.

"You stay here, you die," was all he said.

We ran for the back of the field where the shadow of an outbuilding waited in the dark. Again, the shotgun blast, closer now, seemed to knock the air out of me.

Thoughts raced through my head that I might have already been shot. I had read stories in a history of World War Two of soldiers in battle who had been mortally wounded but fought on because they had yet to realize their pending mortality. I wondered if this were the case with me as we ran for our lives. Had I been shot?

Behind the outbuilding we took a trail that ran down a steep incline through a windbreak of alders. The trail was a trace of moonlight and it was slick with mud from the recent rain. Hitch and I more than once slipped but stopped our fall on exposed tree roots and overhead branches.

We found ourselves on a flat where the county road meandered toward Strand.

"I know this place," Hitch said. "Come on."

We ran through the dark until, like something catastrophic, Nicky Jim's headlights appeared at the high end of the road. It stopped us both dead in our flight. The Dodge engine gunned and its tires shrieked. We could just make out the pipe of the shotgun sticking out the driver's window before we saw the muzzle flash.

Hitch pushed me sideways into the brush at the roadside and fell on top of me.

"Fuck! You all right?"

"Yeah."

I was worn out by all the adrenaline pumping through me. My throat was completely dry. I could hardly peel my tongue off the roof of my mouth.

"Come on," he said.

As we scrambled down a side spar, our boots slipped on the thin gravel. I realized with a sudden optimism that we were running on the earthworks of an old railroad track. The rails and ties had been removed long ago, but the bulwark was still there.

We made it halfway down this straightaway when the Dodge appeared behind us. The headlights burned through the night and lit up the truck's exhaust in a billowing cloud. We stood at a good distance, safe from Nicky Jim's shotgun. Deep woods surrounded us. We knew we could find shelter in the chaos of darkness and underbrush, if it came to that.

"He won't follow us here," Hitch said.

The words were hardly out of his mouth before the Dodge backed up and launched down the spar, illuminating the two of us in the headlights.

"You think?" I said as we turned to run.

Hitch and I separated, left and right side of the spar, not to make a convenient target for his wrath. From the sound the truck made, it was obvious that Nicky Jim was having difficulty navigating the grade. And yet he managed to fire off one or two more shots at us.

Just ahead, light from the moon cast Alder Bridge as a post-industrial site of a long-dead culture, the future having abandoned it. A forest of second-growth trees surrounded the derelict, and I welcomed the sight like nothing I had ever seen before. It was my bridge to safety.

"Hey, look," Hitch said when he recognized where we were.

The muffled roar of whitewater below sounded reassuringly familiar.

We took off across Alder Bridge, picking our way carefully over the rotted railroad ties. At the middle of the bridge, just as I was beginning to feel relieved for having escaped the clutches of Nicky Jim, we saw the truck headlights. The lights reflected off the iron girders and gleamed like a search lamp to expose us above Deep Creek.

"Jesus, the son-of-a-bitch's following us," Hitch said.

The bridge itself shuddered from the weight of the Dodge. We looked behind as the truck lurched forward over each tie, bouncing erratically in a mechanical rage, the engine straining and Nicky Jim shouting above the roar of the rushing creek that he was going to kill us.

We made a nerve-racking dash over the old ties. I could see far below where moonlight burnished the rapids. The thought—*I'm dead*—kept repeating itself in my mind as my lungs rasped to take in the cold air and as my legs went numb with fear.

Halfway across, just as Nicky Jim was about to run us down, his truck wheel caught on a rotted out beam.

The violent cracking sound stopped Hitch and me cold. The bridge gave out an awful aching sound and it trembled. We turned just in time to see the Dodge plunge through the bottom of the bridge and into darkness, the headlights revealing its harrowing plunge toward Deep Creek.

Above the growl of the rushing water, we heard a scream as the truck arced toward eternity.

It shattered explosively against the boulders below, and the lights went out in an instant. The gut-wrenching crash was the impact of glass and metal and flesh against the unyielding ground.

In the midst of this horror came an expectant silence.

We looked down to where the truck had gone in. The moonlight winked in a shard of twisted steel, but for the most part we couldn't see anything. From our vantage, the pickup appeared half-submerged. We waited, searching our eyes over the wreck, for a sign of life that didn't come. Our ears, acutely attuned to the weakest cry for help, heard nothing but the falling creek water. Eventually, the crickets began singing to one another.

After half an hour of standing there in expectation and recovery, Hitch turned to me and said, "Son of a bitch."

"I can't believe it."

Another minute passed before he spoke again. "I'm gonna head back to the Plymouth."

I shook my head. "It's in a ditch. The tire's blown."

"Look," he said. "I can't go back without the goddamned car. The old man'll kill me." He swallowed hard. "I already gotta tell him, I lost his gun."

"Okay," was all I had the strength to say.

"Listen. Nobody needs to know what happened here."

"We've got to tell the police."

Hitch leaned into me and gripped my shirttails. "Nobody. *Nobody* hears about it. Unless you tell."

I gathered up the dryness in my mouth and tried to spit. It was like spitting dust. "Why would I tell?"

"Just make sure you don't."

Chapter 12

By the time I got home, it was past eleven o'clock. What I had assumed were Virgil Stanley's red and green Christmas lights turned out to be the emergency lights on a Strand Police cruiser, idling in the front yard. The car door was open, and the radio squawked like a chicken with instructions from the downtown station. My mother in her bathrobe and Robin Stanley in slacks and a T-shirt, no shoes, spoke to the officer. When they saw my figure tramping up the driveway into the light, my mother shouted my name.

My violation of trust was not going to be addressed by the usual run-of-the-mill punishment. Their punishment would not be meted out piecemeal, not this time, with an extra hour of chores or tighter restrictions on my freedom. This time Robin Stanley and my mother were in agreement over enrolling me in a military academy. My stepfather declared, "It's reform school for you."

I was stood up like the condemned between my accusers. I gave no evidence to support the need for reform school. I made no mention of revolvers or illegal trespassing. I explained my absence "in the middle of the night" as an impromptu desire to go for a walk.

"A *walk*, in the middle of the night?" Robin Stanley said. He looked to the police officer to explain how this boy, his errant stepson, could be such an idiot.

"To Alder Bridge," I said matter-of-factly and wished I hadn't. Thinking of Nicky Jim and Hitch, and our narrow escape.

My mother had her hand at her mouth as though, by holding it there, she could staunch the tears in her eyes. She was shaking her head and repeating, "Oh, Danny… Oh, Danny…"

The police officer shook Robin Stanley's small hand and tipped his hat to my mother in a goodnight bid. The emergency lights were shut off as the cruiser pulled away from the doublewide and made for the county road. It was at this moment, once the police cruiser was out of sight, that Robin Stanley smacked the back of my head. The force of the blow was enough to knock me to my knees.

I sprang up with my ears ringing. I hurled obscenities at him. I think my mother bawled for us to stop when Robin Stanley took a step forward.

It was then, with resolute hatred, I cracked him closed-fisted in a brutal shot to the nose.

He went down immediately like a marionette whose strings were cut. His legs folded beneath and his arms went slack. The shocked look on his face turned to horror when the blood gushed from his nostrils, a tributary blossoming across his T-shirt. The yard lights turned the blood redder than it needed to be. From the front door of the doublewide, Eve Stanley screeched and flew outside to rescue her little boy while my mother stood stock-still, holding her breath amid this absurd theater of our discord.

Within less than half a minute, the world had gone from hostility and voices spoken in anger to a dead calm, leaving the flush of blood in my cheeks and the beating of my furious heart.

Eve Stanley helped her son inside, and we were left alone in the yard, my mother and I, illuminated by the Christmas lights like an antithetical nativity. We listened to the sounds coming from inside the doublewide—water running in the kitchen sink, Eve Stanley's mixture of shrieks and outcries to the Lord, feet scurrying from one end of the house to the other.

My mother's eyes glistened with a Bible-black indictment as though I had convinced her about something that had troubled her for months. It seemed as though the violence of my response to his abuse was all she needed to tip the scales in Robin Stanley's favor. Desperately wanting to take it all back as tears welled up, I knew in an instant that I had lost her. Something had closed, a door was shut, a lock turned. Something like an unstable rock face was shaken, and an entire mountain came down in an avalanche, as irreversible as death itself. Something changed in that instant. She knew it, I knew it. This was what we "said" to one another, what we professed without exchanging a single word. No voices were raised, no "How could you do this, Daniel?" Nothing. Just the unbroken silence like the sound a heart makes when it stops beating at the end of life.

She turned to go.

"Mom…?" I struggled to say that I was sorry.

"No, Daniel." She sighed, an ivory white hand resting on the doorknob, her back to me. "This is no good. I can't take this. Not anymore." And she went inside.

Once again frustration mounted to a fury, and I reached down for a fist full of gravel and hurled it against the doublewide, cursing God and all those who believed in Him.

Virgil Stanley, like an Old Testament prophet, came to the door and stood in shadow. His head shook slightly in silent condemnation.

Glaring at him, with tears coursing down my face, I muttered, "Go to hell." I did not care if he overheard and used my profanity to further drive a wedge between my mother and me.

And then I ran away from the Stanley Farm, down the gravel driveway toward the county road and into the night, believing as all fifteen year olds who runaway believe that I would never return.

*   *   *

Running away from home was something my father would have called a "growth experience." This was how I would come to see it in retrospect, long after I made the effort to look back at who I was at fifteen, when I tried to understand what I was running away from. At the time, I was experiencing a crippling uncertainty and fear of abandonment despite the fact that I was the one running away. My brain hadn't come up with any ideas of where to spend the night or what to do for the rest of my life. My brother Jesse was in my thoughts. I imagined him sitting in a highchair at the kitchen table. By running away, I was deserting him.

He's helpless in that house—I thought.

I hated Robin Stanley. Despised him. Over the past few months, I had wished my stepfather dead many times. On this night I thought of the many ways I might kill him. Strangulation seemed to me the most satisfying means of doing away with him. Or I could do it with a slow poison, although I knew nothing about how to go about getting my hands on a toxic substance. I thought of Nicky Jim's methamphetamine lab tucked away in the Kaysen barn, and I tried to remember information from a newspaper article about how much of the drug could kill a grown man. The article had named a lethal dose in milligrams per body weight, and I wished that I had paid more attention to his specific weight.

Maybe Hitch could loan me one of his old man's guns, I thought, so I could just shoot the bastard.

I walked on. I stumbled through the night, toward the lights of Strand without a secure destination in mind. As I had time to think, and as the rage tapered off, I gave my predicament more serious thought. Punching my stepfather in the nose and running away instead of apologizing only made things worse. I wasn't sure I could go back, not now. I began to worry, what would happen to me? Where would I end up? I wasn't so much worried about my immediate circumstances, but I began to dread the long-term negative effect that punching Robin Stanley in the nose had on my fortune. I knew this was a turning point where the river of fate changed direction. From that night forward, the mistake I'd made would predetermine the remainder of my days.

I wondered if I would ever see my brother again. Would Robin Stanley forbid it or change the locks on the house; perhaps convince my mother to completely reject me? This was an uneasy armistice in the war between my stepfather and me. The more I thought about it, the more I knew that he couldn't possibly keep me from seeing my brother. Feelings of panic gave way to a sense of exile, and it struck me full force and arrested me on that dark road. I could walk no further. *I've lost everything.* In spite of all that I had tried to do since moving to Oregon, everything that I loved was taken from me: my kid brother, my mother, everything.

Life is loss, I said to myself. Life is a brief time between birth and death. It is a process of learning how to let go of the things you love. Life has nothing to do with being *saved* by Christ so you can spend eternity in heaven. If you want to get saved, then do it and change your life now. Don't do it for some pie-in-the-sky promise of a pleasant afterlife. Life is more fundamental and less supernatural than Robin Stanley and his congregation had led me to believe. Life is as elemental as the blood coursing through your arteries. Life is the mere function of your heart and lungs, your guts and sinew. Life is the dance of cells, the play of nerves and the organization of tissues. The way bonds are made and proteins manufactured, the way birth and our deterioration leads to biological death, this is what life is. This was what I thought about on that lonely road, and this is what I believe today.

My revelation was less an intellectual exercise and more of a physical insight into the workings of the world.

The moon winked through a break in the clouds, and I gazed up at it as though for the first time, as if I was the first boy in history to look at it through new eyes. From that moment on, I imagined, I would have a new relationship with everything, with the universe. Now I knew how arbitrary things were and how quickly things could change from bad to worse.

I continued onward.

*   *   *

I found myself on the unlit front porch of Mr. Phelan's house. I had no other place to go. There was no one else in Strand that I could turn to. I hesitated knocking on the door or ringing the doorbell at the late hour. I considered curling up on the porch glider but I discovered the cushions had been removed in preparation for winter. I did not want to lie down on cold steel springs, and so I found myself facing Mr. Phelan's door without options.

I knocked. After counting to ten, I knocked again, this time putting more behind it.

Mr. Phelan had a ten-light door, ten square sleeves of glass set in a wooden frame. Through it I could make out the interior of the living room, the couch, a side table full of books, and the refractory telescope. Emerging through the darkness, a figure in pajamas bobbed rather than strolled to the door.

The door came open in a flash.

"Do you have any idea…?"

He was going to ask if I had any idea *what time it was*, but when Mr. Phelan saw me, his expression softened with a look of heartfelt concern.

"Danny, what in hell…what're you doing? Are you all right?"

He leaned radically on two metal crutches, and I saw that he wasn't wearing his prosthetic leg. I realized, looking down at the missing leg, of course, he wouldn't have worn the artificial leg while he slept.

I winced and scratched the back of my head. "I need a place to stay, Mr. Phelan. My stepfather kicked me out."

He invited me in and shut the door.

"Sit. Sit down. Give me a minute or two."

He shambled off to the back of the house and returned with his prosthesis gripped in one hand. He took a seat at the end of the couch. I watched as he unfolded the pants of his pajamas to expose the white stump of his right leg. The skin appeared tucked inward where the femur had been sawn off just above the knee, traced with veins that spread in a spider's web like a faint blue tattoo. Mr. Phelan glanced up at my barefaced gawking.

"I was fitted right after the amputation. Two or three years older than you are now. You're what?"

"Fifteen."

"I was eighteen, working my folks' farm. Bad age to lose a leg."

"Probably no good age to lose…a leg," I said.

He nodded. From a jar he rubbed Vaseline inside of the soft plastic of the prosthesis, which was molded to perfectly fit the stump. "They applied a plaster dressing right here before this was custom made. Unless I grow a couple inches in the next ten years, it should remain my only fitting." He smiled as he fit the stump into the prosthesis.

"How's it stay on?" I asked.

"Suction. See these diaphragms here? I pull it on…" He grunted as he lifted his body into a suitable position. "Apply the suction. Voila. Good as new. Now…" He slapped the artificial knee and stood off the couch. "Tell me what's going on before I call your mother."

I felt that Mr. Phelan had betrayed me to my enemies.

"She must know you're all right, Danny. She'll worry herself sick—"

"No she won't."

Mr. Phelan checked the time on a wall clock, and sighed. "Tell me what happened."

The version I told differed a great deal from reality. I made no mention of Hitch's gun or revealed that Nicky Jim was a methamphetamine cook and now probably dead in his truck, drowned in Deep Creek. I wondered if Mr. Phelan even knew what meth was. Most of the adults in my life were clueless. I confessed instead that I'd lied to my mother and Robin Stanley, playacting the contrite son whose rebellious friend had led him astray. None of it washed with Mr. Phelan, I could tell.

"Again, why did you go over to Marie's house?" He stroked his chin and reached across the coffee table for his eyeglasses and put them on. "I don't get it. I don't get why you went there in the middle of the night."

I blinked at him, and the truth rose in me like volcanic magma with no place to go but out. I gave a play-by-play of the evening, biting my lower lip frequently in the telling. I avoided looking directly at Mr. Phelan. Instead, I spoke to the carpet and to my muddy shoes, to the worn corner of the coffee table.

"Hitch wanted to teach Nicky Jim a lesson because he's been molesting his girlfriend. One thing led to another. Anyway, he chased us in his truck. And he shot at us with his shotgun. Twelve gauge, I think."

"This is something the police should handle, Danny. Not your astronomy teacher."

I blinked at him. He wasn't my teacher at school, but it was true: I had nominated Mr. Phelan as my life coach. He was my Socrates.

"He didn't hit us. In fact, we got away without a scratch…" I said before my voice trailed off. I was thinking about what Hitch had said, or threatened, that I not tell anyone about what had happened.

Mr. Phelan listened without passing judgment. When I was done speaking, he got up out of the chair and went to a bureau. He returned and handed me the key to the guest cottage. "You'll find the bed already made up. Use the towels. Make yourself at home. You should go clean up and get some rest. It's late."

As I sheepishly got up off the couch and walked toward the back of his house, Mr. Phelan said, "Danny, I'm going to call Karin, call your mom. I don't want her to worry. You can stay the night. It's okay. But tomorrow…well, tomorrow we'll have to put to rights this whole mess."

I gave him the Stanley's phone number—"I've already got it," he said—before I traipsed off to the cottage. Once settled in, I washed up in the sink and switched off the lights and fell quickly to sleep on the bed, too tired to pull down the cover.

I dreamed that I was walking across a dimly lit plain covered with ice as black as a lacquered box. The sky was starless and looked like a featureless slab of green glass. It felt like I'd been walking forever. A bearded old man who accompanied me said, "Through the accident of our birth, we must walk a great distance. From the darkness behind us toward a darkness of a different kind." I did not understand how I got to be there on that dimly lit plain of ice. The old man said, "We learn as we go. Some learn quickly. Some never at all." As we walked together, I could barely perceive my companion. It felt like walking alone. When I grew tired, the old man said, "Don't stop. To stop is to fall through the ice." It was no ordinary ice field, I realized, but more like a frozen lake. The ice in spots was razor thin, and I worried that I might fall through. In one moment the old man walked beside me, and in the next he slipped through the ice and was lost forever. I watched in horror as he floated away into obscurity. Through the ice I could just make out other figures, the pale body of one person here and another there. I counted a dozen, and then grasped that there were hundreds, perhaps thousands, their arms and legs entangled like dead tree limbs below the surface of a river. Among the drowned multitude, I recognized my mother and Jesse…

I woke up with a startled gasp. As my eyes adjusted, I was glad for the unfamiliar surroundings of Mr. Phelan's cottage. I knew the dream to be a dream but also to be true; loved ones can slip away forever. I also knew that I would not let go of Jesse. He was my brother. He belonged with me. I would not let Robin Stanley take him from me. I refused to let go of the last connection to the past of who I was and who my brother and I were together.

*   *   *

My mother came in the morning to retrieve me, but not to forgive. This was made perfectly clear from the moment she said, "Well, good morning." Her tone said it all.

Mr. Phelan and she stood in the kitchen while I finished a late breakfast at the table, having risen from bed around ten o'clock. I looked a sight. The knees of my jeans were stained with mud from the Kaysen farm and our flight across the countryside. A spot of blood stood out on my shirt, Robin Stanley's blood. I recognized it for the emblem it was. I thought of keeping the shirt unwashed as a keepsake to remind me of what was at stake here.

"We have to leave, Daniel. There are things I need to do," my mother said. "Where are your shoes?" Oklahoma came to her voice that morning.

I trotted back to the cottage for my shoes, my feet as brittle as glass on the cold December ground. On my return I came back through the side door rather than retrace my steps across the lawn to the kitchen. In the hallway that was lined with Civil War photographs, I caught my mother twice kissing Mr. Phelan on the cheek, holding his hands and looking into his eyes. "Thank you so much, Audie." She was about to say more before she saw that I had come into the house unexpectedly. They dropped their handholding and pulled away from one another. Mr. Phelan's cheeks were stained with a residue of my mother's lipstick. He lowered his gaze when I squared my shoulders as if to ask, what's going on here? My mother quickly rummaged her purse for the car keys and looked up with eyes imprinted with guilt. She said, "Ready?"

In the Buick on the drive home, the tension in the car was conspicuous. Stopped at a traffic signal, my mother glanced sideways, and caught me staring at her. "You called Mr. Phelan *Audie?*" I said. I faced forward to hide the accusation of my look. The signal changed, and we moved slowly through the intersection amid late Christmas shopping traffic in Strand. I wasn't sure if I was mad at her or jealous. I felt a vague sense of disloyalty not for Robin Stanley's sake, but for my father in California. I had always considered my mother's marriage to Dr. Stanley a sham, an illegitimate union. But her physical affection for Mr. Phelan seemed something adulterous, a violation of my need to get our family back together. She was sullying her relationship with my *real* father, and jeopardizing the possibility for a reunion in San Francisco after this brief mistake with Robin Stanley was annulled.

At last, I said, "He's my *teacher*, mom."

"What are you saying?" She turned the corner for the county road to the Stanley farm. "You're no one to judge me, young man."

She never called me *young man* unless she was trying to hide something. "I'm not judging you." I shifted uncomfortably on the passenger seat. "It's just..."

"Just what?"

"You called him Audie. Mr. Phelan. He's my *teacher*."

After a moment's pause, she said, "We're friends, Danny. That's all. Just good friends."

"Fine." I turned away to look out the window at the monotony of fir and cedar. "You don't have to justify it."

"I'm not justifying anything," she said. With her attention directed at me, the car wandered across the double yellow line.

"Mom—" I pointed toward the approaching intersection.

She corrected and braked at the corner. "I don't have to justify anything."

As we drew near the turnoff for the Stanley farm, I wanted to plead with her to leave Robin Stanley. Where was my courage to tell her that I was secretly glad for her friendship with my teacher? My emotions felt rusted shut like clockwork left out in the rain. *Your life is my life*, I wanted to say. *Whatever you decide to do, as long as it doesn't involve Robin Stanley, is fine with me.* The more I thought about it, the more I liked the idea of her holding hands with Mr. Phelan and kissing him on the cheek. Her simple display of human warmth was another nail in my stepfather's coffin, as far as I could tell. I was glad for it, elated, despite the fact that soon I would be delivered into his unreasonable hands.

She brought the Buick to a stop on the gravel next to the doublewide. As she pulled the handbrake, she said in a soft Oklahoma drawl, "I want you to remember something, Danny." Her eyes brimmed with tears. It seemed she was about to confess the truth, but her eyes caught the movement of Virgil Stanley as he came out of the barn. It stopped her cold, and she reached for my hands. "I love you very much."

We embraced. I could not help but wonder what she was going to tell me.

My kid brother threw open the screen door and ran toward the Buick.

"Dammy! Dammy!" he shrieked.

His little pink palms slapped the passenger side window.

"Dammy. Dammy's home."

I opened the door and jumped out. I gathered his body up in my arms and swung him around once before landing him gently on his feet. He wore the over-sized Nike running shoes that Robin Stanley had purchased for him on our second week in Oregon. They were still too big for him.

"Hey, buddy. I see you got your speedy shoes on?"

"Yeah, Dammy. Watch. Watch how fast I run."

He took two steps and fell down hard on the gravel, nicking the skin of his knees.

Mom quickly crouched next to my brother to reassure him, but Jesse sobbed nonetheless. It was his way.

When I looked up, I was face to face with Virgil Stanley's scowl. This hard, thin man never smiled, but his unbending, disapproving stare had worsened toward me. His hostility brought to mind the reason for my being returned to the farm. He was a reminder of the conditions here and my reason for running away. The old man turned aside without a word.

At the front door, Eve Stanley stood, wiping her hands on an apron, while her son pushed past her for the yard. There was regret in her eyes as well but not the level found in her husband.

My stepfather took a few steps into the yard with difficulty, as though he'd spent a long convalescence from an illness or serious injury. He stopped a good distance away. A large white bandage covered his nose with gauze held down by strips of surgical tape that pressed against his upper lip, making it look swollen. I saw that both eyes were blackened.

I doubted that my punch had done such damage. Surely, after I ran away, he had run into a door or fallen off the roof of the barn, something. I could not be held accountable for all his injuries. They seemed excessive.

The four of us stood there saying nothing with Jesse whimpering in my mother's arms, Robin Stanley's black and blue eyes glaring at me. My mother set her jaw the way she did when something was expected of me.

I knew what it was.

I walked up to Robin Stanley and held out my hand to shake. "I am truly sorry, Robin. Sorry for what I did."

He looked down at my hand without taking it. There would be no truce. He was not man enough to accept my apologies. He said, "What...what you did...." He cleared his throat. "It is so clear to me, what you need is Jesus in your life. Without the Lord, you're lost."

And with that he turned away and walked into the house. My mother followed with Jesse, full of snot and tears, looking back at me longingly.

Virgil Stanley approached, and for a moment it seemed he would hit me in retaliation. He tensed the muscles of his right arm and closed his hand into a fist. A red anger bulged the veins of his neck.

I took a step back and cocked my head. No matter what this old bastard did to me, no matter what consequences were in store, since I had already beaten the son, I was not above striking the father as well. I had been called a godless loser among other invectives in my short tenure on the Stanley farm. Emotional cruelty is one thing, but I was not about to let Virgil Stanley get away with physically abusing me.

He said, "Why don't you boys wear your damn baseball caps like a white man? Turn the bill around like it's 'sposed to be."

I removed my Giants cap and brushed imaginary dust from the bill. Then I fit it on backwards and glowered at him.

He sighed and blinked at the cold daylight. We stood awkwardly in opposition. Without saying another word, he returned to the barn, and I went reluctantly indoors to face a grim reprisal at the hands of my stepfather.

Chapter 13

Christmas came and went on the Stanley farm like a bout of influenza, and the four adults went through the motions more or less for Jesse's sake. My brother could not have understood what had happened, but he was affected by it nonetheless. He occasionally burst into tears and complained to our mother about a stomachache, a clear sign he was internalizing the stress to make it his own. Although I was "allowed" to share in the traditional supper on Christmas day, Eve, Virgil, and Robin Stanley avoided eye contact at the kitchen table. They spoke to me only when necessary. When they did speak, it was in the imperative—"Pass the peas" or "Use your napkin." I had become unacceptable in their sight. Here was the cold porridge of the Stanley's hospitality.

My mother gave up her role as family mediator. Instead of her usual impulsive chattiness to cover the tension between Robin Stanley and me, she subjected us to sullen discontent. Ever since divorcing my father, my mother rarely smiled, but over the course of the week between Christmas and New Year's, she seemed grimly resigned to having to spend the rest of her life with a difficult son and emotionally unavailable spouse in the cramped quarters of a doublewide.

My war with Robin Stanley had reached a stalemate. Over the holiday he seldom spoke directly to me. In his version of Christianity, forgiveness was not the highest moral virtue. He expressed his opinions by muttering remarks: "Who does he think he is...that boy is Satan's issue...it's military academy for him." On one particularly ugly night, I overheard Virgil Stanley arguing with Eve. "Kid like that ought not to live here, hitting our Robbie. I say, throw 'em to the dogs. That's what my folks woulda done." As long as Robin Stanley found it rewarding to wear his badge of courage, which he did long after it became unnecessary, the bloodied nose bandage reminded them of the pariah in their midst.

And so, I spent most of the Christmas season alone in my room, writing letters to my father.

Dear Dad,

Howzitgoin? Merry Xmas. Sure wish we all could ~~ge~~ be together right now. Jesse says "hello." And that he loves you. I know Mom misses you, too. She won't say so, but I just know it.

You haven't written or called and I know you must be very busy with the Practice. Oh, by the way, I really liked the Sony Walkman. Sorry, but I already have one. You gave it to me ~~lsat~~ last year. That's okay. Jesse broke his and doesn't have one right now. He takes mine to listen to tapes. ~~He's~~ His favorite is "The Little Mermaid." He sings along with the songs. Still gets the words wrong but that doesn't matter. Anyway, thank you tons. Hey, did you get my present yet? Did you like it? I won't say what it is and spoil the surprise in case you've been so busy you haven't had a chance to open your gifts yet.

I really miss you, Dad. I called ~~lsat~~ last week but got the machine. Wished you'd call. You know the number here, right? I'd call more often but Robin Stanley won't let me. I really hate him, Dad. He treats me bad. Hecka bad.

I have ~~to~~ a confession to make. Mom will probably tell you anyways. I'm sorry but I hit him. I hit Robin Stanley in the nose. He hit me first though. I know what you'll say, you'll say that it's no excuse, but you just don't know what it's like. I hate living here. I hate Oregon. It sucks.

I really want to come home, Dad. I miss my life. I miss <u>you</u>. You'd let me come home and live with you, right? I swear I wouldn't cause any trouble. <u>I swear.</u> Please! I can't take living here another ~~week~~ day.

Sorry about begging like a little kid but things aren't good up here. And I figured you should know. I love you.

Your son,
Daniel

A few days before New Year's Eve, I planned to sneak out of the house to go see Hitch McDonough. I wanted to talk to him about Nicky Jim, about going to the police or at least reporting that we'd found his truck in Deep Creek. Every morning I checked the obituaries in the paper, but Nicky Jim's death was never mentioned. I watched the local television news shows at night, anticipating the report of a local man's death in a bizarre accident but none materialized. I wanted to ask Hitch if it was possible nobody missed the son-of-a-bitch.

The opportunity to slip away came when Eve and my mother drove into town with Jesse to take advantage of the after Christmas sales. They were looking to fit him with a winter jacket. Before they left, I asked my mother to mail a letter to Dad, and I watched her slip the envelope into her purse. Robin Stanley went with them. Somebody named Mrs. Proctor was scheduled for a frame adjustment at his optometry office. As soon as Virgil fell asleep in the recliner, while football highlights played on ESPN, I slipped out of the house through my bedroom window.

We had received a light dusting of snow the previous night, and in spite of a warming trend, patches of the stuff clung to shadows on the forest floor. The wind caught handfuls and tossed flurries across the driveway. It was so cold that I wished I'd thought to wear my new woolen socks, the pair Eve Stanley made for me before I punched her son in the face. Giving me anything was the last thing either Stanley wished to do, but I think she felt obligated because she'd made a point of measuring my feet the month before.

To escape the cold and get back before they discovered me gone, I hurried to the McDonough place. Their unnamed hound greeted me with barking the moment I approached. I tossed a small rock, and the dog yelped in retreat under the sagging porch.

"Hitch!" I called out. "Hey, you home?"

I was struggling to form the words in my mind, to ask Hitch what we should do about Nicky Jim at the bottom of Deep Creek. Also, I was looking forward to bragging about giving Robin Stanley a nosebleed. I wasn't sure I wanted to ask how Annette was doing now that she was pregnant.

Wallace McDonough came to the side door and complained that I had disturbed his nap. He leaned out in a pair of filthy briefs and one sock. He spat a comet of chewing tobacco that splattered like tar in the snowy weeds.

"What do you want?"

I grimaced. "Merry Christmas, Mr. McDonough—"

"I asked what you want."

This was not a person to stir to anger. Wallace McDonough was more like a hornet's nest than a human being. He did not possess his son's muscularity, but the roughness and size of his hands, the squint in his eye, and his hard round belly spoke of the potential for homicidal rage.

"Is Hitch…is *Greg* here?"

From beneath the porch, the dog barked. The old man rolled a gob of spit around his tongue and lobbed it at the dog. He mumbled for the goddamned dog to shut up. Even from a good distance away, I could smell liquor on him.

"He's gone." His eyes narrowed as though he blamed me for something as yet unnamed. *"Gone!"* he shouted. "You deaf or something?"

I glanced sideways at the yard between their tumbledown barn and the house, where Hitch ordinarily parked the Plymouth Duster. All that remained were several wide bruises on the gravel where oil had dripped from beneath the engine.

Hitch was gone.

"Where'd he go?" I asked.

"Don't see how that's any your business."

Did I have to explain who I was? Why was I suddenly forced to tell Wallace McDonough that his son and I were friends? Didn't he remember me from my last visit to the house?

From the look on his face, Wallace McDonough would just as soon shoot me than talk. As I turned to go, he spoke in a stutter. "He's gone to his grandpa's."

I stopped and looked back.

"Down Arkansas way. The good-for-nothin' stole my car." The creases around his eyes deepened when he steadied himself against the door. "Don't know anything about that, do ya?"

It was less of a question than a conclusion drawn through the illogic of booze. In Wallace McDonough's mind, I was somehow responsible for the loss of his automobile and for his criminal son's running off. I retraced my footsteps through the scattered patches of snow. "If you hear from him," I said, "tell 'em I said howdy." Wallace McDonough observed me as one would a hateful insect. I was halfway to the county road before I heard him holler once again at the dog.

Rather than return to the farm, I took a circuitous route toward Alder Bridge. I had to see for myself what had happened to Nicky Jim. There was part of me that wanted to believe he had survived the crash. "It's not possible," I told myself as I made my way across the bridge.

I stopped well short of where the Dodge had broken through the rotted-out railroad ties. It was like a gaping flesh wound with shredded cable dangling at the edges. I leaned against the catwalk railing and peered down.

Far below, the waters of Deep Creek roiled over the pickup's rear bumper. One wheel, the tire still attached, sat partially submerged. The rest was underwater. With the cab completely flooded, there was no way anyone could have survived the accident.

But I had to see for myself.

I picked my way down the embankment toward the swollen creek, through the tangle of denuded alder and maple. Near the bottom I lost my footing and slid the rest of the way on my ass, down a chute of wet leaves. I twisted my right ankle on a round stone at the bottom but walked off the pain.

Winter rains had turned Deep Creek into a muddy torrent. Gone was the picturesque jade-water of summer and early fall. I could not see below the surface, but the calamity of whitewater raging around the truck convinced me—Nicky Jim was dead.

*   *   *

Returned to the farm, I laid in the semidarkness of my bedroom and thought about the new direction my life had taken. I felt like an accessory to a murder, and my best friend, my accomplice, was gone.

Hitch had honored his pledge to drive the Plymouth to Arkansas, to live with his grandfather. He was out of my life like so many other people that I had depended on. One more loss to add to a long list of losses.

When the sound of the Buick returning from town filtered up the driveway, I listened as they returned noisily—almost happily—to the kitchen. My mother looked in on me, but I pretended to be asleep. I overheard Robin Stanley speaking adamantly to my mother. At first, I was unable to identify the main point of his argument, but it became clear when he said, "Family planning is the fate of whores, Karin. Birth control is abortion, don't you see?" Here was the continuation of a quarrel that had gone on sporadically since our arrival in Strand. In support of her son, Eve Stanley suggested my mother join a wife-mentoring group at the church to "instruct her in biblical wifehood." I strained to hear my mother's response but heard none. Robin Stanley used the phrase "race suicide" two or three times along with a word I had never heard before—abortifacient. It was a word I could not define but which would be repeated in church more often than my mother liked. "We can't afford to have a baby, Robin. Please...we've talked about this," my mother said. "God," my stepfather replied, "will provide his flock. Don't worry about the money."

At last, Eve Stanley said, "The number of children you have is the gauge of your holiness, dear. They are arrows in your quiver. I only wish we had more."

I overheard my mother say "Jesse" as if to convey her overwhelming sense of guilt for the last time she had delivered life into the world, a life damaged by her irresponsible drinking. Robin Stanley told her it was "judgment for past sins. Jess is your cross to bear..."

"My brother's no cross," I muttered into the pillow.

When Jesse burst into the bedroom and jumped on my bed, I kept my eyes shut.

Jesse pushed at me with his pudgy hands. "Wake up, Dammy. Wake up."

"Don't, Jesse. Dammy's tired. I just want to sleep, okay, buddy. Leave me alone."

Eventually he grew bored with my unresponsiveness and he fled the room for the kitchen where Eve Stanley called that she was about to serve lemon meringue pie and put on the kettle to make hot chocolate.

*   *   *

On the following night at eight o'clock, as I sat at the kitchen table reading an astronomy book, Mr. Phelan called my mother to let her know that Annette Kaysen had been admitted to the county medical clinic in Strand. She was waiting for an ambulance to take her to a hospital, fifteen miles away.

"What happened to her?" my mother said. There was a weight to her look as I glanced up to find out whom she was referring to. "Did the police come...? But he *beat* her...?"

"What's going on?" I said, closing the book. I was afraid that the news from my teacher somehow involved me.

She raised her hand for silence as she listened intently to the caller. His voice came through the receiver tinny and distant. "Okay. Yes. Okay." And then her countenance fell and my mother's glare drilled into me like a mining auger. Something that Mr. Phelan and she spoke about, something about me, had terribly disappointed her. A verdict seemed quickly decided without a fair trial or witnesses called for the defense. I stood as though for a gallows walk, condemned on circumstantial evidence. My mother hung up the phone and pressed her back against the kitchen wall. She would not look at me and she would not explain what Mr. Phelan had said. I was not given the benefit of the doubt.

"Get your coat," was all she said. "We're going for a ride."

With its frontier fantasy architecture, Clackamas County Medical Clinic was an easily ignored structure on the corner of McGrath Street in Strand. You could overlook it unless you were without medical insurance. On this night, as my mother's Buick pulled into the parking lot, three parishioners from Valley Shepherd Community Church stood outside to protest the county plan to expand the clinic with family planning services. They held placards showing grotesque pictures of late-term aborted fetuses. The placental blood was noticeable even in the dark. "Family planning" was classified by the evangelical mind as abortion.

My mother said, "Don't look."

At first, I thought she referred to the photographs of fetuses. I thought she might think that the pictures would harm my psyche, but soon I realized she had meant to hide from the protestors. She knew them and didn't want to be recognized. We belonged to the same church. Driving into the clinic would raise embarrassing questions that might stigmatize her. Why was she there, after all? What possibly could have drawn her to such an "unholy" place when Dr. Stanley provided adequate medical insurance for his family? Was Karin Stanley a supporter of *Roe v. Wade?* Was she seeking an abortion?

"Do you think they saw us?" she asked when I pulled open the front door.

Hispanic families lined the walls in the waiting room, standing against the wall and sitting in the few available plastic chairs. There were stocky men in cowboy hats and worn denim, their faces lined by labor in the nursery stock fields. Their women were almost universally overweight from an impoverished diet. They had more children than seemed likely to belong to so few adults.

"Karin?" Mr. Phelan greeted us. "I'm afraid the news is not good."

He told us that a county sheriff deputy had admitted Annette Kaysen to the clinic with multiple abrasions and contusions. "Her mother's boyfriend beat her up." I doubted this could be true. Last time I saw him, Nicky Jim was plunging toward Deep Creek.

"Where's Marie, Mr. Phelan? She all right?" I asked.

"She's with county services, Danny. She's been taken into the foster care system." He told us that Nicky Jim had not been arrested in the assault. "The police can't find him. He may have left town."

My heart skipped a beat when I heard this. I knew it couldn't be true. I knew that Nicky Jim was dead, but now was not the time to confess my failure to report his death. Still, I knew for certain, someone else had beaten Annette.

"Anybody give her mom a call?" I asked.

Mr. Phelan shook his head and ushered us to a less crowded corner, keeping his voice down. "That's the saddest part in all this.

She's been *arrested*. They found a meth lab on her property. She can't help Annette, not from jail. There'll be a hearing and probably a trial. She'll end up in prison."

My mother shook her head. There was something she did not understand.

"Audie, why did the girl call *you?*"

He shook his head. "She has no family other than her mother. Not any living relatives, far as they can tell. At a school health day, Marie...her sister...put my phone number down in case of emergency. It was the only number the police had. So, they called me. Annette was home-schooled," he said, more or less as an afterthought.

Throughout the drive and on our arrival, despite my mother's telling silence, I could not help but wonder why we had been asked to join Mr. Phelan at the clinic. Yes, it was true that I knew Annette, and that I had been friendly with her sister Marie, but how was their dysfunctional family my concern? Had Mr. Phelan called my mother as a Good Samaritan? Did he expect her to adopt Annette? But the question *why am I here* nagged at me from every corner of the evening.

"As I told you," Mr. Phelan said, "Annette's pregnant."

"And the baby...?" my mother said, hand at her mouth.

"The baby's fine." He looked at my mother and then at me when he said, "She says you're the father, Danny. Is that true?"

Bingo. Here it was, the reason I had been asked to come along— Annette's Big Lie. She had accused me of fathering her illegitimate child. Any number of thoughts raced through my head, but paramount was the name of my best friend. I knew Hitch to have done the deed. The notion, however, that I should dishonor our friendship by branding him the culprit was out of the question. Despite the scandal sure to follow, in spite of Robin Stanley's wrath that would undoubtedly rain stones upon me, I refused to tarnish for a single moment my friendship with Hitch McDonough, even if it meant my mother's bitter disappointment and her eventual rejection.

They wanted to believe the worst in me without giving me the benefit of the doubt. My mother would rather believe a damaged girl from Dover than her own son. And Mr. Phelan had overturned everything he knew about me in favor of the lies of the pregnant daughter of a meth addict. It hurt that they thought so little of me.

Both Mr. Phelan and she waited impatiently for a response.

"Are you...did you...with that girl, Danny?" my mother said.

"If you are responsible, you need to do the right thing." There was disappointment in Mr. Phelan's tone, an emotional detachment that said he had given up on me, that his efforts to improve my mind had been, in the end, a waste of time.

Neither admitting nor denying guilt, I asked, "May I see her?"

Mr. Phelan looked to Karin for direction here. He would allow my mother to say whether or not I could visit my accuser. She nodded regretfully.

Annette Kaysen shared a room with three other patients where retractable curtains were drawn between the four beds. A nurse stood at the bedside and adjusted a shuttlecock in the intravenous line and counted the drips against the secondhand of her wristwatch.

"Excuse us?" Mr. Phelan said. The nurse looked up, and he pulled her aside and spoke in a whisper. Although I did not hear what was said, the denunciation in the nurse's eyes spoke loudly enough. "We have five minutes before the ambulance gets here," Mr. Phelan told my mother.

She sat on the edge of the bed and took Annette's limp hand into her own. When she opened her eyes, Annette asked, "Mom?"

"You just rest a spell, darlin'." My mother smiled, bringing on tears along with her Oklahoma accent.

Someone had given her an awful thrashing. A few blotches of dried blood stained the clean bed linen, but the treating physician had swabbed the source, a deep slash on her chin, and applied stitches. Annette's upper lip was swollen to twice its normal size, and she had a lump—the nurse called it a hematoma—on her forehead, on the right temple. This injury caused the most concern among medical staff who had requested transfer to the east county trauma center where Annette would undergo a CAT-scan to rule out brain injury or swelling.

"How're you feeling now, Annette?" Mr. Phelan asked.

"She's received something to relax her," the nurse said.

"Is there any danger—" My mother caught herself and pulled away from Annette to speak more privately with the nurse. "What about the baby?"

It took the nurse a moment to process what my mother had asked. "You mean…oh, she's fine. As far as we can tell, the patient is only eight weeks along. She's been given a brochure on abortion services—"

"Absolutely not," my mother said. "I won't hear of it." She went protectively to the bedside. "We're talking about my first grandchild."

In a drugged state, Annette focused her glassy eyes on me. I was standing there in anticipation of what was to come next.

"Hullo, Daniel."

Through the gauze of her confused speech, it sounded as though she said *Damn You* instead of Daniel.

"Hey, Annette. How you feelin'?"

She sighed. "Been better."

My mother began to weep into a handkerchief. The nurse abruptly parted the drapes to assist another patient, seemingly glad to escape my mother's melodrama. Mr. Phelan gave excuses to see what was holding up the ambulance.

Sitting on the corner of the bed and taking up Annette's hand in hers, my mother said, "Darlin', I want you to know…I want you to know." She struggled to find the right words. "I'm going to adopt your baby. Do you understand? You simply cannot have an *abortion*…." The word caught in her throat like bile and made her shudder. "You simply can't."

The nurse pulled back the drapes and announced, "The paramedics have arrived." She turned to my mother. "I'll need to take it from here."

"Can't we go with her?" my mother asked.

This request was impossible, she was told. We could visit the patient after she was admitted to the hospital, but now we must vacate the room and wait in the waiting room.

The interruption of my mother's plea to Annette to give up all thought of getting rid of the baby tightened the cords in her neck. She clutched at her purse and worried the clasp. Mr. Phelan came in and took my mother by the arm and led her out of the room. I followed like a lost lamb.

At the front door, my mother thanked Mr. Phelan. I took note, no kisses were exchanged under these circumstances, and I hated myself for having so cynical a mind. *Don't give cause*, I thought. *In spite of their double standards.* They were two of the last three people on Earth who still loved me or thought kindly of me. And I had done just about everything possible to discourage their genuine affection. When Mr. Phelan bid us good night, my mother and I walked separately through the parking lot to the Buick.

"Can we talk about this?" As I tried to explain the situation, my voice cracked. "Mom...would you slow down? We need to talk."

Fumbling the key into the door lock, she said nothing.

"I want to tell you something in confidence. You can't tell *any*body—"

She rushed around the car to the passenger side, towards me, her high heels clacking against the asphalt. She shoved her finger in my face.

"Now...I see...where we stand," she said through a stutter. "Everything, *everything* Dr. Stanley...said about you, it's true."

"Mom—"

"Don't!"

"It isn't true."

I did not see the arc of her swing but felt the sharp sting of her open-handed slap. I nearly fell down. It wasn't from the force of the blow, but more from the shock of it. My mother had never raised a hand to me until that moment in the parking lot of the county medical clinic in Strand, Oregon.

"Don't you *ever* lie to me again, you hear me? Don't you *ever!*"

I had no recourse. I made no reply. None was requested, none given. The jury was in. And the verdict? Guilty beyond a shadow of doubt. Sentencing would be delivered at home, or in what passed for "home" on the Stanley farm. We drove there in a palpable silence, the tender threads of our attachment torn apart. Our hearts were broken by the falsehoods of another that brought about the unremitting loss of a mother's faith in her son.

I was heartbroken by this, but my final defeat would come later where a kind of living death awaited me, a kind of dark night of the soul without benefit of dawn.

*   *   *

Two days after New Year's Eve at around seven in the morning, Robin Stanley answered the telephone. I was at the kitchen counter, awkwardly making a peanut butter and jelly sandwich for my return to school. We were not on speaking terms, he and I. The tension between us was thicker than the peanut butter I spread across Eve Stanley's homemade bread.

After exchanging false pleasantries, Robin Stanley called out to my mother that it was her "ex" from California. He left the receiver dangling from the cord. My mother trotted into the room with only half her makeup on, a mascara applicator in hand.

"Yes? Hello, Ponce. No. No, it's not." As she listened she frowned upon my activities at the counter and covered the receiver to tell me to be sure to clean up the mess. "Yes, Ponce, we got it. No, I…well, Dr. Stanley and I…." She sighed and turned away from me. "No. Listen. Okay, but how can you expect me…expect us…we can't afford to hire a lawyer, you know that. No? Well, what's changed…okay, I'm listening."

From the far side of the kitchen, I could hear the timbre of my father's voice, his raspy lawyering baritone, through the telephone.

My mother's expression softened and her shoulders lowered as though a great weight had been lifted. "You're not then, it's dropped? Then we're in agreement…I'm relieved, yes." She sighed and wrapped the telephone cord around her finger. "Ponce, Ponce? I have something to say. When you have the time, there's something we must talk about. It's Daniel. That's right…" Her glance said that I could never make her smile again. "Yes…yes, he's here. You want to speak with him?"

She gestured with a nod of her head and handed the phone to me. "It's your father," she said and turned and walked out of the kitchen without offering to explain what my dad and she had spoken about.

"Hey, Dad." I tried to sound upbeat.

"Hello, Bucko. What's going on?"

"Did you get my letter?"

"Danny, I've got some good news I want to share with you, okay?"

I don't remember the exact words my father spoke that morning. They were delivered one at a time, formed into declarations like bricks set in an impenetrable wall, separating me from the future I had hoped for.

"You remember Clarisse, my secretary? Anyway, congratulate me, son. We're married. Last night. Justice of the Peace, an old friend of mine from Boalt Hall days. You remember him, tall guy with the white beard...?"

He continued but my mind could not get past the words "Clarisse," "congratulate me," and "we're married."

"Are you there?"

"Yeah. Dad. Still here."

"You don't sound so happy for me. What gives? Come on. This is your old man. Throw me a rope, okay?"

"Congratulations, Dad."

"Thanks, son."

"No, I mean it." I lied.

I could hear a smile in my father's voice. "Listen, hey, I've got to run. Honeymoon stuff."

"Oh yeah...?" I said, again feigning cheerfulness.

"We're flying to Maui tomorrow. We'll send a postcard, would you like that?"

"Great."

"Danny," my father said. "You're okay with this, right? I mean, I really love this lady. The love of my life." He paused. "This doesn't change anything between us...you know that, right?"

"No. No, Dad." I fought a sea of emotion. "I'm glad for you, really."

"Thanks, Danny. I knew I could count on you. Well, gotta run. Got packing to do, pick up crap at the cleaners. Hey...here's a thought. When we get back maybe we can, I don't know, have you and Jesse down for a weekend or something? Give you boys a chance to meet your new sisters."

Sisters.

"Clarisse's girls'll be living with us...well, you know, when they're not at their dad's place. Anyway, hey, love you. Take care of yourself, buddy, okay? Hey, I gotta run."

I told him that I loved him, too, but by then my father had hung up.

Where in the course of my life did my father become a hoped-for promise, the savior, the hero of my rescue? The world of a fifteen-year-old boy is one full of expectation. My childhood ended when I recognized the false hopes of expectation, when I finally managed my misdirected anger, when I finally saw rebellion as something futile against my opposition. Adulthood does not come upon us as the result of a sudden insight—it is more a process, incremental and deliberate. In my case, the gradual acceptance of my more or less permanent residency in Oregon came at the price of seeing my biological father for what he was, a remote false hope. One reaches a milestone on the way to maturity when we say, "The past is over." Well, the past *is* prologue. Hanging onto blighted hope is an unhealthy alternative to moving on with your life.

Chapter 14

In the dead of winter, snow softened the hard edges of the Stanley farm like a blanket on a cadaver. The doublewide and barn poked out of deep drifts in raw-boned defiance, the roofs quaintly frosted. The evergreens were as well and stood in chilled silence. Virgil's gum maple sapling in the front yard was the last to lose her rust and golden leaves. It was an incongruous mark of vegetation in an otherwise lifeless landscape. The bare branches of dogwood, pear and crabapple stood against the snowy backdrop like squiggles on a blank canvas.

This was the hour of my discontent when the world seemed gripped by something bleak and sodden.

Robin Stanley made good on his threat to send me away to an Idaho military academy for troubled teenagers. I was registered for September enrollment, which dissatisfied him that I should not depart sooner. To hurry matters along, he called my mother, Jesse and me to the kitchen table, the venue of many "family" meetings, where he became enlivened by the mere idea of my removal.

"How will I get there?" I asked, opening the tri-fold brochure.

My stepfather's eyes were inert black pebbles that glittered on this day, in the hour of his victory.

"A Trailways bus will take you as far as Boise. From there, arrangements have been made by JMA to pick you up," Robin Stanley said.

"JMA?" I asked.

"Jesus Military Academy."

I glanced across the table at my mother but found no sympathy. She looked away.

"And don't think, not for one minute, you can get away with…that you can shirk your responsibility. Not for one minute." Robin Stanley waggled his finger in the space between us. "This child, the baby…." He reached out and grasped my mother's hands.

They shared the look of a couple shouldering a duty not of their making. "You will take responsibility for what you did. We expect you to make an honest woman of this…girl…?" He could not recall her name.

"Annette." My mother's voice came sweet and dripping with Southern drawl.

"Yes, Annette."

"Nanette," Jesse parroted.

My mother shushed him.

"You will marry her."

"Robin?" my mother said. "I want this child. You know that. We talked about this."

Gently, he turned to her. "I know, Karin. But your son has to do the right thing. This has nothing to do with the baby." He returned to me. "You will marry her. Do you understand?" Robin Stanley took great joy in issuing this invective. "And when you turn eighteen, when you come of age, I expect you to join our armed forces. To make a man out of you. It's your only option." His eyebrows were arched for emphasis. By then, the second week of January, his swollen nose and blackened eyes were almost completely healed. Only a greenish yellow smear below one eye remained. Listening to him, I could not help but think that he wished for another Middle East war like Desert Storm to crush me beneath its boot. He prayed for my extinction.

We had lost power earlier in the day, plunging temperatures inside the house into the fifties. Virgil Stanley had stoked the woodstove, but it didn't heat the back rooms. We sat at the kitchen table in our winter coats. Eve and Virgil Stanley were in the barn boiling water on the propane stove for our midday meal. Earlier in the day, the doublewide had sprung a leak in our bedroom, but rather than fix the roof, Virgil rearranged our beds and set a plastic pail on the floor. The weather and fate conspired against me. I fell under siege, what with the bitter treatment at the hands of my stepfather.

Over the previous two weeks, Robin Stanley had lain down the rules after Mom handed over responsibility for my upbringing. She had yet to decide what my role would be in raising the illegitimate child she hoped to adopt despite her husband's disaffection, and in spite of my getting shipped off to the Jesus Military Academy. While her submission to Robin Stanley and indifference towards me were her daily reprimands, my stepfather centered his battle against my disobedience on God and the Valley Shepherd Community Church. He forced me to attend church *every* Sunday. He added in an extra measure of cruelty by insisting that I regularly attend a Wednesday evening youth group called Rise Up.

A soot-eyed college kid named George Latimer, a former state-wrestling champion, ran the youth ministry at church. He had short legs and foreshortened arms that earned him the nickname The Dwarf. Every kid who attended Rise Up was given a nickname, usually taken from scripture. Mine was DT for Doubting Thomas. The Dwarf supervised our activities and facilitated questions during our Bible study group, In The Word.

Soon after I had joined, we watched a video that debunked the science of evolution. When the lights came up, I asked how the world could be a mere five or six thousand years old when you considered the Grand Canyon. The Dwarf said, "Read your Bible, DT. You never heard of the Flood?"

Rise Up entertained speakers, a Christian stand-up comic, a Christian college counselor, and a self-styled professional who addressed the more serious topic of homosexuality. Rev. Sty Onslow was a retired minister and evangelical missionary from Alaska. A robust man with thick white hair, Rev. Onslow taught us to "hate the sin, love the sinner." It was a phrase calculated to separate what the evangelical church saw as aberrant sexual behavior from the individual's soul, which we were told, was redeemable through the gift of Christ, the Son of God. The Reverend concluded his talk by saying "AIDS is God's response to the gay lifestyle."

We were seated in the all-purpose room, in the basement below the church sanctuary. Rise Up had few attendees that night because the weather service had accurately predicted a snowstorm. Those few who had shown up resembled Eskimos in their parkas and boots. Rev. Onslow stood at a podium, facing the unoccupied folding chairs.

"Reverend?" I asked. "What about, you know, people with that bleeding disorder I saw on PBS...?"

"You mean hemophilia?"

"More like *homo*phelia." A boy seated behind me snickered at his ugly pun.

I shook my head. "There's something I don't get because, well, does God punish us for having bleeding disorders, too?" I was not stupid; I knew how provocative the question was.

"What's your name, son?"

"DT."

"No, I mean, your real name."

I hesitated. I was in enough trouble as it was without kindling the ire of an out-of-work fundamentalist.

"Daniel. Daniel Aiken."

The Good Reverend noted my name on a slip of paper, folded it, and put it in his coat pocket. He said, "Let's not confuse the two, shall we. I didn't say AIDS was God's way of punishing gays because of their lifestyle." He showed us his crooked teeth in a broad smile. "It is not for us to know what the Lord's intentions are."

As he proceeded to quote scriptural verses to demonstrate God's judgment against homosexuality, I raised my hand again.

"I'm sorry, but you said AIDS was God's response to the gay lifestyle, right? Is the disease itself something people *deserve?*"

He shook his head. "I didn't say that, Daniel—"

"Because if AIDS is God's response to being gay, then I have to wonder if cancer is God's response to, say, smoking. Or a heart attack because we ate too many Big Mac's?"

The Dwarf came to the Reverend's rescue by sidling over to me. "Hey, DT," he said, tightening his grip on my shoulder. "Give it a rest."

In what proved to be my last Rise Up class, I stated an extreme view of the history of religion. I said that in the beginning we humans sacrificed people to the gods, the so-called blood sacrifice. In our middle stage, ascetics sacrificed their desire for our sake, as though to purify themselves as mediators between the gods and us. And in the end, we sacrificed God in Jesus by executing Him on a cross. "Wouldn't you say," I asked our speaker, "that we've gone from sacrificing people to sacrificing God?" The Dwarf telephoned Robin Stanley to complain and clarify why my behavior was considered objectionable. He turned down my stepfather's petition that I be accepted back in class.

*   *   *

During this time my kid brother's health suffered. I outwardly blamed Robin Stanley for his refusal to register Jesse at the Boring School because the cost was "too high," but I knew my brother's heart defect had nothing to do with his not attending school for the developmentally handicapped. His symptoms seemed to worsen as a consequence of the growing hostility between Robin Stanley and me.

My mother worried constantly about him. In early January when Jesse grumbled about headaches, she took him to the pediatrician in town. Kids with fetal alcohol syndrome often have hearing and visual problems. To our relief, the doctor said that Jesse might have a slight hearing problem, but his vision was perfect. The doctor named the unnecessary eyeglass frames as a source of the headaches—they constricted his temples. He underwent a battery of hearing tests, and his "auditory acuity" was shown to be a little below normal. Had Mom asked, I could have told her that Jesse's hearing was fine. He selectively listened to what he wanted to hear, that's all. Since we often raised our voices in anger at the supper table, Jesse compensated by shutting down and refusing to reply when asked a question. It was his defense mechanism, not deafness.

The pediatrician found something else. Jesse had a hole in his heart, what the doctor called an atrial septal defect. She asked my mother if Jesse tired easily, if he complained of shortness of breath upon slight exertion, that sort of thing. He was always suffering some kind of respiratory infection. When we lived in San Francisco, my parents hospitalized Jesse once for treatment of pneumonia. He chronically and needlessly took antibiotics for colds and the flu along with his regular Dilantin to prevent seizures. But in January, on the Stanley farm, when the weather turned foul, my kid brother's health deteriorated.

At Oregon Health Sciences University in Portland, over a two-week period, Jesse's heart function was evaluated in a series of noninvasive tests. The tests were painless to him but unbearable to our mother. The commute to the hospital took over an hour each way. Her first appointment with Jesse was relatively uneventful, but once my brother figured out that Mom would wear her dress-up clothes on a day scheduled for a cardiology test, Jesse protested vehemently. At breakfast, if Mom entered the kitchen in her go-to-town outfit, he screamed. He refused to eat his "bowl of stupid." He refused his vitamins, and he would spit out the Dilantin tablet. Mom couldn't get Jesse to sit in the car seat without a battle. She invited me to come along as a solution since I had a calming effect on my little brother. I was happy to oblige because it meant no school on medical appointment days.

Jesse's pediatric cardiologist was a petite woman named Rose Offenbach. She navigated us through the choppy seas of a health crisis with her unflinching good humor and sensitive manner. Jesse underwent electrocardiograms, echocardiograms, and CT imaging, and the worst of all, magnetic resonance imaging, an MRI. My little brother has always been afraid of enclosed spaces, especially tunnels. The MRI procedure with its jawboning mechanical clangs inside the tunnel proved a nightmare for him, as well as for the technicians who had to strap him down.

On our final appointment, a consultation with Dr. Rose and a pediatric cardiac surgeon, we got the bad news. They recommended that Jesse be scheduled to undergo a surgical procedure to correct his heart defect.

Robin Stanley did not join us on the day they presented Jesse's prognosis. Only my mother and I were with the doctors in the office.

"It's called a transcatheter closure, Karin," Dr. Rose said. "A closure of the ASD...that's the name for Jesse's heart defect." She had a very high-pitched voice. Her habit of clicking a ballpoint pen was annoying, but on this day Dr. Rose appeared less compulsive and more composed. She walked us painstakingly through what Jesse was facing.

"The procedure will involve the use of a single-disc prosthesis," the surgeon said. The pediatric cardiac surgeon was younger than my mother and looked as though he hadn't started shaving yet. He wore a powder blue surgical cap with dancing cartoon animals, tigers, elephants and pink pigs.

My mother asked, "What is a single-disc prosthesis?"

The surgeon made a circle with his thumb and index finger. "It's about this small. Folds up like an umbrella. After proper placement, the prosthesis is released and the defect closed."

My mother sighed. "What are...?" Her emotions stole her voice, which she struggled to regain. "What are my boy's chances, I mean, on the operating table?" She blinked at the horrible thought of Jesse's little body under the surgical knife.

Dr. Rose shook her head and gave us one of her celebrated smiles. "That's what's so great about this, Karin. Jesse doesn't have to undergo a lot of trauma...there is no need for open heart surgery, if that's what's worrying you?"

"Yes, it is my biggest concern."

"The procedure, Mrs. Stanley," the surgeon said, "is done in the cath lab. Jesse is given what we call conscious sedation, and the prosthesis is introduced from the femoral vein and advanced upward across the defect to the left atrium. We call it interventional therapy. Not surgery."

"Will you have to cut my son open?" my mother asked.

The surgeon shook his head. "This isn't something where we have to put your child on by-pass."

"The heart-lung machine," Dr. Rose interjected, shaking her head. "None of that is necessary here." She smiled reassuringly.

"We make a small incision in his leg, about here, to introduce the catheter. Once we have placed the prosthesis, your son will have a little scar. A few stitches, is all."

I was glad that Jesse was not in the room. We'd left him with the hospital daycare service on the ground floor. He would not have understood most of what was said, but he would have sensed my mother's anxiety, and this would have brought on a tantrum.

Still, after everything had been explained and shown to involve a minimum of trauma to her son, my mother trembled from relief. She brought a handkerchief to her mouth.

I reached across the arm of my chair and said, "It sounds okay, Mom. Really. Jesse's gonna be fine. Don't worry."

For the first time in weeks, as her eyes searched mine in an emotional appeal, it felt good offering support and being needed.

When tears of relief flooded her eyes, they had an empathetic effect on my own heart. I gave her a hug, and she cried on my shoulder.

On the drive home to Strand, I sat in the backseat to comfort Jesse. My mother asked if I wanted to listen to music on the radio. She had never before offered a choice of radio stations. It was always what she wanted to listen to, which was usually an incomprehensible Classical Music station. When Robin Stanley rode with us, we were subjected to talk radio, Rush Limbaugh, or the local Christian station.

"Sure. Whatever you want," I told her.

"No, I don't mind. Really. We can listen to whatever you want. Pick a station, Danny."

I picked the least parent-offensive station I could come up with, one that played Golden Oldies, to please us both. When Jim Morrison of The Doors sang "Light My Fire," I managed to get Jesse to sing along. As the station signal began to dissolve in static, and as the highway climbed the grade toward Mt. Hood, Jesse sang, "Come on, bubby, light my fi-*yah*. Come on, bubby, light my fi-*yah*," until our mother lost patience. "Danny, could you please keep him quiet. I've got a splitting headache," she said, and the radio was switched off.

Robin Stanley waited for us in the kitchen. From his expression, and from the torn envelope and school grades spread across the table, I knew that the sweetness of our time together—just the three of us alone once again—was over. My stepfather clutched my report card and glowered at me.

"What is it, honey?" my mother asked.

He handed her the grades. She clicked her tongue and took a deep breath. My grades were awful. That my stepfather had intercepted my mail did not seem to rouse her sense of fair play or rights to privacy. What bothered her was the downward trajectory of my abysmal school career. What bothered Robin Stanley was something I had not anticipated or prepared to argue against.

"You've been lying to us again," he said.

Taken aback by the accusation, my mother looked up from her study of my failure and said, "Danny got bad grades, Robin. Doesn't mean he's a liar."

He faced her, eyes blackened by self-righteousness. "What do you see…what's missing there? Why don't you see it?" His mouth tightened as my mother read the column made up of C's and an undeserved D. "*Your Mr. Phelan!* He's not listed, is he?"

My mother looked at me, again with disappointment.

"Danny," she asked. "You aren't enrolled in Mr. Phelan's class?"

"He's been *lying* to us, lying all *along!*" Robin Stanley spoke loud enough for his father to complain from the living room. We were told to hold it down so he could hear the television.

My mother held up my report card. "I don't see Mr. Phelan's class listed here. Can you explain yourself?"

Robin Stanley huffed as though my explaining anything would be another opportunity for me to lie.

I had no choice but to confess. "I am not enrolled in Mr. Phelan's class."

"*So you lied!*" Robin Stanley shouted.

"Look." I began in a forceful tone that softened when my mother raised an eyebrow of suspicion. "I'm not enrolled in Mr. Phelan's physical sciences class—"

"See, I told you," Robin Stanley said. He shrugged and shook his head. "I told you."

"*But*...but he lets me help him out on fieldtrips. They're for extra credit—"

"Extra credit? You can't get extra credit. Not if you're *not* taking the class."

"Please, Robin, let him finish."

I surrendered the point. "I'm Mr. Phelan's...assistant. I carry the equipment, set up the telescope, stuff he can't do."

"Such a liar. What did Mr. Phelan do before *you* showed up, huh? What, was he completely helpless? Is that what you expect me to believe? Nonsense."

"Danny," my mother said, closing her eyes and slowly opening them to search mine for the truth of the matter. "If I call Mr. Phelan, if I call him right now, will he say the same thing you've just said? That you're his...what did you call it, his assistant for these outings?"

I nodded, calling her bluff.

"Well, if I call, and Mr. Phelan says...if he denies what you're saying, what am I supposed to think?"

"I don't know, Mom. Think what you want to think," I said, turning to leave the kitchen for my bedroom.

"You're not excused," Robin Stanley said. "Don't you walk away when your mother's talking to you."

I faced my stepfather in the kitchen galley to measure my strength against his. I'd already proven that I could beat him on his best day. Yes, he reigned supreme in the pathetic doublewide trailer he called "home." Yes, he was my mother's second husband. But he wielded no power over me, not really. Facing one another in yet another occasion where Robin Stanley put me down, the thought crossed my mind to open his desk drawer and dump his secret stash of pornography on the Bible. I considered exposing him for what he truly was, a sanctimonious hypocrite.

But as soon as the thought crossed my mind, doubt nibbled at my confidence. What if Robin Stanley had moved the perverted material to a new hiding place? I imagined myself, shouting accusations, unlocking the desk only to find the drawer empty of evidence. What if the brass key to the drawer were no longer hidden between the pages of his "Good Book"? I think my stepfather sensed my doubt when he squared his shoulders and said, "You've got nothing. No future, no leg to stand on. Nothing. What kind of boy do you think you are? You lie to your mother. You forge my signature. *Yes!* Yes, I remember. Remember all of it, Daniel. You impregnate some girl, and now *this*." He sniffed at the scent of victory. "You are forbidden from going on any more of these fieldtrips. Do you understand? *Do you understand!?*" he shouted.

Because I said nothing, my mother retaliated in her most disciplined Southern drawl. "Go to your room."

*   *   *

Before the calendar came around to the day of his operation, Jesse ended up on a therapeutic teeter-totter. His pediatrician told us that he seemed more prone to seizures, for which I again blamed Robin Stanley. But the doctor said it had something to do with his worsening condition. Yet, she cautioned against increasing his pills. To protect Jesse against an allergic reaction to anesthesia, Dr. Rose recommended a gradual reduction of Dilantin and Ritalin. "We need to wash out his chemical burden." The doctor warned of what she called "rebound hyperactivity." But rather than an increase in hyperactivity, it was during these days that Jesse napped often without complaint. In the hours when he was awake, he moped around, sometimes pushing his toy trucks on the indoor-outdoor carpeting of the doublewide. More often than not, he watched television like a zombie. He tired easily and lost his appetite, and I became even more protective of my little brother.

A few days before the surgical procedure, Robin Stanley laid down the law: I would attend my classes at school rather than accompany them to the hospital. Both my mother and he were in agreement. Dr. Stanley would shut down his optometry practice, which he could ill afford to do, and my mother would take time off from teaching in order to be there for Jesse. But to get my grades up, I was ordered to attend my classes.

"So, you can go, but I can't? What about the classes *you* teach?" I said. My mother replied that she had made arrangements with the principal for a substitute. "The school's gonna get a substitute for the substitute? Why can't I go?" I demanded. Robin Stanley forbade me from joining them. My father would have called his contempt for my rights a *fait accompli*. At a time when Jesse needed me most, my stepfather strove to divide and conquer. The thought of being separated from my brother was unbearable.

When I demanded to be with Jesse at the hospital, Robin Stanley shook his head and clinched his teeth. "Nope. I forbid it."

"It could go bad for him," I said, "if I'm not there…Mom, you see how much Jesse needs me. Come on. I've got to be there."

"He'll be fine, Danny."

"You don't even know his dosing schedule."

"Don't talk to your mother that way." Robin Stanley frowned.

I narrowed my eyes at the man. "This has nothing to do with you, Robin. He's not *your* kid."

He turned to my mother. "See how he talks to me?" His right hand groped for the Marlboro Lights in his shirt pocket. He sighed and shook his head in exasperation. He could not have been more thankful that I was scheduled to attend the Jesus Military Academy, and yet he wished for an earlier departure. He stepped outside, onto the back porch for a smoke. With the door ajar, he continued to reiterate why he was prohibiting me from being with Jesse on the most critical day in his life, exhaling his acrid smoke.

Speaking to be heard above my stepfather's bromides, I said, "Mom, you can't do this. Jesse needs me."

"You said yourself, it's a simple thing the doctors are doing. Jesse will be fine. I want you to concentrate on bringing up your grades, okay?"

"You're not going!" Robin Stanley shouted from outside, his cigarette smoke slipping into the kitchen through the open door. And then my stepfather did something my mother had never heard him do before. He cursed me, using the Lord's name in vain. He said, "You're a goddamned godless bastard." These were the exact words he used, and their effect on my mother was striking.

I think, the "godless" part was what she found most offensive, because years ago I'd heard her call my dad "bastard" every other night. So I don't think Robin's calling me one rattled her chain. On the surface, Robin Stanley's profanity was not a tipping point in their brief marriage. But it had a sudden, negative effect on my mother. It was as though certain founding assumptions on which she'd based her marriage were yanked out from under her. By calling me "godless," Robin Stanley had overstepped his authority with her boys. Yes, it was true: as far as my mother was concerned, I had violated her trust. I had been caught in more lies than poor old Richard Nixon. As far as she knew, I had impregnated a girl with an illegitimate child—her first grandchild—but we were blood, and blood was thicker than the water that ran in Robin Stanley's veins.

Without a word to me, she stepped onto the porch and shut the door. At first, they kept their voices low as they walked away from the doublewide, toward the barn, to keep the argument private. But as soon as my mother's anger wore down her timidity, I followed the fight by eavesdropping on their shouting as they paced the property. When they reversed direction, my mother's voice came loud and clear from the front yard. There, Robin Stanley said he deserved more respect as the "head of household." He had every right to exert his authority, he said. "It's in the Bible, Karin. Maybe you should read it more often." My mother said something I could not hear, and my stepfather shouted back, "And now you want to bring that illegitimate baby into this house? That's ridiculous!" More muffled arguing, and then my mother shouted, "Don't you dare call it a *bastard*, Robin! It is *my* grandchild!" They dragged their battle into the house, to their bedroom. Doors were slammed, which awakened Jesse from his nap. I went to him and carried him to the kitchen, the warmest room in the house. There he sat on my lap, wrapped in a blanket. Whenever my mother shouted, Jesse opened his eyes, and I had to reassure him again. Eventually, he fell asleep.

At this point Eve Stanley entered the kitchen and fit into her apron. Tying the strings behind her back, she said, "How'd you two like some fresh cookies?"

"Tanks, Gammy," Jesse said rubbing sleep from his eyes.

My stepfather's mother had invented numerous ways to avoid conflict in her life. Eve Stanley's answer to disagreements, to raised voices and slammed doors, was to bake cookies or bread or pies. During our residency we were never without bakery goods.

My brother and I sat at the table to watch Eve Stanley stir a tall wooden spoon through thick cookie dough. She mashed eggs and sugar into a ball of butter and flour. The warmth of the oven and our companionship must have had an intoxicating effect because she began to talk openly of a fondness for her previous daughter-in-law, Robin Stanley's first wife. She made unfavorable comparisons to my mother. "Your mother does not like it here," she said. "That's clear enough. She resents living under our roof." She continued as though I was not sitting there, as though Daniel Aiken were not Karin Stanley's first-born son; as though we all were impartial observers in what Eve Stanley described as "these awful times" in her boy's life. And when the cookies were pulled from the oven and served hot, I left mine untouched on the plate. After Jesse ate his, and after I cleaned up the crumbs beneath his chair, I offered him my share. I refused to eat something so full of denial and petty jealousy.

Three days later, Jesse underwent the surgical intervention to correct his heart defect. It was a complete success. Robin Stanley and my mother were at his side when he recovered from the anesthesia called conscious sedation. The first thing he asked for was me. "I want Dammy, Mommy." When he would not stop screaming my name and sobbing uncontrollably, my mother decided to give the school a call and have me paged to come to the phone. A senior in her cheerleading uniform strolled into my third period biology class, fingering a note from Principal Horvath. When the teacher, Mr. Grayson, read the note and gestured that I come forward, I thought my heart would stop. *It's got to be about Jesse*, I thought. My kid brother must have died on the operating table. I don't remember taking a full breath until Principal Horvath explained in the privacy of his office what was going on. He handed the telephone receiver to me and said, "It's your brother." I spoke with Jesse on the phone for over half an hour, until he finally calmed down and my mother came on the line. "Thanks, Danny," she said. After I hung up, Principal Horvath handed me a box of Kleenex. I had not realized that I'd been crying.

Chapter 15

I had been thinking about getting a tattoo. A good number of kids in first period PE had at least one, but no red and blue ink marked my skin. Even some of the Christian kids that I remembered from Rise Up had discretely tattooed iconography on their ankles and wrists. I never saw a tat on Hitch, but he and I often dared one another to get inked at The Illustrated Man in Strand. Now that my best friend had run away to Arkansas in a stolen car, it was up to me to get the job done on my own. To this end I studied tattooing magazines in search of an icon, a beautiful sign or single word, an image that identified who I was and how I wanted others to see me.

Half the fun of getting a tattoo was making a choice among the endless possibilities. A tattoo should be personal—because it will be with your forever. It should say something about what you care about or what you believe in. It should bring to life a dedication or life-long romance. Many older veterans of foreign wars who attended our church had "Mom" needled into their skin or the name of their wives or girlfriends, names like Nancy, Betty, and Gloria. Some chose an illustration of a cartoon wolf, Wily Coyote or Bugs Bunny above their nicknames. Others had the Stars and Stripes or their branch of the armed services' emblem. The less imaginative among my generation had standard Maori symbols, jagged snakes encircling biceps, or a cloverleaf representing an Irish heritage; the Om symbol for New Agers, a marijuana leaf for the Stoners. A tattoo should make a statement of your independence, of nonconformity, in spite of everyone my age having one.

But after my preparation and anticipation, I chickened out.

I made it as far as the side street where Strand's illustrated man himself sat in a wicker chair set in the window of his shop, shirtsleeves rolled up, smoking a cigarette that he rolled himself. In early February, I found him reading a bodybuilding magazine. When he glanced up, he recognized me from my previously missed appointments. He shook his head in disgust. His name was Magnus, no last name, just the one, like Cher or Sting or Bono. When I visited the shop for the first time, I made the mistake of complimenting the scrawling tattoos on his arm. He corrected me.

"Body art," he said. "It's called body art."

For my edification, he ran through an abbreviated history of *body art*. I learned that the Egyptians had perfected tattooing about five thousand years ago. "Some of them mummy Pharaohs had 'em," Magnus said. The back wall was covered in photographs of Maori warriors. "The original people of New Zealand," Magnus said, tapping a photograph of the Maoris. "They invented color body art." When I expressed concerns about infectious disease—my mother had fueled my phobia of hepatitis and AIDS—Magnus described his practice in detail. "Never work with old needles. I use disposable points like this. Fresh out of the box." He assured me there was no risk of infection. And what if I want it removed later, I asked. "Laser beam," Magnus said. "Wipe it clean off. No sweat." I was sold until he ran down a column of figures and cited cost per square inch. Twice the price for two-color body art, higher for any tat not found in his Catalogue of Standards. "You bring in something, picture out of a magazine, book or something, it's twenty bucks the first hour, fifteen after that," Magnus said. He charged more for original art because of the hassle. "Stenciling is a pain in the ass."

I decided on an image of Earthrise as seen through the camera lens of the Apollo 8 astronauts who were the first to orbit the moon. Magnus warned how geometric designs would fade and get out of shape over a lifetime. "Something like that'll end up looking like a Bartlett pear. And you'll end up having to explain yourself to every swinging dick you run into." I returned home to think it over and came up with a second choice. I wanted our solar system in miniature, up the outside of my right arm, Mercury, Mars, Neptune, all the planets, with a sunburst as the central theme on the back of my hand. Magnus went to his calculator and came up with an astronomical figure to match my idea. Out of the question. Next, I narrowed my choice of planets to one that most intrigued me— Jupiter. Of all the planets, with the exception of our own, Jupiter with its Great Red Spot has a unique appearance. Yes, Saturn has its rings, but Jupiter has size and color. After Magnus cautioned once more that oval tattoos would distort as skin aged, I picked the gaseous giant in a two-color depiction, blue with a red blotch. It was a stroke of genius, I thought, until I came across photographs in *Time Magazine* taken the month before by the Galileo orbiter spacecraft. Jupiter was not blue but like polished agate with bands of ochre and veins of rust. I showed Magnus the picture, and he just shook his head.

Finally, I decided on the astronomical symbol for Jupiter, which looks like the number 4 superimposed over 2 in curlicue fashion. It is also the alchemical symbol for tin. When I showed Magnus a Xerox copy of the symbol, he said, "What's that, your sign?" I worried that others might see it as an astrological sign and think me uncool.

When I was fifteen, the worst thing in the world was to be labeled *uncool*. Cool was everything. It was what most teen-aged boys worked hardest at, not schoolwork or even sports, but acting cool; an elusive behavior that we sought to reinvent ourselves as something less foolish or awkward. Many decades ago, when the Supreme Court debated the definition of obscenity with an eye toward censorship, Justice Stewart had said he could not define pornography "…but I know it when I see it." Well, it was the same with *cool*—it was ill defined, but we knew it when we saw it. Although most of us sensed when someone had it and when someone didn't, nobody referred to it as "cool." We rejected the hackneyed slang of previous generations. To infuse your everyday speech with the word "cool" was about as uncool as the word "groovy."

Only a few kids in the student body, who occupied a social niche outside the mainstream, ever spoke the word. These were the total nerds, the pocket-protector types and the Goth-retros, whose rebellion rejected not merely parents and established authority but the popular kids at the top of the high school food chain, the *coolest* among us. Where did I fit in? Nowhere and everywhere. It is simplest to say that I was invisible. But had I picked Jupiter's symbol for my tattoo, I would have had to explain astronomy versus astrology to all the cool kids. Tattooing the symbol of Jupiter on my arm ran the risk of banishment among an already elite, inaccessible student body.

I decided against a permanent tattoo. And so, while sitting in bed in the dark with Jesse snoring across the room, I stuck a black pen to a penlight with duct tape and sketched Jupiter's symbol on my forearm as best I could. I figured, if one of the kids in first period gym laughed at it and mocked, "Is that your sign, Aiken? That's so uncool," I could always wash it off with soap and water.

*   *   *

"Here is the church, here's the steeple…."

My kid brother loved when our mom played this game. She would wrap her arms around him and intertwine her hands, making a pyramid shape with index fingers and closed thumbs. "Open the door and look at *all* the people." Every time Mom enfolded her hands and wiggled her fingers, Jesse was delighted as though each occasion were the first. I suppose, for his limited aptitude it was. He eventually learned the trick, and every chance he got, he showed me—"Where're all the pebbles, Dammy?" To cheer him on, I pretended shock or dismay, depending, but after endless performances of full and empty churches, I got fed up and sent him away. I regret doing this. Today, I wish Jesse were here to show me "all the pebbles."

We attended service every Sunday at the Valley Shepherd Community Church. The site looked more like a military compound than the campus of a religious organization. The most striking aspect was the American flag that waved day and night in the eternal luminescence of floodlights. By comparison, the cross on the steeple looked puny. Of course, churches are not made up entirely of brick and mortar but by people. The congregation makes the church. Valley Shepherd's three thousand members could not worship all at once, and so they attended four different services. With youth activities such as Rise Up, Bible study groups, workshops and the like, the campus was never empty of "all the pebbles."

Valley Shepherd was made up of a social sampling of the Strand Township. That is to say, it didn't reflect America's diversity of races, creeds and social values, as it would have in San Francisco. You would not have seen a lesbian couple praying next to a middle-aged man and woman, as you would have at a Unitarian church. At our church everyone looked and acted alike. It was uncanny. Blond-haired children were the rule. Northern European stock for parents usually paired up along heterosexual lines. Valley Shepherd gave every appearance of what Jerry Falwell and James Dobson called the "moral majority" and "value voters." They were working- and middle-class white people who had escaped urban America for the relatively crime-free Oregon countryside. For me, going to church was like taking a walk through another century.

On a Sunday in February, my mother invited Annette Kaysen to worship with us. Oregon rainfall and flooding had reached biblical proportions, and Annette's foster parents lived along a vulnerable stretch of Deep Creek, in a ravine where Robin Stanley parked the Buick behind a makeshift wall of sandbags.

"May I run down to get her?" I asked my mother. I had hoped for two minutes alone to confront Annette over her bogus claims that I was the father of her illegitimate child, but my mother declined. She preferred to be the one to fetch her since she had called the foster mother to make the arrangements. On the car ride to church, Jesse sat between Annette and me, squirming like a sea otter at the sight of the pretty girl in a white miniskirt and heavy makeup, this new addition to our "family." Other than saying "howdy," I said next to nothing in Annette's presence, preferring instead to sulk and give sidelong looks of self-pity.

At church, while Robin Stanley and my mother ushered Jesse to Sunday school, she and I had a chance to talk.

"So, how've you been?" Annette asked.

I scowled at her incredulously. "Why'd you tell 'em it was my kid?"

She took a breath. "I'm sorry, Danny. After Hitch left town, I mean, what could I do?"

"Tell 'em the truth."

"But Hitch isn't here to defend himself," she said.

In the foyer where the congregation gathered before the service, Annette and I stood side by side like examples of immoral behavior. We could almost sense the thoughts of the other teen-aged girls standing nearby. They looked at us askance as though we were carriers of the Bubonic Plague. It united us as nothing else could have, and despite my complete lack of responsibility for her pregnancy, I felt protective all of a sudden.

Trying to hide how I felt for contributing to his death, I asked a question to deflect my guilt. "So, you ever hear from Nicky Jim?"

Annette shook her head. "Nah, he's been gone for, like, couple months now."

"So, what do you think, he ran off after beating you up?"

"Nicky Jim didn't beat me up."

Earnestly, I said, "Didn't you tell Mr. Phelan that Nicky Jim beat you? Didn't you tell me—"

"You can't say anything, Danny." Her hazel eyes were watery with fear. "My mom beat me."

"Your mom?"

"It wasn't her fault. She was high. You have to promise, you won't tell no one."

I was digesting this new fact when Robin Stanley and my mother returned to escort us to the sanctuary.

Homosexuality was the principal theme of our sermon. The former head of the music department faced the congregation and suffered the equivalent of a public stoning. In a lapse in judgment, the music director had confessed to an affair with a male member of the choir. He did so in confidence to a "friend" on the worship committee, but word got back to church leadership. He was stripped of his official duties but allowed to remain a member if he publicly decried the immoral behavior. The music director was married and had four children. On this day of her husband's atonement, his overweight wife wept into a handkerchief in the front row of the service we attended. They had to endure the public humiliation again and again, at each of the four services, until the music director's reparation satisfied church leadership. It was the last time any of us would see the music director. For the complicated act of his having sex with his own gender, he lost his family, his church community, and self-respect. When I raised my objections with George Latimer who happened to be sitting nearby in the sanctuary, he explained that the music director would have been chastised for the affair had it been with a woman. "It broke the bonds of wedlock," he said in a harsh whisper. But I knew their censure had more to do with the homosexual aspect of the indiscretion than the adultery of the matter.

The culture of hate was so pervasive that I was not surprised to overhear kids from Jesse's Sunday school call the music director a "fag." Little kids learn words that hurt others from their peers who in turn hear the words from adults. As Annette and I waited at the schoolroom door to pick up my brother, I wondered which of the Sunday school teacher's had expressed the derogative. This was the church in years to come that would urge its congregation to vote "One Man, One Woman," for the Oregon anti-gay-marriage amendment. This was the church where the leadership, an all-male club, said legalizing a civil union between homosexuals would make a "mockery of marriage." This was the bastion against secularism. This was where the culture wars were fought, in the trenches between the pews, in the Bible study groups and biblical wifehood classes, at Rise Up. This was where *We*, the benevolent *Us*, were members in good standing of the Christian Club, while *They*, the malevolent *Them*, the nonbelievers, those not baptized, the unsaved, they were the enemies of God. Valley Shepherd Community Church made every effort to instruct me, and my kid brother, that we were at war with *Them*, at war for the very soul of our country.

"Here is the church, and here's the steeple. Open the door and look at all the people...."

*   *   *

On our way to Elmo's Eatery for our customary Sunday brunch, Annette Kaysen declared herself "born again" in the backseat of the Buick. My mother reached to pat Annette's knee. Robin Stanley repeated, "Praise the Lord, praise the Lord," so many times that he sounded insincere. Then again, my stepfather always sounded as though he was compensating for an unsteady faith. Jesse clapped unwittingly and got caught up in the enthusiasm of our mother's Amen's.

"This is so wonderful, Annette," she said. "Amen, Amen. Oh...here's a thought. We should be baptized together. Reverend

Vickers does a whole bunch of believers every spring, down Deep Creek somewhere. Wouldn't that be wonderful?"

When my mother overreached, it made her affections sound fake. The proposal put Annette in an anxious temper. After all, she may have been born again but that didn't mean she was willing to be dunked in snowmelt.

"Maybe she doesn't want to get baptized, Mom," I said.

Her expression reddened from the test of patience. "Just thinking of the baby," she said in a quieter voice. "Just thinking of the baby."

I hated it when she played the martyr as though my rough blood were too much for her sensibilities and her Southern rose wilted like something out of a Tennessee Williams play. She played unfairly but effectively. It was time to give something back, by my estimate, in the balance of our relationship. Our emotional separation, at the hands of my stepfather, had gone on far too long. I decided, then and there in the back of my mother's old Buick, to build a bridge to span the chasm between us.

"Tell you what, Mom," I said. "Tell you what. I thought about it long and hard. And I decided, I'll get baptized with you."

I had shocked her, clearly from the look on her face.

"If this is what you want, we can do it together," I said.

"Do you mean it?"

Robin Stanley interrupted. "You can't just get baptized because you...out of the blue like that...just because you want to." We came to a stop at a traffic light, and he turned partially around to address me. "You have to be born again, Daniel. You have to accept Jesus into your life."

I said, "I know."

My stepfather and mother exchanged glances, the light changed and we proceeded through the intersection.

"You know what?" my mother said, shifting her weight to look directly at Annette, smiling. "I think we should discuss plans, you know, for the wedding?"

It felt as though I had opened Pandora's box. All manner of creepy things crawled over the car seats in the form of, of all things, wedding plans. By my agreeing to the baptism, somehow my mother saw it as an occasion to push for more concessions on my part. I wasn't in love with Annette, never had been. Heck, I hardly knew her. And now my mother was suggesting that we discuss wedding plans. I tried to keep my feelings to myself, but when I glared at Annette, she must have seen the heartache behind my mask. She leaned toward me and whispered, "You don't have to look so mean at me."

My mother clicked her tongue. "You should be happy for your future bride, Danny? Why aren't you happy?" She looked to Annette. "It means so much to me to have you all here with us today. I can't tell you." Her voice cracked theatrically in a Southern mannerism. "And with a grandbaby on the way. I don't know when I've been so happy."

My mother's mind must have tripped over an upturned stone on her way to declaring how happy she was.

"Mrs. Stanley," Annette said. "Dr. Stanley. I got something to confess."

"Oh, sweetie…" My mother reached around again, this time to touch Annette's face.

"Lord Jesus doesn't ask that of you," Robin Stanley said. "You're thinking of Catholics. They're the ones with the confessionals." He pulled into the restaurant parking lot. "You're saved. You're one of the chosen now. That's all that counts."

In the rearview mirror, I caught my stepfather's eyes. He looked genuinely pleased with himself.

"No, I don't mean that," Annette said nervously.

"Well. What is it, sweetie?"

"It's Daniel," Annette said quickly. "I think you should know. *Daniel's not the father.*"

She might as well have set off an explosive inside the car.

I have to be honest—I don't remember details of our brunch at Elmo's. I do remember my mother's ambivalence over the loss of her first grandchild and over the rehabilitation of her son. Her emotions were tricky, uncertain about how she felt that the baby Annette carried was not her relation. But she seemed relieved that her son had not done the deed. I remember Robin Stanley's dissatisfaction that the filthy mark against my character was wiped clean. I have a picture in my mind of Annette, sitting across from me in the restaurant booth and acting contrite as she sipped water and pressed a ring of lipstick on the glass. It is peculiar in life how we remember the little things like lipstick rings on cups but forget the bigger picture, things of greater importance. For over an hour, I seldom spoke unless addressed, preferring to let the redemption simmer a while longer, before another false accusation was hurled my way. As they ordered cheese omelets and blueberry pancakes, coffee and orange juice, I got lost in a mesh of thoughts about the past few months, about Hitch and Marie, about Nicky Jim, Mr. Phelan, about my father and his bride on their Maui honeymoon. I imagined the surgical device in Jesse's heart as he giggled at Annette's attentiveness, as surely she pondered the life growing inside her womb and the changes it foretold. I watched stone-faced as my mother teased Jesse by stealing a piece of sausage off his plate. I listened to Robin Stanley's complaints about an aching molar in the back of his mouth. My thoughts, like an overwhelming congestion, got caught in my throat, and I excused myself from the table. In the empty restroom, in a booth with the door securely locked, I wept into a wad of toilet tissue, a kind of quiet weeping, from the relief of it all and for the desolation that had become my life.

*   *   *

In the week that followed, after school hours, I visited Mr. Phelan in his classroom. The school administration had set aside an hour once a week for teachers to meet with, counsel or tutor students. Mr. Phelan's class schedule was too full to allow an hour in the middle of the day, and so he took his administrative time after the last bell.

I had never been in his classroom before, in this inner sanctum of the most popular teacher at school. It was nothing special, but I supposed our perception of classrooms, the surface of things, has nothing to do with their true substance. Still, I knew I would never have the benefit of sitting at a desk and listening to Mr. Phelan's lectures. Getting into his class would be impossible now that Robin Stanley had enrolled me at a military academy. Another blighted hope as remote as Jupiter, shattered as surely as my dreams of returning to live with my father.

Mr. Phelan was sitting behind his desk as he corrected papers. Wire-rimmed eyeglasses perched on his nose. Without looking up, he said, "Hello, Daniel."

"Mr. Phelan."

The legs of the chair ratcheted against the linoleum when I pulled it and set down my book bag.

He glanced up only briefly as though he did not have time to spare.

"What is it?"

I sat carefully in the chair, blinking, afraid to make another sound.

Mr. Phelan removed his glasses and dropped the ballpoint pen on the stack of papers. He raised his eyebrows and shrugged. "You want to talk to me about something?"

"I want you to know," I started to say but cleared my throat. "I want you to know, it's not my child."

He replaced his eyeglasses and went back to correcting papers. "Glad to hear that, Daniel." And without looking at me, he said, "Will there be anything else?"

"So...now will you let me come back, you know, on the fieldtrips to help out?"

Mr. Phelan looked at me over the rims of his glasses. "I never stopped you."

"Okay, but my stepfather won't let me."

He shook his head and returned to his papers. "That's between you two. Something you have to work out yourself."

I listened as his pen scratched the papers and the clock on the wall ticked away the seconds.

"Your stepfather did call me about something, though, just yesterday," he said.

"He did? What did he call about?"

"He wanted to know if I or someone I knew would be interested in buying a transilluminator with two rechargeable handles."

"What's a transilluminator?"

Mr. Phelan shifted a short stack of papers and aligned them by tapping them against the desktop. "Something to do with his optometry practice, I would imagine." He lifted a paper from another stack and set to work on it. "Guess he's selling his business. I'm sure he's talked to you about it."

I shook my head.

Some kids outside ran past his window, and in spite of it being closed, we could hear their profanity and mockery. Mr. Phelan got up from his desk and opened the window. He shouted, "Is that you Jake? Ulrich. I don't like that kind of language, not in the least. And I especially don't like it outside my classroom. You hear me?" One of the kids said something that I didn't hear clearly. "That's right. No more of that." And he shut the window.

After he sat down, he looked up from his papers and said, "Is there anything else, Daniel?"

"Mr. Phelan, are you and my mother...?"

He understood my incomplete thought and took offense.

"Don't insult your mother. Or me." He rubbed the creases around the corners of his mouth. "You're talking about a married woman. Your mother."

Something in his voice spurred me to ask, "Do you like her?"

Mr. Phelan pushed back in his chair, and his hands came to rest on the papers. "Your mother and I are *friends*. And frankly, I don't think that's any of your business. Does that compute?"

I nodded and reached for my book bag. At this time in my life, my stores of courage had been spent on nonsense, leaving very little nerve for my everyday encounters, especially with a favorite teacher. I stood to leave.

"I heard your brother...I'm sorry, I've forgotten his name," Mr. Phelan said.

"Jesse."

"I heard Jesse had an operation. Is he all right?"

I nodded. "Doing much better now."

Mr. Phelan looked away thoughtfully and then returned to his papers. "Someday," he said. "Someday you'll understand. Men and women...adults can be friends without all the rest of it. The problem comes from the small minds of others. Not from the simplicity and beauty of the friendship, but from the duplicity of closed-minded people." He pushed his glasses up the ridge of his nose. Finally, he said, "Good afternoon, Daniel."

Chapter 16

"How do you feel," Robin Stanley asked, "after you asked Jesus into your life?"

I adjusted my baseball cap, having worn it forward this day to please my stepfather. How should I answer without giving away my secret?

Walking against the east wind, we wore parkas zipped to the neck as we found our way down a row of desiccated raspberry canes to the fence line. We stood at a distance of two hundred yards from the doublewide, to talk privately. We had walked away from the family dynamic of Virgil watching television and Eve's interminable baking. As my mother coined it, "So you two can have a nice chat about your future." Before us, visible through a thin mist, Mt. Hood had a ghostly look under a shroud of snow in the darkening afternoon.

"Because, you know, if you're lying, Daniel..."

"I'm not lying."

"There are cases in the Bible of what happens to people who say they've been born again when they're not."

I nodded. "Haven't got to that part yet."

My personal beliefs were sacred to me. As unformed and naïve as they were, I was determined not to forfeit what I believed to please him, no matter the consequences, but I was willing to pretend being born again if it meant a return of house privileges and fewer "family" meetings at the kitchen table.

For the first time in our relationship, Robin Stanley acted the father, as though he cared, as though everything that had come between us was forgiven. This manipulation of the facts put me on guard. He straightened his shoulders and gazed eastward toward the mountain. He spoke and postured with a hardened squint like Clint Eastwood, not like the narrow-shouldered optometrist I knew him to be.

"It's just that," he began. "It's just that I want to make sure you're not making all this up." He faced me. "This bit about being born again. You'd better look into your heart. Make sure you're sincere." He looked away, leaning against the fence in a cowboy pose. "Because what you're messing with is very powerful. More powerful than you can imagine."

Jupiter came to mind, that and the hidden influence of its gravity on the evolution of our world. I had gazed upon Jupiter and counted its moons through the lenses of Mr. Phelan's telescope. I had stood at an unimaginable distance from the sheer vulgarity of its power, a gravitational pull strong enough to strip my bones of meat, its atmospheric gases condensed into something between ice and liquid petroleum. Jupiter did not know of my existence. Nor did it care. It was an inert unfeeling mass, and yet from what I knew, the giant planet wielded far greater power over me than anything Robin Stanley had ever talked about. Why should I fear the wrath of an unseen God because of the universally inherited guilt of Original Sin, which was something I found impractical and archaic? It seemed to me that Jupiter was a force in the universe to be reckoned with. In my life I had yet to see any evidence of the god of my stepfather.

"And of course…" A triumphant smile came to him. "You do know that you'll still have to go to the Jesus Academy next fall, right?" He exaggerated a furrowed brow as though he were talking to a child. "You wouldn't just be *saying* you're born again to get out of that, would you?"

I wore a mask of contrition as I shook my head.

"Good. Good."

He took a breath before he said that my mother was pleased by my commitment to baptism. "You're going to heaven with us now." He said that those who believed in Jesus would be saved to live for eternity among the host of the chosen. "It's like being admitted to a very exclusive Country Club." It seemed to me, Robin Stanley's version of Christianity was all about counterbalancing the fear of death. Having faith was a trade off—if you accepted Jesus, then death was conquered. My father down in California would have called this *quid pro quo*. In my heart, I was not ready to compromise my honesty for promises made by a supernatural being.

"We're all sinners," Robin Stanley said. "God does not distinguish between greater and lesser sins. Even if you accept Jesus, Daniel, you're no better than the heroin addict who repents. Or some degenerate or homosexual. No better than the lowest of the low, do you understand?" All that one could do, according to his reading of scripture, was to accept without question and be fearful of the wrath of God. My stepfather was obsessed with the "End Times," which he believed were upon us from his study of the *Left Behind* series. "The Rapture," he said, "is coming. Make no mistake about it."

He winced when he inhaled through his mouth and the arctic air bit his sore gums. At the beginning of March, he had undergone a root canal. I was told that my punching him in the nose had caused a dental emergency. The dentist had explained to my mother that Dr. Stanley would require deep teeth cleaning to treat advanced gum disease—he rarely flossed, and he smoked regularly—but my stepfather refused to make an appointment. "The Lord's coming back soon, Karin. I don't think we have time. Why should I spend the money?" After the Second Coming and the Rapture, after Jesus made good on His promise to return to Earth, Robin Stanley firmly believed he, a small town optometrist on the verge of bankruptcy, would reign supreme in heaven like a mini-god. "In heaven," he said, "we will all wear diademed crowns, Daniel. Can you believe it?"

He patted my shoulder as we returned to the doublewide, and I wondered if Robin Stanley sensed my distaste for him in the knotted muscles of my shoulders and neck.

"Yes, Robin," I said, stepping behind him. "I can believe it."

I didn't accept any of it as true, but the bond between my mother and I had improved because both she and my stepfather believed I was saved and because I had agreed to be baptized. I had agreed not because I was saved—far from it—but in order to get back in my mother's good graces now that Annette had told the truth, now that my reputation had been restored. After they gave a student Bible to me, I carried it everywhere to please my mother. I would often strike the pose of a novice Christian. I let her catch me "studying scripture" in my bedroom, but what my mother failed to see was the paperback copy of William Burroughs' *Naked Lunch* behind the ramparts of the Bible. Had circumstances been different, had my mother not married a man who compensated poorly for feelings of extreme inadequacy, had Robin Stanley considered religion a personal choice, not some kind of vendetta, and had I been accepted for who I was and not been told every day what kind of person I should be, perhaps then I would have developed a sincere interest in Christianity. But as it was, I feigned curiosity to safeguard my mother's love.

When I look back at the boy I was, I refuse to judge my dishonesty. Consider the stress that I was under to conform to Robin Stanley's worldview. I was being forced to live passively under "his roof." He claimed authority over me, and my deviation from the "righteous path" had resulted in his campaign to send me away to military school. From the beginning he had intended to separate me from my mother. And so, I challenged his authority by promising to join my mother in the baptismal waters of Deep Creek. I lied because, if I had learned anything at Valley Shepherd Community Church, it was to beware of people who hold a claim on absolute moral authority.

*   *   *

Winter had not yielded its grip on the world, and Easter was weeks away, the summer a distant hope. Spring hinted its promise in the farmers' fields, furrowed and spread with lime to sweeten the soil, where green shone at the edges and in pockets of warming earth. Branches of alder and maple had yet to burst with new growth, orchards of cherry and apple trees stood still, waiting for the blossoming. It was the time before the greening of a world full of cold sunshine.

The Deep Creek that I knew came from the rugged violence of the Cascades. It was a cataract rushing for the sea through volcanic ravines. Lower down, where the creek met the Clackamas River, before joining the greater Willamette, the alluvial land affords a broadening into harmless eddies and quiet pools along sandy banks. This was where my mother and I were to be baptized, on a deceptively peaceful shore.

We rode together down Highway 11 in the Valley Shepherd School bus, a yellow wreck with bad brakes. The flock wore ceremonial white robes over street clothes for extra warmth. We sang praise songs, and Pastor Sonny Vickers, also dressed in white, stood in the aisle and steadied himself by gripping a stirrup. He cradled the Bible in his free hand. Shouting to be heard above the shrieking brakes, he told us that life was a battle between spiritual forces of good and evil. Life was a conflict in which he warned, "You must gird your loins. It is good to be saved, but prepare yourself for war against the secular world. *This* world is an illusion. What we see, smell, taste and hear is not real. The world isn't real, not like heaven. And when we get to heaven, the difference will make us all stand up and sing praises to the Lord. The colors, the music! The heavenly host praising the Lord God Almighty. Only then will we see, truly *see*, this world..." He nearly lost his balance when the bus lurched against a pothole. "We will look down and see, this world is a place of shadows. A battlefield against evil. Where the Lord gave us a choice, to be saved...or not." He wrenched the stirrup in his hand, and smiled. "And *you*..." He pointed the Bible at us. "*You* made the right choice. You are about to be *saved!*" He asked that we join together in singing another praise song.

My mother leaned toward me and said, "I'm thinking of lightening my hair to bring out the auburn, with some henna. Do you think that'll be all right with Dr. Stanley?"

Her question was incongruent. Here she was, poised in an important step on her spiritual journey, and she had chosen to talk about dyeing her hair. The subject was at odds with the gravity of what we were about to do. Besides, why should her personal choice of hair color need Robin Stanley's approval?

She and I sat next to one another, and Robin Stanley sat next to Jesse. Earlier in the day, my brother had thrown a conniption fit at church where we stood in line for the bus. We calmed him down by letting him wear a white robe "like the other pebbles." It was right for us to make him feel that he belonged. Jesse struggled with compulsive behaviors. To make certain that his big brother had not abandoned him, he swung around repetitively to look for me among the parishioners on the bus. Each time he did so, his flat features were riddled by fear until our eyes met and he grinned. Only then would he be satisfied that I was nearby, only to repeat the behavior a minute later. Robin Stanley had run out of patience trying to muzzle Jesse. My stepfather stared straight ahead and clapped to the music, as though, by paying no attention to my kid brother's compulsive behavior, it would go away. When it did not, Robin Stanley reprimanded him. Had he laid a finger on Jesse, I would have surged up the aisle and reacquainted my stepfather with his first punch in the nose. Damn the baptism. Forget the ceasefire. Nobody came between my kid brother and me.

We arrived at a Boy Scout staging area near Deep Creek and disembarked the bus. My mother and I paired up, which left Robin Stanley in charge of Jesse. They joined the group of friends and family off to the side, who had come to observe the baptism and provide towels. We strolled down the gentle embankment to the creek side where Pastor Vickers told us to remove our shoes while he read from Matthew 3:11:

> *John the Baptist was preaching in the desert. When he saw the Sadducees and Pharisees coming, he said, 'You brood of vipers! I baptize you with water for repentance. But after me will come one who is more powerful than I…He will baptize you with the Holy Spirit and with fire….' "*

Pastor Vickers said, "Let us pray."

Those of us about to be baptized held hands in a circle with Pastor Vickers at the center, leading us. I gave a sidelong glance at Robin Stanley, who was grinning fawningly at a young woman standing next to him. Jesse had wandered off a ways to poke a stick in the shallows. My stepfather's irresponsibility disturbed me, and I wanted to shout out that he more closely watch my brother.

As we reached the end of the prayer and as amen's were spoken, Pastor Vickers quoted from Matthew once more:

> *"When the Son of Man comes in his glory…he will sit on his throne in heaven in glory. The King will say 'I was hungry and you gave me something to eat, I was thirsty and you gave me something to drink. I was a*

stranger and you invited me in. I was sick and you looked after me, I was in prison and you came to visit me. Whatever you did for one of the least of these, you did for me.'"

He invited the first believer forward. We were to be baptized in a relatively calm pool at the waters edge. This was along a narrow strand of small stones made smooth and flat by the creek.

It was back on the farm that Jesse had said to our mother, "I'm bored again jus' like Dammy."

Whether or not he understood the seriousness of being born again, in our church Jesse was too young for baptism. The Evangelical Charismatic Christian Fundamentalism practiced at Valley Shepherd was firm on adult baptism. They argued that only adults were guilty of sinful acts, and only adults could repent and understand salvation. Pastor Vickers' favorite phrase was, "It all comes down to Jesus." But my little brother wasn't good enough for their brand of Jesus. Had he been a few years older, Jesse would have been with me and not placed under the inept care of Robin Stanley. I would never have let go of his hand or lost track of his whereabouts.

Pastor Vickers and a church elder stood up to their knees in Deep Creek. Each believer stepped forward, one at a time. They were blessed from a silver chalice of water poured out over their heads, and then the two men, one on either side, lowered the believer backwards into the pool. There were repeated phrases of "praise be to God" when the saved were delivered unto their families. They were dried in towels and wrapped in the blankets and kissed on the cheek. My mother and I were at the end of the line. I could tell, my mother was anxious. When I squeezed her hand, she smiled her Oklahoma smile meant to reassure me that everything was okay, although I knew everything wasn't. We waited together as members of the congregation were baptized.

I marveled at how each individual approached the dunking uniquely. The younger women worried about their hairdos and squealed when pulled out of the creek. Most men faced the immersion in the very cold water stoically and without complaint. The older women pinched their noses before submersion, and they clung modestly to their white robe should any female parts be exposed.

When it came time for my mother's baptism, she gave me a hug and mouthed a silent "thank you" as she stepped down, into the water. I was happy for her. This was something she believed in, and I would be the last person to challenge or harm her faith. We clapped to keep a beat and we raised our voices in a praise song—I've forgotten which one, although after a dozen weeks of regular attendance you'd expect me to have remembered. Pastor Vickers encircled my mother's small waist as he poured the blessed water over her head, ruining her hairstyle. Then they lowered her into the creek.

As my mother was pulled out, and while we sang so that heaven could hear us, I remember smiling at her and looking around to see if Jesse was watching. I wanted to make sure that he saw his mother's benevolent face. But he was not at Robin Stanley's side. Rather than watch Jesse, as he'd been asked, rather than "witness" his wife's baptism, my stepfather was chatting up one of his customers, a woman in a tight knit sweater.

I called out. "Robin, where's Jesse?" But he did not hear me above the singing.

I shouted. *"Robin!"*

He turned, distracted, scowling at me for interrupting his business.

The choir of voices trailed off.

"Jesse? *Where's Jesse?"*

My mother took a few steps up the embankment, the white robe clinging to the form of her body and dripping. She wiped her face and smeared her mascara. Her mood instantly changed from elation to terror.

"My little boy. Where's my little boy?" she said in a voice too soft for anyone to hear.

I ran up the strand of river rock, yelling Jesse's name. I went no more than fifteen yards and turned to look downstream. There, beside the creek, beyond the confused faithful in their wet robes, where the elevation dipped and the current strengthened, I saw my kid brother's Nike shoes. Jesse's "speedy shoes," the shoes Robin

Stanley had said he'd grow into. The shoes that had been too big for his feet.

"Jess?" Robin Stanley called. "Come here, Jess. Come back here right this instant."

I pushed him aside in my rush downstream. I came to the tumble of discarded socks and shoes. I reached down and picked up Jesse's favorite Winnie The Pooh T-shirt. The waterlogged robe was there, twisted together like rope.

"*Jesse!*" I called. "Where are you, buddy?"

My mother stumbled and clung to me, black mascara running with tears now, trembling uncontrollably. In the midst of this tragedy, she had not sought her husband's help to find her second-born son. She had come to me with eyes begging that I take away the horror.

"I'll find him. It'll be okay. He'll be okay."

She looked at the jumbled pile of shoes and clothing and fell to her knees. She threw her head back and screamed. The anguish of the sound she made clenched my chest, and I hollered Jesse's name again. My eyes darted below the surface of the creek, afraid to see beneath the glassy swirls and maelstroms, scanning the stampeding cascade as the creek ran away from us for the Pacific. I was praying not to see his body floating farther down, beneath a nest of roots or circling face down in the black eddies.

Robin Stanley came to my mother and lifted her up, held her tightly as she struggled for release. She flailed at his chest and cried, "No, no, no…" He spoke to her about everything being okay, that it was God's will, that her son was in the hands of the Lord, that Jesse was with the angels now.

She stiffened in his arms. She pushed him away. She screamed in a harsh guttural voice from a place deep inside, from a profound depth she never hoped to plumb, out of a panic no one, regardless of intellectual or spiritual strength, is prepared to comprehend or defend against.

"Why didn't you watch him," she said, her teeth rattling from the chill of the baptism. "You *knew* he'd wander off. *Why!* Why didn't you watch him?"

Startled by her accusations and by a vague sense of guilt, Robin Stanley said, "Honey, I was…you know how he is. It's okay. It's okay…"

By now, the baptized, Pastor Vickers and members of the flock assisted in our search. The pastor approached two fishermen in a float boat tied off upstream, asking if they'd seen a child, giving a description, pointing downstream at the three of us near his discarded clothing. Those who carried cell phones tried to call 911 but found themselves out of range. Others went into the surrounding scrub along shore, calling versions of Jesse's name—"Jesus" and "Jessica"—while others stood gaping at our trauma like spectators at a catastrophe. Most were helpless in the crisis.

I went into the creek and gasped at the glacial cold, feeling the enmity of its current against my legs. There was a spillway where Deep Creek burbled over a bed of round stones that flashed white in a steep cascade to lower, calmer water. Behind a moraine, an ancient pool had formed. The surrounding alder kept half the pool in shadow, and something below the surface at the deep end flared in the dappled sunlight like the bloodless flesh of a small body. I thrashed and half swam to the spot, and when I dove into the frigid water, the thing proved not to be my brother's body but a waterlogged tree limb stripped of its bark, slimed and eerily soft to the touch.

I burst through the surface, choking for air. I heard my mother screaming from the shore. She was inconsolable, on her knees, wailing Jesse's name. Robin Stanley stood helplessly behind, mute with an expression of hopeless distraction.

I remembered my nightmare and wished I could have taken back the thought that Jesse had fallen through the ice. In this moment when misery was already being written on our hearts, where the world was transforming before our eyes from a land full of sunlight and hope to something flat and dead and gray, where just now I was becoming acquainted with the true meaning of loss, of the irreversibility of death, I heard my brother's voice.

"Dammy?"

"*Jesse!*"

Out of a bramble on the inside bend in the creek, my kid brother crawled on hands and knees, nearly naked except for his Mickey Mouse underwear. He came out of the shadows and into the hard sunlight. My mother and I ran to him, leaving Robin Stanley alone to retrieve the oversized Nike's and damp clothes. My mother picked Jesse up and kissed and held him to her breasts. Her tears commingled with his as she pleaded, "Where were you? Didn't you hear us calling? Jesse, Jesse, Jesse my darlin'."

And in that way we had, he and I spoke without words. Here was something in my life that I had taken for granted, a charmed and sweet connection that I thought forever-lost just moments before. I asked him, "Why'd you take off your shoes, buddy. What in hell did you think you were doing?"

"Sorry…Dammy," he cried. "Hadda go pee."

We bundled Jesse in a towel, and others offered their blankets. My mother would not lessen her grip on him. She held him and alternatively kissed him and wept from relief. My greatest fear, as she carried him to the school bus, was that my kid brother might have a seizure. I returned to Robin Stanley, to ask for the prescription bottle, but he had neglected to bring it. He'd left the Dilantin at home, on the desk in the living room, next to his Bible.

Chapter 17

On the drive home from church, Robin Stanley took a wrong turn, and we ended up in ranch country on a bluff where an empty mile of hayfields was interposed by the carcass of a homestead barn. He pulled to the shoulder to check the map. None of us spoke. In the front of the Buick, he and I sat opposite one another while my mother was in the backseat with Jesse wrapped in a blanket.

The image of my brother's discarded shoes at Deep Creek stayed in my mind, but I kept quiet for fear I'd lose my temper and blame Robin Stanley. It was a clear case of intentional neglect. He would have liked nothing more than to have gotten rid of Jesse now that I was destined for an Idaho military school. He wanted our mother all to himself. I wondered about my stepfather's children from his previous marriage, wondered why their names never came up in conversation or in Robin Stanley's prayers. Why hadn't he seen or spoken to them in over a year?

I glanced at my mother in the backseat. She looked as though she had survived a traumatic ordeal, which she had. Her hair, which looked thin on her best days, was plastered to her scalp. Smudges of mascara underscored her eyes. She rocked Jesse and asked, "Would someone please turn up the heat?" These were the first words spoken since we'd left the Valley Shepherd parking lot.

Lost in a nest of back roads, Robin Stanley eventually found his way to Strand. We rolled slowly through the deserted town, most citizens being elsewhere, at church functions and Sunday afternoon suppers. The bank and library were closed along with the majority of businesses. A lone police cruiser was parked in front of the station. I gazed at the Dairy Queen and thought of Marie. I looked at the Strand Farm & Feed that was fashioned after a romantic notion of the Old West.

When we stopped at a traffic light, Robin Stanley said, "Would anyone like to get something to eat?"

My mother muttered a response neither of us heard clearly, although "you've got to be kidding" came through plainly enough. My stepfather got the gist of it. The light changed, and he made for the turnoff to the county road.

At the farm, Eve Stanley took care of Jesse so my mother could take a shower and put on some dry clothes. In the midst of all the confusion, with Virgil asking repeatedly how in blazes it could have happened, and while Eve hurried from one end of the house to the other, fussing over Jesse, I managed to get my kid brother to swallow his Dilantin before they gave him a hot bath. Then Eve Stanley put Jesse to bed, and I watched over him until he closed his eyes and fell asleep.

I was sitting at the table, wrapped in a quilt, still in my damp clothes and waiting for my turn in the shower, when my mother came into the kitchen in a pair of dark slacks and an old sweater. She'd brushed her hair straight back in a style I'd not seen on her before. She was without makeup for the first time in a long time. The determined set of her jaw dropped a hint of the decision she must have made in the bathroom while staring in the mirror, searching for answers.

"Where's your stepfather?" she asked.

She and I were alone, a rarity within the confines of the doublewide. Eve Stanley had heated me up a cup of soup to "take the chill off your bones" and had gone off to check on Jesse. I glanced up from stirring a spoon through the soup.

"Don't know. Barn, I guess."

A moment later my stepfather entered the kitchen through the side door and admitted a residue of cigarette smoke.

"How did this happen, Robin?" my mother asked immediately.

He looked surprised as though caught unawares. He was unprepared for a cross-examination.

"How did *what* happen, Karin?" he said, knowing full well what had been asked. He shut the door, didn't slam it exactly but closed it like an exclamation point closes a sentence.

My mother took the chair next to mine and frowned from exhaustion. Ordinarily, she deferred to the men in her life, to my father and her second husband. In most instances she was servile when it came to Robin Stanley, at least until now.

"Jesse," she said. Nothing more.

My stepfather blinked to discern this new attitude in his wife. He struggled to find a means of dismantling the disobedience in her voice, in her manner.

"He got away from me. You know how he is. Just impossible at times."

"He. Could. Have. Drowned."

She smacked her open palm on the table, and Robin Stanley jumped at it.

"I could have lost him. You were supposed to keep an eye on him—"

"I did."

"So he wouldn't wander off."

"*I did.*"

"No, you didn't! How could you let this happen?"

"Nothing happened." He shrugged. "He's in his room, Karin, sleeping. Jess is fine, in case you hadn't noticed."

"Hadn't *noticed?*" She looked as though suddenly she understood something about her husband that she hadn't understood before. "You bastard!"

"Karin…!"

"You're an absolute shit," my mother said in her best Oklahoma drawl. "I despise you. Positively despise you."

Dissolution was taking place before my eyes. The honeymoon, the marriage, their feigned intimacy, all of it was dissolving in the alchemy of my mother's ire. Her anger seemed only to build the more my stepfather tried to deflect blame or explain away the inexcusable.

"I don't think I deserve that, do you? Name-calling. Have you forgotten you were just *baptized?*" His mouth tightened. "You have no reason to hate me, Karin. I'm not at fault in this."

It was as though a dynamite fuse burned between them.

"Nothing happened. No harm came to the boy." He huffed.

"My son could have died today. And I'm just supposed to be, what, happy about it? Just go on? No." My mother ran a hand through her hair. "No. The least you could do, the *least*, is admit you were wrong."

He counterpunched. "I could just as well accuse you—look to your own heart, Karin. What's gone on over the past few weeks? You…and your *Mr. Phelan.*"

"What in the world are you talking about?"

"I hear rumors. People talk. I'm not blind. I see what's going on."

His accusation nearly robbed my mother of speech.

"I cannot believe, *cannot believe* you are accusing me of having an affair. Why am I even having this conversation?"

I stirred my soup like the bystander at a street brawl.

Robin Stanley said, "We shouldn't argue with your son in the room."

"If he's old enough for military school, he's old enough to hear this."

I could see a sudden change in Robin Stanley's posture. It was as though the weight of the world bore down on him. He yanked out a chair and sat dejectedly between us. "Well. You made your point, but none of it matters. Not now." He avoided looking directly at either my mother or me. "There's something you should know about the practice." He seemed to be addressing the walls and not us. "My practice…the business isn't doing well."

"I know that, Robin. It hasn't done well for weeks. For months."

"No. You should know, we're bankrupt. There, I've said it. I'm closing the business. Selling everything." He cleared his throat.

I looked to my mother. It was as though I could watch her mentally digest this news. The stated loss of his optometry practice, the innuendo about Mr. Phelan, these were raised like bricks at a barricade, as meaningless distractions from the subject at hand. Finally, she said, "Does this mean we'll lose the farm?" She was lost in thought momentarily. "What will happen to your parents?"

"No. No, I'll work it out." He propped up his head in his hands and hid his brow.

"*How?*" she demanded. "You used the farm as…what's the word? *Collateral.* The bank owns it, Robin." She picked up a saltshaker. "They own everything." She threw the saltshaker on the table, and I reached out to right it. "But that has nothing to do with what you did. Jesse could have died because you weren't watching him. "

"Your idiot son ran away. We found him. End of story." Robin Stanley said this without looking up.

"And that's how you think about Jesse? *Idiot son*."

He lowered his hands, and my mother looked at him expectantly. He was at a loss to answer now that his ruse was out in the open. Nothing in his argument had anything to do with anything. He'd only accused her of having an affair with Mr. Phelan to deflect attention from his carelessness. He'd admitted to an impending bankruptcy only because he lacked a proper defense against his negligence. Through an act of self-preservation, the secret of his business failure was now exposed. The entire applecart of lies seemed upended, and Robin Stanley's feeble sleight of hand had proved inept. He had come up empty in his battle to reassert authority by belittling what she valued most in the world, the safety and well being of her children.

My mother got up from the table and left the kitchen. We could hear her movements coming from the back bedroom, the jangle of car keys, and the rustle of her putting on her coat. Robin Stanley stood up but did not go to her. He called out her name but did not move toward the door. It was as though his shoes were fused to the kitchen linoleum.

I listened to the clickety-click of my mother's high heels cross behind us, toward the front door. We heard the latch open and then close as the door was shut. Within a minute, the Buick's engine started. My stepfather sat down in his chair, blinking at the glitter of spilt salt on the table. After the crunch of car tires on gravel and the purr of the engine faded down the driveway, without saying a word Robin Stanley got up from the table, carefully replaced the chair, and left me alone with my cold soup.

*   *   *

Night comes early to cities above the forty-fifth parallel, but this night came to the Stanley farm earlier than expected. The Oregon countryside around the town of Strand was quiet and dark. It is a silence emphasized by the hooting of an owl, a darkness strengthened by a light burning in a farmhouse window not unlike the light of a ship at sea. Traffic noise and police sirens, sounds that I'd grown used to living in San Francisco, were all but gone here. Far removed from the trappings of civilization, from the effects of what Mr. Phelan called "Edison's invention," night in the country still holds the power of the primeval. It is the way the world appeared before the industriousness of humankind, before *homo fabricanus*. Before we tainted the natural aspect of night. Here, there was no more deep or profound a thing as the dark and the hope of a solitary light burning in the distance.

The house fell into a dull quiet, bereft of life. The Stanley's acted as though someone had died. At dinner, Jesse asked after his mother, but none of the adults replied. "She'll be back soon," I told him. "It's okay. She's gone out." No television came on at the usual hour, just the murmuring conversation between Virgil and Eve Stanley in the living room. A single reading lamp was lit between their recliners until they went to bed. I retreated to my bedroom.

At nine o'clock I was reading on my bed when my stepfather walked in. He said, "You're coming with me. To look for your mother." Then he turned and walked out.

I had been lying on my bed, dressed in clean jeans and a warm sweatshirt, worrying that I might be coming down with the flu. My legs ached, and I wanted to be left alone to brood. The last thing I needed was to leave the house on a cold night, on a wild goose chase after my mother.

Jesse raised his head off the pillow. "Dammy?"

"It's all right, buddy. Go back to sleep."

I grabbed my boots, jacket and cap, and I joined my stepfather in the living room. He sat cross-legged in a recliner, nervously tapping the heel of a shoe.

"Robin," I said, "Mom took the Buick. You don't have a car."

He shook a set of keys. "We're taking Daddy's pickup."

I sat in the twin recliner to tie my shoelaces. "Why do I have to go? I'm not feeling very well."

"She's your mother. Let's go. Put your coat on."

Virgil Stanley's pickup truck was pieced together from parts scavenged at an auto dismantler. My stepfather and I, neither of us speaking, rattled down the county road where the lights from a few manufactured homes shone in the night. The weak yellow headlights from the pickup were all the light in the world. They barely revealed the road between the nursery stock farms until we came to the state highway and to a string of streetlights. Robin Stanley worried the steering wheel with his thumbnail by crosshatching a rut, and at the stop sign, he slowed the pickup to take the corner on a bad front tire. We drove through Strand proper, searching for the Buick. A police cruiser passed us, and I caught the hesitancy in my stepfather's eye: should he flag down the officer and request help in locating a misbehaved wife? The notion to ask for assistance in a small town where everyone knew your business, where everyone knew where you lived and what you farmed, was counterbalanced by Robin Stanley's indecision. He hesitated until the opportunity drove away.

"Where...?" he said. "Where would she go, your mother?"

I shook my head, the gesture lost inside the dark cab. When he asked again, I replied, "I don't know. She's probably home by now."

"No, we would've seen her. If she's in town, I'll find her."

I was thinking the obvious, that my mother had sought Mr. Phelan's company to talk things out, to bounce her argument off an impartial observer, although Mr. Phelan was far from unbiased. He was trustworthy and probably my mother's confidante, but he was not disinterested. Robin Stanley must have had the same thought. He jammed the heel of his shoe on the brake pedal and took the first left turn into the residential neighborhood.

"I know where she is."

When we turned up the familiar street, my mouth went dry and my heart hammered in my ears. The lights were on in the house, the blinds open. Through the front window I saw a figure, probably Mr. Phelan, seated in a chair, clearly not expecting or entertaining company. Robin Stanley drove partway up the sidewalk before coming to a stop and yanking the emergency brake like he meant it. He climbed out of the truck, and he banged the door shut. This encounter would not go well, I knew. I watched Mr. Phelan through the window, alerted by the clanging door of the truck. He marked his place in the book he'd been reading before closing it.

Robin Stanley went up the front steps and was pounding on the door when I came up behind him on the porch. He bent down and gripped an empty ceramic flowerpot, but I stayed his hand before he smashed it against the glass.

"Hey, hey, hey, don't do that. Don't. My mother's not here. She's not here."

Mr. Phelan opened the door and leaned forward on his crutches. He wasn't wearing the prosthesis. With a free hand he cinched the knot of his bathrobe.

Without a word, my stepfather rushed inside and nearly knocked Mr. Phelan down. I charged past Robin Stanley to rescue my teacher, reaching desperately, but luckily he regained balance on his own and hobbled to the center of the living room.

"What in hell do you think you're doing?" he demanded.

"Where's Karin? Where's my wife?"

Not in the short time we'd known each other had I seen my stepfather so agitated. The fairness of his skin had gone from pale to crimson. He faced my teacher straight on and flexed his hands into fists and he shifted weight from one shoe to the other.

"Is she missing?" When Mr. Phelan got no reply from Robin Stanley, he turned to me. "Where's your mother?"

"I don't know."

"Don't lie to me, dammit!" Robin Stanley shouted.

He shoved my teacher openhanded against the chest, acting the angry schoolboy.

Mr. Phelan lost balance and fell backwards, upsetting the floor lamp and tumbling over his reading table. His books toppled to the floor, the leaves of pages flapping like the wings of dead birds. I rushed forward but was too late. The sconce of the lamp shattered against the fireplace, and Mr. Phelan crashed to the floor, the stump of his leg wobbling in a muscle spasm. He cried out when the palm of his hand caught the bright edge of broken glass near the fireplace.

Robin Stanley stepped forward to do my teacher more harm, but I put myself between the two, squaring off, measuring the jealous fury in his eyes and countering it with rage of my own. When he hesitantly took another step, I shook my head.

"Don't do it."

My eyes never left his so that my stepfather would make no mistake about it.

This time I was prepared to do him serious damage. He blinked at my determination, the flex of my arm, and he backed down.

"Stop it. Stop it!" Mr. Phelan shouted.

He pulled himself up by the arm of the chair. Standing now, he leaned on the chair for support, grimacing at his bleeding palm. He pulled a handkerchief from the pocket of his robe and pressed it against his hand. "Danny, would you? Please. My crutches." I stood the crutches up and steadied them to make his recovery more convenient. "Thank you."

He turned to my stepfather and said in a steady voice, "Let's forget for the moment, shall we, that you've violated the law. Breaking and entering. Assault, property damage, to name just a few." He was upset over the broken lamp, and his precious books scattered on the floor. "If you leave now, Mr. Stanley—"

"That's *Doctor* to you."

Mr. Phelan laughed modestly. He wrinkled his brow and leaned down to pick up his eyeglasses. Fitting them over his ears, he said, "If you leave now...*Doctor*...I won't press charges, and we can forget the whole thing. But if you persist, I'll see you thrown in jail. Surely, a simple choice even for a doctor of optometry."

My stepfather turned and left the house, just like that.

"I'm sorry, Mr. Phelan," I said. "Real sorry."

"Go find your mother, Danny."

Before I stepped through the door, he added, "Danny. Call me. Let me know everything's all right. With your mom, I mean."

"Sure, Mr. Phelan."

Back in the pickup, Robin Stanley had some trouble turning over the engine. When it caught, he said, "Well, you're certainly *not* a Daniel come to judgment, are you?"

"I don't know what that means." I was finding it hard to hold my temper.

"It's from Daniel in the Old Testament. If you had read your Bible, like you said you did, you'd know what I was talking about." He shifted gears. "Rather than help your dad out, you helped my enemy instead. Pretty rotten judgment, if you ask me. Says a lot about your character."

We turned the corner onto the state highway, and he ran through the gears. I looked out the passenger window. Seeing the two men together in the same room had me thinking about how dissimilar they were. Both men, though vastly different, used lenses and magnifiers in their vocation and avocation. This they had in common. Robin Stanley, of course, focused his lens on the acute and narrow, whereas Mr. Phelan directed his outward, across the heavens, at the stars and planets. This was where the comparison ended. One had every manner of lens available to him to improve his sight, and yet he was blind. The other was disabled, yet he could see forever.

I turned to him. "You hit my teacher, Robin. I'd say that says a lot about your character."

"*Your* teacher?" He laughed haughtily. "That jerk isn't your teacher. Don't pull that on me."

I took a breath, and gathered what little spit I had in my mouth, and I swallowed.

"He's only got one leg, case you didn't notice."

My stepfather's expression seemed self-satisfied as though he'd come up against adversity and come out the other side unscathed.

"Hardly a fair fight, wouldn't you say, Robin?" I wanted to add something provocative, something about stopping the truck so we could go a few rounds under a streetlamp. I wanted to kick his ass one last time.

Robin Stanley rolled down the window and removed a crushed pack of cigarettes from his shirt pocket. He shoved the lighter on the dashboard and glanced at me. How was I to judge a bad habit that we shared? He lit the cigarette and exhaled out the window. The smell reminded me of Hitch McDonough, and I almost asked for one but laid off. I wanted nothing more from the bastard.

As we passed the Tollhouse Saloon, my stepfather made an inarticulate sound, not so much a grunt as an *ah-ha!* He worked the steering wheel hard to the right, and the old truck bounded into the parking lot. He straddled two parking spaces and shut off the motor, and I wondered if he were going to leave the truck like this. He took a final drag and flicked the cigarette out the window. I looked from his face to the guttering neon sign that advertised the tavern, and looked back at him. What were we doing in the parking lot of the Tollhouse Saloon? Was my stepfather alcoholic? I had never seen him take a drink before, but there is a first time for everything.

He gestured at a sedan parked between two trucks. "Your mother's car," he said casually. "She's here. Fallen off the wagon, I suspect."

He got out of the pickup, and I followed at a few paces to the saloon door.

The Tollhouse was a rustic saloon that took after a Hollywood set for a Western movie. You half-expected John Wayne to walk through the swinging doors. It was a bar dominated by men, and almost everyone smoked. The place smelled like an ashtray and of rotting fruit from all that sour mash filtered through livers. Searching for my mother, I squinted from the bar to the booths along the walls, hoping not to find her there. Among all that testosterone, my stepfather acted less aggressively than he had at Mr. Phelan's house. He slinked sideways like a fiddler crab, careful not to upset the brutes that stood shoulder to shoulder. Mostly they drank beer and cheered on a basketball game playing itself out on a set over the bar. When he bumped one of them, the man turned, scowling, and looked down at the half-pint intrusion. "'Scuse me?" the man said, and Robin Stanley excused himself. He ingratiated himself. For a second there, I thought he might prostrate himself. "Sorry," he said. "I'm looking for my wife." Rather than let the intrusion go, the man sipped from his beer mug and grinned as he enveloped my stepfather's shoulders in a powerfully built arm. "Hey!" he shouted. "Hey, this guy's lookin' for a wife. Anybody see a wife round here?" Laughter cackled from all quarters. A pool game in a far corner came to a halt when someone shouted that the son-of-a-bitch had walked into the wrong tavern, looking for a wife. More laughter.

And then my mother turned round on the barstool with a look of surprise that matched Robin Stanley's shock. Her surprise also matched the look of my disappointment and defeat. In a voice weakened by shots of bourbon, she said, "Danny, is that you?"

"Mom?"

On either side of her, two men, whose broad backs stretched their flannel shirts, with baseball caps pulled down over mullets, played liar's dice and drank from longnecks. Another man stood nearby, wobbly from inebriation, glassy eyed, his face like a roadmap.

"Karin?" Robin Stanley said.

One of the men swiveled around to look cockeyed at us. To my mother he said, "You know this pipsqueak."

She smirked and brought her highball to her lips. "This pipsqueak…" she said, Oklahoma conducting her voice. "He's my husband." The men laughed, and so did my mother at first until her eyes fell on me and she read my regret. Her lower lip trembled, and she replaced her drink on the coaster. "Danny," she whispered. She sighed. She looked beaten by the alcohol and the rest of it. She was lost down some dark tunnel of her own choosing without the light to guide her. I nearly broke into sobs. "Robin?" she said, as though just now recognizing the two of us, as though finally conquering her deviant behavior and overcoming the specter of multiple personality. Her true self in control once again, she saw us standing there. The lenses in her eyes filled with emotions brought on by too many drinks. She mouthed the words "forgive me."

But by then, my stepfather had exhausted all paths of mercy. He held such vileness in him that all nature of goodness had fled. The tonic of rage whipped him while the background laughter of men and the cheering of sports fans worsened the humiliation. Robin Stanley stepped closer to my mother with a look of resolution that I had never seen before. He formed the four words that I had prayed to hear ever since the day we moved to this miserable town.

He said, "I want a divorce."

He turned on his heels and walked briskly out of the Tollhouse Saloon.

Chapter 18

On the following day, Alder Bridge granted an escape from my mother's remorseful recovery. Alone, I hiked to the middle span to dangle my legs above the void where Nicky Jim's truck had broken through. This was where I could think about things.

A river of low-lying fog submerged Deep Creek and veiled the rear bumper of the wrecked pickup. The fog could not silence the creek's rush through the foothills where the tops of alders were showing green. Spring would make good on its promise. The sun through the fog was no brighter than the Moon in its ascension and race for equinox. The woods were alive with birdsong. The jays scrabbled like clowns in the branches, and curious finches lighted on the bridge struts only to dart away. My immersion in nature put my heart at ease, for the time being.

I hadn't gotten much sleep, and I don't suppose my stepfather slept well either. After my mother and I had returned home in the Buick, I put her in my bed and I laid down on one of the Stanley's recliners, under a thin blanket. I may have dozed off once or twice, but the trials of the day kept me awake. I should have been grateful for being spared a deep sleep and given free reign to nightmares of my kid brother's drowning.

I could not sleep for remembering my mother falling apart outside the Tollhouse Saloon. I had lain awake in the recliner and listened to my memory of her arguing that I was not old enough to drive the two of us back to the farm. Finally, after she had relented and I got behind the wheel, she stayed my hand as I shoved the key in the ignition. I recalled her mumbling something about the death of a baby that had happened years ago. This was something she had kept secret but felt compelled to confess. When my mother drank she told secrets; her speech became slurred and words tended to run together, but alcohol illuminated her mind. Drink freed it from the chains of a real or imagined wifely submission. Booze brought out the articulate in my mother.

"I'm sorry to have to tell you this, Danny," she said. Slurring her words, she told me the story about her first-born child, a baby boy that the hospital staff had taken away moments after she gave birth. The nurses had taken away the baby because there was something horribly wrong with it. "Hours later, after I nearly lost my mind, the nurse brought me a little bundle of joy wrapped in a blue blanket, like an angel."

I told her that the hour was getting late. "We should think about getting back, Mom."

"No, wait." Her eyes glittered in the neon sign of the Tollgate. "You don't understand. You don't understand. The nurse, that nurse in the hospital brought me *you*." She attempted to smile through two tears that fell from her eyes like diamonds.

Over the years in my previous life in California when my mother drank heavily, I had grown accustomed to her rambling mind. I had grown used to words that floated on a sea of alcohol, to her dirty secrets told in the dark that the morning light sterilized. In our Buick, as I listened respectfully as possible to her drunken rant, I had discounted these statements as nonsense. Still, I could not disregard the story about the death of a first-born son.

"What are you saying?"

"I'm saying," she said emphatically through her Southern drawl. "I'm saying you are an imposter."

She must have seen my distress at the word because she hastened to add, "Not that I love you any less than I would my *own* child, Daniel. Love you so much. But…I had to tell you. I have kept this from you. I know I shouldn't have. The nurses and even my obstetrician, that stupid old fool, none of them would admit to it. They lied to me. My baby boy died, and they saw how upset I was. They made arrangements to give me a new baby, and so they gave me you." She shut her eyes and fell back against the car seat. "I know. I know. I should be happy. I should be happy for such a strong, handsome boy. You are, after all, my very own Savior, my Miracle Child." Suddenly, she sat up with her eyes wide, in the blunt theatricality of a drunk. "Your father says I don't know what I'm talking about. A man like that is in denial. Can't see the truth…for all the rest of it." Again, she fell back against the seat, exhausted by this fantasy, this delusion of dead babies and imposters and wayward husbands. She said at last, "Your father got married, the dreadful shit. His *secretary*. Did he tell you that?" She glanced at me and rolled her eyes.

I told her that I knew, that my father and I had talked about it on the telephone.

"I can't believe it." Her voice cracked with emotion, and she rummaged her purse for a hanky in anticipation of more tears. Defeated, she gave up and shut the clasp, and she willed the tears away. She battled emotions that trembled at her fingertips. "Ponce knows nothing of this. What I've had to endure. This stupid town, those stupid people." She waved her tremulous fingers in disgust at a man and woman, their arms entwined at the waist, who were making their way between the parked cars toward their automobile.

"Do you know them?" I asked. I was thankful the couple had not noticed my mother's gesture inside our car.

"No. Don't be ridiculous. *Do I know them?* How can you tell one from the other?" She laughed. "I can't tell you how much I *hate* teaching their stupid children."

For a short time, she said nothing but stared straight ahead through the fogged windshield. I could see her mind turn over all the disappointments in life. I was afraid to agree that the present circumstances were unacceptable. For all those past months of holding my tongue and putting on a good show at the Stanley farm, I now had the opportunity to get agreement from my mother, now that she was willing to admit the mistake of marrying Robin Stanley, as she had been willing to admit disgust for the people of Strand. But I kept quiet because the inebriate forgets promises made. Had my mother turned to me in the Buick and suggested that we gather our belongings and leave the farm that very night, by tomorrow she would have remembered none of it. All forgotten, all forgiven.

Finally, she said, "Please, Danny, would you, please, drive me home? Thank you." Before I took the turn onto the county road, her eyes closed. She fell into a stupor, breathing shallowly, and her head came to rest against my shoulder.

In the morning, she remembered none of it. She had called me an *imposter*. What statement could possibly be worse to hear from your own mother? But I questioned that she truly believed her biological baby had died at childbirth and that I was its replacement. I wondered if she remembered that Robin Stanley had asked for a divorce. Without thinking, husbands and wives say things to hurt the other, only to regret it later. I wondered if Robin Stanley regretted having asked for a divorce. He probably hoped his wife would not remember hearing it.

For the first time since we'd moved to Oregon, the future was undecided. Our living situation in Medford and later on at the Stanley farm had always appeared uncertain. But now the future seemed even more vague. The Jesus Military Academy loomed less menacingly, leaving me to wonder, what was next? Would my mother stay in Strand after she divorced Dr. Stanley? With my father's recent marriage, my returning to our old San Francisco house was not an option. It was something that I had held as a blighted hope. All chance of reconciliation seemed lost. Timing is everything, as my father often said. My mother's timing, in light of the apparent change in circumstances, was way off. She had always been an easily distracted woman, but I worried for her emotional stability after our conversation in the Buick. Was it bourbon or the truth?

A son often overlooks his mother's flaws. After Jesse was born with FAS, when I was ten-years-old, she pulled me aside to explain how "special" my brother was. On my thirteenth birthday, she confessed her responsibility for Jesse's condition, making it clear that alcoholism had caused it. In the current case, I could not ignore my mother's shallowness. She worried about the inconsequential. Yes, she was in successful recovery (with the exception of one slip), but for the most part, my mother lived a life in denial, denying that her son Jesse needed professional help; denying that the family's situation in Strand—living in a doublewide trailer with Robin Stanley's parents—was untenable; denying that I was spinning out of control in this small town, that I'd fallen in with a dangerous crowd, that I sneaked out of the house to smoke and drink; that I was an accomplice to theft and the death of Nicky Jim, among other things. My mother denied the truth while trivial matters preoccupied her.

She was the kind of woman who, when she was about to be baptized, had turned to me and said something about getting her hair dyed a new color, and she had asked what I thought Dr. Stanley would have to say about it.

After drinking excessively, she called me an "imposter." She said that her biological child had died, and that the medical staff replaced the dead baby with me. This is a dangerous thing to tell a child, made worse for the fact that it was not true. For a good part of her adult married life, my mother clung to the delusion about a lost dead baby. It was a story that she told herself when she wallowed in self-pity during her unhappily married years in San Francisco. It was a story she repeated when self-medicating rather than face the facts; when she chose to ignore their broken matrimony and instead soothed the rough edges with alcohol. My mother was a dualistic woman who had struggled to do away with a regional accent, but Oklahoma came through loud and clear in times of stress. It was as though she wore an invisible mask, one that she hoped would deceive the world but through which the world saw who she really was.

*   *   *

On Alder Bridge, I heard the doleful call of a locomotive in the distance. It was the fruit train making its way up the mountain grade. I recalled the first time I had heard it when Hitch McDonough and I sat in the cemetery to talk about girls and to swig beer. I listened for more evidence of its climb, but Deep Creek would not permit anything to intrude on the blustering serenity of waters coursing through the rock and the ruins of a pickup truck. From my backpack I ate two muffins taken from Eve Stanley's breadbox and I drank a bottle of water. I decided to delay my return to the doublewide, in spite of the fact that Robin Stanley and my mother would have left for work by now. The old man would still be there to freely register his dissatisfaction with me as though I was solely responsible for his son's troubled marriage.

It had been Virgil Stanley who awakened me this morning. It was still dark when he came in from the barn with his boots crusted with spring mud as he tossed lengths of firewood into the iron stove.

When he saw me rise up from a night spent in the recliner, he had said, "What're you doing in my chair?" Not good morning or how are you today but an allegation that I had infringed on his property. "And good morning to you, too, Virgil," I had said mockingly, not caring if he took offense at my scorn.

In the bathroom Robin Stanley stood before the mirror in his pajama bottoms and a white T-shirt. He had lathered his face in cream and was about to shave. With the straight razor poised over the sink, he glanced at me in the doorway. Without a word, he leaned back to kick the door shut, but I held it open.

"You left my mother last night, Robin. You left her there to fend for herself. At that bar. What kind of husband does that make you?"

He managed a single swipe of the razor before he replied. His eyes were bloodshot. "This isn't any of your business. It never has been. This is between your mother and I." And with that, he pushed me out of the way, slammed the door shut and locked it.

I remember walking into the kitchen with the lingering impression of his bony hand on the skin of my chest. Eve Stanley was at the stove. My kid brother was in his Spiderman pajamas in his highchair. "Hi, Dammy. It's my birfday. Wish me Happy Birfday, Dammy."

I checked the wall calendar. The actual date of his birth was circled in red, nearly two weeks away. I leaned down and kissed his forehead. "Mornin', buddy," I said. "It's not your birthday. Not yet. See the circle. *That's* your birthday." Jesse insisted once more that it was his birthday, and I touched the side of his face. He seemed close to tears, and I saw him as an unknowingly empathetic little boy who digested my mother's grief. He internalized the tension in the house. To calm him down, I said, "Okay, okay. Happy Birthday."

"He's been going on like that all morning," Eve said. "Take a seat. Breakfast'll be on the table soon."

I took two muffins from the box instead. "Just coffee, if there is any."

She poured a cup from the percolator and placed it before me at the table. She pressed the back of her hand on my forehead and said, "You feeling all right?" I nodded but gave no reassuring smile while I stirred sugar and cream into my cup. When Virgil walked into the kitchen, still wearing muck boots, I carried my cup of coffee to the living room and sat before the stove. At that hour my mother still slept and probably would not be up until her husband had left the house for his optometry office. As was her custom years ago, I knew she would get up late. She would take over an hour to shower and dress before making an appearance in the kitchen. Heavy makeup would conceal wounds from the previous night. A shaky hand would lift the cup of coffee. She would hold her head regally and make no reference to whatever had happened the night before. She would deny words that had been spoken in anger and she would not take credit for broken crockery or a shattered wineglass. I resolved to get out of there. I couldn't watch another one of her performances, not this morning, not after everything that had happened.

Robin Stanley walked briskly across the room to the kitchen. I overheard him say something about seeing a lawyer. I guessed that he'd meant a divorce lawyer until he said the word *bankruptcy*. My stepfather would be seeing a bankruptcy lawyer this morning for legal and tax advice, to learn of his options. I heard the side door close after Robin Stanley said good-bye to his parents. I finished my coffee and thought about the day.

They would have expected me to go to school. They would have expected me to return to my chores. The Stanley's would expect a seamless continuation of routine, regardless of squabbles and threats to livelihood. The world still revolved on its axis, and as far as Virgil Stanley was concerned, that was enough incentive to go to work and for me to go to school and for him to complete the pointless tasks that he'd set for himself. I did not disappoint. I left the house at the designated time to catch the school bus at the bottom of the driveway, but I did not go to school. Instead, I hiked across Alder Bridge. I was determined to spend the day alone, there.

At noon as the fog lifted, I removed my jacket and used it for a pillow. I stretched out between the creosoted planks to bask in the vernal sun. I fell asleep and must have slept for over an hour before someone kicked my boots to awaken me.

It was Hitch McDonough.

The sun was behind him. He cast his wide gloomy outline and put me in his shadow. Still, although I could not make out his face, I knew it was Hitch. I sat up.

"Thought you went to Arkansas."

He did not answer right away but sat down at his usual spot. He glared at the world and condemned everything in it as corrupt and unworthy.

"You didn't go, did you?" I said.

By reason of the past twenty-four hours, indeed the last few weeks, I minced no words for fear of offending him. Much of what I had suffered in his absence was due by and large to his deficiencies, due to his not taking responsibility for his actions. And here we were, all of a sudden, out of the blue, taking a meeting at our usual location high above Deep Creek on the rickety planks of an obsolete railway bridge. Sitting there with him, it struck me as though nothing had happened and all was forgiven. The world was made new again. It was as though I had been baptized; as though I had not been accused of impregnating Annette Kaysen; as though my half-baked sense of loyalty had not landed me in more trouble than a renegade; as though he and I had not been the cause of Nicky Jim's death. Here was the return of my reckless friend with nothing more to offer than his own wretched example of how to screw up a life, and yet I welcomed him. For reasons founded on my mother's failure and that of my stepfather, it seemed enough at the time.

"I heard what you did, for Annette and all," Hitch said. A breeze came up, and he steadied himself by holding onto a rusted cable. He leaned forward and looked down. "You suppose his body's still in the truck?"

Without looking down at the horrible reminder of my moral failures, I said, "The water washed it out the night he crashed. I'm sure of it."

"Think they'll ever find the body?"

I shook my head.

He pulled out a smoke and clenched the filter between his teeth while searching the pockets of his jacket and jeans. "You got a light?"

"Lost your Zippo?" I asked.

He said nothing. He just looked at me with those hard eyes as if to question our friendship over a lost lighter. I kept a box of matches in my book bag. I tossed it to him. He in turn offered a smoke but I declined. He touched the flame to the end of his cigarette and exhaled thoughtfully. "I didn't want to go before I had a chance to say so long."

"Where you been then, if you didn't go to Arkansas?"

He shrugged. "Around."

There was an unfamiliar world-weariness to him. It was the same fatigue I used to see in the eyes and haunch of the homeless in San Francisco, the dog-eared scruff that bone-chilling exposure and paucity would do to a person. Hitch would never admit defeat or surrender, but for whatever had happened to him over the course of his disappearance, the world had handed him a comeuppance.

"Don't take this the wrong way, but you look all beat up."

Hitch nodded and sucked at the cigarette. As he exhaled, he glanced at me with a wry smile.

"Got your car nearby?" I asked.

He recoiled at my off-the-wall question. With a half-hearted gesture, he said, "Yeah. On the other side of the bridge. Why?"

"You hungry?"

Taking a drag, he mulled over my meaning. I watched him ponder whether or not to accept the charity, despite the offer coming from a loyal friend. Rather than cause further humiliation, I got up and brushed the splinters from my jeans.

He shrugged and said, "What gives?"

"I haven't eaten all day. I could use a burger or something. You mind driving me to town?"

The Diary Queen was nearly empty of the noon rush in the time between lunch and after school when students came in for a snack. A skinny kid with a pronounced Adam's apple and a rash of acne stood at the counter. I ordered a cheeseburger, fries and milkshake before turning to Hitch. "Aren't you gonna order something? I'm buying." I had said it offhandedly with no hint of boastfulness or brag that might offend. When Hitch declined, I told the kid at the counter to double the order. At our booth I pushed the extra food tray across the table. "Here," was all I said. It didn't take Hitch long to unwrap the greasy paper and take his first bite of the cheeseburger. We said nothing while we ate. Without letting on to Hitch, I scanned the faces at the counter for Marie Kaysen, hoping to see her. I wanted to find out how things were and learn where she'd ended up. Was her foster family to her liking, if not superior to living with Nicky Jim amid the debris of a meth lab? Before I'd finished my milkshake, Hitch ran his finger inside the French fry container for the extra grease and salt. When I stood up, he said, "Where you going?"

I looked past him, at the order counter, pretending an interest in the menu. "I'm still hungry. You want something?"

"Whatever."

From the same skinny kid, I ordered another cheeseburger and an apple turnover. As I opened my wallet and pulled out five dollars, I said, "Say, does Marie Kaysen still work here?"

"Who?"

I pushed the bills across the counter. "Marie Kaysen?"

He returned the change with a shake of the head. "Never heard of her."

At the booth when I handed Hitch the burger, I said, "Let's get out of here."

We drove the Plymouth Duster to the cemetery for old times sake. From the looks of it, the Duster had been Hitch's home away from home. Discarded fast food containers and rumpled piles of clothes littered the backseat. Empty Marlboro packs had been scattered across the dashboard. There was an air to the old car, borne of infrequent bathing and the rancid excess of chain smoking out of boredom. I made an effort not to mention any of it or complain of the biting odor of piss.

"So," I asked him. "What now? Where you headed?"

Hitch crumpled up the burger wrapper and rolled down the window. He tossed it out.

After living in Strand over the last few months, I had developed a strong aversion to the thoughtless disrespect of littering. It was something practiced unconscientiously by locals on county roads. I bristled at how people abused the landscape as if it were their own personal ashtray or trashcan, how fast food packaging and empty aluminum cans scarred the roadside. I had paid for his meal and felt responsible for the trash. "Hey, don't do that." I got out of the Plymouth, circled round to his side and picked it up, and returned to the car.

"What, is this part of your Christian shit?" he said, as I shut the door. "Save the planet?"

"That's got nothing to do with it."

He smoked his last cigarette and crushed the empty pack. He faked like he was going to throw it out the window only to grin crazily and toss it among his dashboard collection. We said little to one another for a time, and I began to recognize the waning of our mutual enthusiasm. The friendship had changed. Things had changed. Nothing we did or said to one another was quite as simple or nonchalant as it had been. Everything was weighed down by insinuations. The burden of the past, a kind of prologue, was like a storage locker carried between the two of us. Each of us was willing to bear the load but we waited for the other to quit. My heart was not in it, but I couldn't be the one to end this, whatever *it* was.

Still, I saw him from a different angle. Not only did Hitch have feet of clay, but I was hard pressed to name a single sterling quality. How had I seen him as anything but a diversion from my predicament at the Stanley farm?

"So," I said, "you seen Annette? She know you're back?"

Hitch shook his head. "I called her." He sighed and looked away. "I can't say she'd be better off with me, you know?"

I asked him about his old man. "Did he call the police on you? You know, for stealing the car?"

Hitch shot me a look. "I didn't steal this car. I own it. It belonged to my mother, and she give it to me before she died." He roughed his hands through the discarded cigarette packs on the dashboard. "Shit, I'm out of smokes."

We drove back toward town with the intention of stopping at a convenience store for a pack of Marlboros, but I spoiled Hitch's plan. As we reached the corner of the state and county roads, I said, "Hey, drop me off here, okay?"

"Why?"

"I got to get back home."

He was disappointed but resigned to it. "No sweat. I'll drive you."

At the bottom of the Stanley driveway, Hitch stopped the Plymouth and pulled the emergency brake. I lifted my book bag onto my shoulders and climbed out of the car. I leaned in through the open window. He extended his hand, and I took it. There was something to his look that said I wouldn't see him again. It wasn't a casual good-bye. This was different. This was farewell.

"So, where are you headed?" I asked.

"Don't laugh but I am gonna try for Arkansas."

I laughed, and so did Hitch.

"There's nothing here to hold me, you know?"

I nodded and pulled back. I told him to take it easy, that I would see him when he returned to Strand, but we both knew his departure was of a more permanent nature. Home is not some place revisited without consequence. The Plymouth Duster pulled away, and Hitch popped the clutch in second and scratched the tires. As he raced down the road, I imagined that I could hear his laughter. When the car turned the corner, I shifted the weight of my book bag and hiked up the gravel driveway for the farm.

Chapter 19

Hours after saying good-bye to Hitch McDonough, I declined Eve Stanley's call to dinner. Jesse sat in his highchair and Virgil was enthroned at his place, but neither my mother nor Robin Stanley came to the table. Their paroxysms and war of words had been sustained throughout the day, according to the Stanley's. My mother had locked the bedroom door, and my stepfather worked late to avoid confrontation.

In the early evening, I spoke with my mother in her room. She made no reference to imposters. We didn't bring up the slip from the previous night. I had received a postcard from my dad with a Maui postmark that she solemnly handed to me. I didn't have the heart to read it in front of her. Without my asking, she brought up how miserable Dr. Stanley looked when he'd rushed home two or three times that day. He'd come home looking for legal documents, and after upsetting everyone in the house, found them locked in his desk drawer. The mere mention of papers locked in his desk brought on a shameless smirk. "Why are you smiling?" my mother asked.

No reason, I told her.

She went on. "He was slamming doors and cursing all over the house." She described her husband's profanity as a symptom of what she called his *religious insincerity*. "I told him to stop making such a fool of himself. That whatever the problem was, God would fix it. I tell you, we fought like cats and dogs. His hands shook, Danny, like Mrs. Gleason's. Remember?" I reminded her that our old neighbor, Mrs. Gleason, had Parkinson's disease. My mother would not listen to what I had to say. She was too intent on relaying her version of the fight. "His eyes, they were, I don't know, dead flat. Glassy, you know? Like he'd been drinking. (She was no one to talk.) I think it's much worse than he's letting on." She lowered her voice in a way that meant she was about to reveal secrets. "The bankruptcy, I mean. There's no telling what'll happen. We may have to move soon."

When I dared to suggest San Francisco as a destination, words that she forbade me from ever saying again, her complexion darkened. "We talked about this. Your father's married. This you must accept. Period. Get *San Francisco* out of your mind." Her face became drawn with a twist of doubt as if she had yet to admit to the end of marriage with my father.

For her boys, my mother always covered herself in a veneer of studied hopefulness. It was a thin shell, if you like, that made her the image of contentment. However, should the slightest disturbance occur, the shell cracked like an egg and my real mom emerged. My real mom pouted for hours. She broke down our resistance by subjecting us to an unrelenting self-pity until we gave in and did what she asked. The veneer was not my mother, but it was the mother I wished she were, unfairly I suppose. I should have mustered the compassion to accept her inconsistencies as she accepted mine. But what boy does not want Donna Reed or June Cleaver for a mother, faithfully at home, wearing pearls and sensible shoes while she serves home-cooked meals? That day I saw past the veneer. Given time, my mother would restore the façade, once again making herself into the picture of contentment. Having her for a mother was like living along an earthquake fault, never knowing when the Big One was going to hit and change your life forever.

The old saw *the truth shall set you free* was nonsense or at least inapplicable to my fifteen-year-old mind. Had my mother been honest, been her true self, where would that have left my kid brother and me? A minimum of social veneer is necessary for a happy home. In our brave new world, pretense and Victorian pose may very well be passé, but a bit of masquerade, a modicum of good manners no matter how bogus, puts us in good stead. It fools us into believing all is well with humanity so that we can go on with the business of living. In my own life, the truth has proved a cruel teacher. Little tender loving care did I receive from its telling. In point of fact, copping to the truth has often put me in dire straits. The truth got me into more trouble than had I stuck to my guns and lied. The liar is, after all, a happy man. He may live an unrealized existence by never knowing himself, but the liar is seldom found in detention at school or put on restriction at home, seldom suspended, expelled, or imprisoned. Some of our most famous men in history have been unconscionable liars, so good at it that their names make it into history books. At their funerals, companionable first-class liars speak eloquently on their behalf and tell elegiac lies, which to my mind is like tossing the truth on the pyre. No, the truth will not set you free, not in every sense of the word. In the example of my mother, lying was a way of life.

"Will you be coming to dinner?" I asked. She shook her head, and I kissed her good night and left her alone.

Late in the night, before Robin Stanley came home, I rose from bed in the dark and made my way to the kitchen for a snack. On my return to bed, I stopped. My stepfather's desk glowed in the moonlight that was drawn down through a skylight. I cannot say what made me stop and consider the desk, but my hands searched for and found the tiny brass key tucked between the tissue-thin pages of the Bible. What sort of boy is it that regards the sweetness of revenge under the grim circumstances of this day? I should have left well enough alone and let my mother work out her differences with Robin Stanley. Things would fall apart of their own accord without my interference. But meddling in their affairs had been an irresistible urge of mine throughout their brief marriage. I was not about to change my ways before committing one last crime.

Inserting the key, I opened the drawer and, to my amazement, found the pile of Robin Stanley's pornography just as I had left it months earlier, undisturbed. After I had stuck in his Bible a picture of two women in the throes of sex, the exposure of which should have mortified him, he had not bothered to remove the explicit materials from the drawer. He had perhaps added pictures to the collection, which spoke to the seriousness of his fixation. Dr. Stanley proved the gambler. Gambling against the odds that I would not divulge his secret. On this night, the probabilities turned against him as I removed the drawer and dumped its contents on the Bible in a disheveled heap. Where I found an upside down photograph, I righted it. For a place of prominence, I selected the more graphic pictures of monumental erections and hideous bestiality as frosting on this cake of unclean behavior and lies.

Satisfied that the damage was done—or soon would be by morning—I returned to my room. I didn't feel smug about what I'd done. Revenge is not the sweet elixir it's made out to be. Rather than gloat, I laid on the bed in the moonlight and observed the sporadic moths land on the window screen in their suicidal hunt for the brightest light and the hottest of flames. And I mused, isn't this what all the little living things strive for through instinct and force of habit? Isn't what we desire the thing most likely to kill us?

I heard my stepfather come home at one o'clock in the morning. Because he turned on no lights, he didn't see the mess I'd made of his desk.

*   *   *

I was awakened by my mother screaming *Robin!*

Into that gauzy membrane separating dreams from reality, I awoke to the conscious thought that she had discovered her husband's pornography strewn across the desk. As I got out of bed, I constructed a scenario in which she had gone to the kitchen for a glass of water, and on her return to their bedroom, had discovered the filth. But this proved not the case.

Light in northern climes becomes critically important to those who have endured winter. For the Californian, especially San Francisco natives, seasonal change is scarcely noticeable. Oregon has distinct seasons; California has none. Here winter solstice heralds the dark days of long shadows under the rare clear sky, and the sun sets at four o'clock in the afternoon. Our nights wait for the belated sunrise. And so, on the Stanley farm, spring's approach was something I had raised high hopes in. This morning, as my mother screamed and the doublewide was thrown over to great commotion, the gray edges of my window showed that there would be another hour *in extremis* before daylight.

A light was on in my mother's bedroom and the door was ajar. Through the crack I saw the Stanley's and my mother standing beside the double bed. Robin Stanley was in the bed snoring loudly, but it wasn't snoring exactly. More like the thrashing of a drowning man. I stepped through the door to ask what was going on when Eve

Stanley desperately called out her son's name. She couldn't believe what was happening. We were in our pajamas and bathrobes. Does Robin have narcolepsy, my mother asked. My stepfather's mouth was open, gasping for air. Virgil gripped the mattress and bounced the bed, shaking it. "Wake up, son! Wake up!" My mother pressed three fingers of her hand against Robin Stanley's neck. She turned to me and yelled, "Call nine one one."

"What's going on?" I said. There's something wrong, she said. Go, she yelled. Go!

I have heard the term "fog of war," and I cannot know its meaning because I have never been in combat, but *fog* best describes my state of mind over the course of this hour. I remember the gist of what I told the 911 dispatcher. I remember her confirming our address and saying that paramedics "have been alerted. They're on their way." She asked if anyone in the house knew CPR. I told her I didn't know. She asked if I wanted her to walk me through what I would have to do, to save the person's life. I made the call from the kitchen, I explained, our only telephone. The "victim"—this was what I called my stepfather—was at the opposite end of the house. "The cord won't reach," I said. This absurd discussion about telephony escalated when the dispatcher asked if it was a "walk-around" phone. At that moment, my mother rushed in, said something I did not hear, and yanked the receiver out of my hand. "Go help," she told me.

"Sorry, Mom," I said.

She covered the mouthpiece and said she thought Dr. Stanley had been joking before he struggled for breath. "We were chatting, laying there." She said that all of a sudden he had started snoring. She thought that he was making a joke, that her conversation had bored him, but when she shook him, he didn't stop. He just kept struggling to breathe. There were tears in her eyes. "Last thing he said, he was sorry for...*everything*."

My kid brother walked into the kitchen, dragging his favorite blanket and sucking his thumb. My mother dropped the telephone receiver and her legs gave out and she fell in a seated position on the linoleum floor. "Mommy?" Jesse cried. I spoke into the phone and assured the lady my mother was okay, that she was just shocked by it all. The dispatcher said the paramedics would be arriving shortly and to hang on. I told her that I was going to hang up and take care of my mother. I wrapped Jesse in the blanket and lifted him into my arms and carried him out of the kitchen.

Eve Stanley howled in hysteria in the darkened living room. I put Jesse on the couch and told him to stay there. Virgil was still with his son, and when I rushed into the bedroom, he said, "He just keeps up that noise. He won't stop." It was *râle de la mort,* a death rattle, and within half a minute it stopped.

The paramedics arrived. They worked on him for nearly an hour. We were ushered out of the bedroom to the living room where we shivered from emotions and the chill. My mother sat on the couch next to Eve Stanley to comfort her, but the old lady was inconsolable. Virgil stood in the doorway, his gnarled face reflecting the swirling blue and red lights of the paramedic rig. After a long time, they "called the code" and the coroner was notified. On their two-ways with dispatch, the paramedics noted the time of death. I watched from a recliner, holding Jesse on my lap, as they removed the scattered equipment—a defibrillator and tackle boxes full of drugs and syringes—and one of them returned to the house with what looked like a yellow slicker. It was a body bag.

"No no no," Eve Stanley shouted. My mother held her and kept her from inhibiting what the paramedics had to do. They fit the body bag under Robin Stanley's remains and zipped him into it. Urine dampened a dark circle on the bed sheet. One of the paramedics asked Virgil Stanley a few questions, but he was too dazed to reply. He kept repeating that this had happened before, when his son was much younger. There was no sense in stuffing him into that bag, he would be coming awake in a few minutes. "I'm sorry, sir, but your son has expired." I got out of the recliner and walked up to the old man. I asked if he wanted me to answer the questions for him, I wouldn't mind, but he repeated again that he had seen just such an "epileptic fit" in his son years ago, that everything would be fine if they would just let him breathe, if they would just take him out of that "damn bag."

I turned to the paramedic and answered her questions as best I could, pointing out my mother as next of kin. "She's his wife," I said.

Had the deceased complained of any chest pain or shortness of breath earlier in the day, the paramedic asked. I had to tell her that I didn't know, that I hadn't been around for most of the day. "He could have," I said. The paramedic kneeled before my mother and Eve Stanley on the couch, and although I could not hear what was being said, she was tender and kind to the grieving women. The paramedic had gone through similar scenarios many times before where shocked family members could not come to grips with the sudden death of a loved one. At this point, Jesse sobbed into his blanket, not understanding the gravity of the situation but responding to his mother's tears.

"He was fine, he was just fine," my mother said. One minute they were talking about what they had to do today, and in the next minute he had some trouble breathing. Just like that. And so this was how the Stanley's, my mother and I received a brutal instruction on the arbitrariness and irreversibility of death. How tentative were the strings that held the living aloft.

The coroner explained to my mother that her husband had died of cardiac arrest that resulted in sudden death. He was dead within three minutes. Since he'd lost consciousness at the onset of the attack, and never regained it, my stepfather did not suffer, which was a small comfort to his parents and my mother.

After the coroner removed the body, my mother and the Stanley's stood outside in their bare feet. Virgil held Eve, my mother stood alone with her arms across her chest. In the kitchen I put Jesse in his highchair and he asked for a "bowl of stupid." I poured a bowl of Cheerios. On my return to the living room, the pornography on top of Robin Stanley's desk stopped me cold.

They should not see it.

I scooped up most of the photographs and clippings and threw them into the woodstove. I returned to the desk for the rest until all of it was removed. I put a match to the corner of a picture and the wrinkled mass caught. I shut the iron door and locked it. I quickly inspected the drawer to make certain all evidence of my dead stepfather's obsession was destroyed. I opened the door on the stove again, this time to admit a gust of oxygen to disinfect a man's past of minor mistakes in judgment, mistakes best relegated to dust and ash.

*   *   *

We held Dr. Robin Stanley's funeral at the end of the week, on a Friday, at graveside in the Strand cemetery. It rained, and all those black umbrellas recalled my mother's wedding on the previous summer, in Medford. Mom dressed Jesse in a pair of black slacks with the cuffs rolled and a white shirt that was too big for him. Despite my mother's ministrations—she put him in the highchair to keep him "presentable" but Eve fed him toast and jam—my kid brother had stained the shirt with an abstract raspberry smear. I wore black jeans and my Sunday school shirt. I had asked Virgil to help me with the tie, but he refused. "Do it yourself. Can't you see I'm busy?" He wasn't preoccupied by anything but grief, and I respected that. But the tie ended up with an irregular knot, a granny knot never to be seen in the pages of *Gentleman's Quarterly*. My mother wore her Laura Ashley dress. It was the last time she would wear it, she told me. "Tomorrow, I'm getting rid of this old thing."

For the most part, the service was lightly observed. Few people from our church attended along with a scattering of townspeople, the pharmacist, Mr. Oja Palmquist, and two ladies from the bakery. One of the bakers offered her condolences to my mother. "Dr. Stanley was such a nice man." Evidently, Robin Stanley had a weakness for pastry, another of his habits he kept to himself. The eulogy was delivered by Sonny Vickers. It struck me, sitting between my mother and Jesse on metal folding chairs, the pastor knew scant about Robin Stanley's personal life. Much of what he said centered on the proof of divine love "because our brother, on this day, is seated in the Kingdom of Heaven, with our Lord Jesus Christ." I wondered, where was the proof? How could we know for certain? For the sake of my mother's faith, I let Rev. Vickers have his say without raising an iota of doubt.

They rested the coffin, a simple affair, on slats of oak. Scattered on the grass around the grave were clumps of coarse red clay dug up from two-yards down. Four men, two on either side holding canvas straps, lowered the coffin into the hole. We were silhouettes behind a line of red cedar below the fortress sky, huddled against the brisk spring air. There was denial in the eyes of Eve and Virgil Stanley. Eve murmured, "Where is my boy?" Sonny Vickers prayed for birds at night whose wings are tipped by heaven, that grace us with the sweet brevity of life. "Before we know, they fly," the pastor said. He commended Robin Stanley's body to the earth, and stones prattled on eternity as the four men worked their blades.

To the cemetery and back to the farm we had driven separately. Mom was behind the wheel of the Buick, and the Stanley's drove their old Ford pickup. I don't know if Virgil and Eve had anything to say to each other, but my mother and I became lost in thoughtful silence. Jesse snoozed, wrapped up in his jacket and baseball cap, his head lolling on his small neck. My mother glanced at him in the backseat and told me to check his muffler, make sure it wasn't too tight. These were the only words we spoke until we pulled next to the doublewide and my mother set the emergency brake. She shut off the motor but just sat behind the wheel and stared off at the distance. Her expression was set in something like contemptuous resolve. I think she was feeling contempt for her husband's unexpected desertion but she looked determined to change the situation. I imagined she resolved to remove us boys from what had become an unworkable state of affairs, living on the Stanley farm. Whether or not this was on her mind is impossible to say. She never let on. But it occupied my thoughts in the logic that death brings to survivors. Common sense told me that our time with the Stanley's was at an end. What could possibly hold us there?

"Stay in the car," she said as she got out just as the Stanley's drove up in their pickup. The three adults spoke to one another in the yard. Virgil did most of the talking. His ruddy face was flushed. After my mother gestured for us to stay in the car, the three adults went inside, Virgil followed by Eve and my mother. Jesse woke up, and I had to keep him occupied for the quarter of an hour of his mother's absence. The keys were in the ignition, and I knew how to turn on the radio without draining the battery. It was set to a station playing a James Taylor song, and I was about to change the channel when the lyrics sang something about *hard times, hard times come again no more and many days you have lingered round my cabin door.* That cello and voice struck me as profound. It so finely captured the moment of sitting there in the car that I wished the song never to end. When a commercial came on, I switched off the radio, and my mother came out of the doublewide. She paused to wipe her face, turning away from us, keeping true to her practice of shielding us from her emotions as though the toxicity of tears would prematurely turn her boys into cynics.

She opened my door. "Come on. Come with me. We have things to do."

Jesse and I followed her, holding hands, into the doublewide. Beside the door, Virgil had stacked a pile of empty boxes, the same ones that had occupied our bedroom all these months. My brother and I stood stock-still in the doorway while my mother went to her room. She turned round. "Don't stand there. Come over here. I can't be expected to do this all by myself."

It became suddenly clear what *it* was that needed doing—we were being evicted. Jesse and I would need to pack our belongings into the empty cartons and carry them to the trunk of the Buick. This chore elated and demoralized me. Leaving the Stanley farm had been my long-term goal, but the circumstances left me feeling ambivalent. Victory was not sweet but offensive. I worried for my mother. How was she taking this? What had the Stanley's said to her? She was a widow and had been married to Robin Stanley for less than nine months, less time than it took to gestate a baby but long enough to be considered "family," surely. I knew Virgil Stanley as a man without any generosity of spirit, but his wife…how could she have allowed our eviction? Eve Stanley had welcomed us, fed us, clothed us and kept us warm and gave more than a fair share of what little they had to offer. I knew this as Virgil's doing, kicking us out on the street on the day of his son's funeral. This was not how I had envisioned victory over my adversary, to be bushwhacked by the father.

Within the hour we'd removed from the doublewide all that we owned. We packed under Virgil Stanley's scrutiny that we not take what belonged to him or his dead child. For the most part, Eve remained out of sight, in the kitchen, which was her customary realm. Finally, with Jesse clipped into his seatbelt and the trunk tied down with twine for all those boxes, my mother carried a small suitcase, one that I remembered her buying at a San Francisco department store years ago, something she called her overnight bag. It was the last item removed from the doublewide. Virgil Stanley stood in the yard, his arms crossed like a sentinel, glowering at me in the passenger seat. When my mother took the two steps down from the front door, I got out of the car and circled around to help her. She refused to let me carry the overnight bag. She quickly threw it on the front seat and got in the car. "Come on, Danny. Let's go," she said.

I hesitated. This was not how I wanted it. This was not how it was supposed to go down. Something needed to be said, not just a fare-thee-well or good riddance, but something more to the point of what was going on here.

I went up to Virgil Stanley and faced him. He straightened his spine and narrowed his eyes at me, working his jaw like he had something distasteful in his mouth that needed chewing. For the longest time, I waited for my brains to cough up an insult to yell at the old man. For months I had lain on my bed in the dark imagining this moment, inventing a flourish of abuse to hurl at Robin Stanley and his father on my final departure from their lives. Here it was happening and my mind was a blank.

"Shouldn't you be going?" Virgil said. His thin mouth was smug in triumph. Recognizing his contempt was all the incentive I needed.

"You can think whatever you want to think, old man. About me, I mean."

"Like I told the wife, just want that bitch and you brats off my land," he said.

"My *mother*, she did everything she could to make this work."

He turned his head and spat sideways. I let the mist of his spittle clear before I took a step closer.

"But let me tell you something. You're gonna lose the farm, old man. Your precious son gambled it away, do you know that? In his stupid business venture. That's right. It's gone. All of this. All your work, and all those years. Gone. So, you can spit and curse me all day. Enjoy it, because the bank will foreclose on your goddamned ass soon enough."

I returned to the car. From the passenger seat, as my mother drove away, I couldn't help but observe Virgil Stanley in the side-view mirror, staring after us, standing in the middle of his desolate homestead, the plum sapling in the yard showing blossoms of a false spring.

Chapter 20

Life isn't a novel whose loose ends are tied into a pretty bow in the last chapter. My father was right—life *is* messy. People come into and go out of it. You make friends, they move away. You relocate to another state. People die. Babies are born. The innocent suffer and the guilty go unpunished. It's the same old rhythm played out since the beginning of time. But as a fifteen-year-old I had yet to gain the perspective of age. My youth felt like a permanent condition despite evidence to the contrary.

In college, I wrote a short story about my life in Oregon and opened it with the following: "In the spring of my fifteenth year, after a stretch of disappointment and trouble, I had a surprising bit of good luck. My stepfather died." Back then, we were instructed to create appealing opening lines. The creative writing instructor labeled mine "biting irony," but I knew that it came at the expense of Robin Stanley. It was a story of loss and gain, as most stories must be. Although I should have begun at the beginning, I could not have imagined when that was. My life had an uncertain beginning followed by a vague ending because my life really started when my stepfather died. And so each time I sat down to write the story, I began at a time when I felt dead and concluded when life began, with the death of Robin Stanley.

I saw Strand one last time after graduate school. I'd decided to take time off from the academic grind to kick around the West "before it was gone," as I explained my *wanderlust* to my mother. I had a close friend in Walter Harbrace who owned a Volkswagen bug. He shared my naiveté for seeing wildness before the developers bulldozed everything. We also shared a love of books and a passion for fly-fishing. We had feral ideas about driving to Alaska, of surviving by our wits in wilderness, but the engine sucked a valve in Bellingham and made goulash of our plans. The mechanic took a week to replace it, which put us back nearly five hundred bucks. So much for Alaska. We ended up nursing the VW around the Olympic peninsula before we headed east. We fly-fished across the Cascades, through the Idaho panhandle and into the great basin of Montana and Wyoming, Yellowstone country.

When either of us was too tired to drive we slept in sleeping bags under tarps on the shoulders of highways. On one night in particular, I remember looking up at the clear sky of spectacular firmament. The stars brought back everything to memory, the Stanley farm, Hitch, the Kaysen sisters, Mr. Phelan, everything. I had forgotten what stars looked like, and that night I got very little sleep.

On rainy nights, we checked into cheap motels and flipped a quarter for who got the bed. We returned to California by the odd road, long forgotten highways, taking digital pictures of derelict gas stations, feed supply stores and road signs peppered with buckshot. We aimed for the landmark of Mt. Hood, and that's how we found ourselves on a warm summer's day motoring through Strand. I hardly recognized it for all the growth. We didn't stop.

Harbrace went on to earn a Fulbright to Oxford, and he ended up teaching irony to comparative literature students at Columbia. I returned to Berkeley but never finished my dissertation and ended up teaching high school science for a time, before I got married. For years I guessed that my friendship with Audley Phelan had inspired my teaching science to kids more interested in iPods and virtual Internet cultures than beakers and dissected frogs. For a time I liked to think that I was my students' Mr. Phelan. I would hope that someday, by helping a kid in trouble, I might be able to repay what he did for my mother and I.

On the afternoon of Robin Stanley's funeral, after we left the farm, Mom had driven to The Cozy Corner, a breakfast cafe off the main highway. We had no other place to go, and she needed time to think. We ordered, and Jesse ate strawberry pancakes while my mother and I brooded over endless cups of coffee. What were we going to do? We could not leave town right away, although I would have preferred doing so. My mother had signed a contract to teach at the middle school, and I had to finish out the freshman year or repeat it in California, where I hoped we would eventually end up. Our choices were few. At first, she rejected my suggestion that we see Mr.

Phelan. "It's our only option," I told her. We didn't have a place to live, and Strand was not replete with boardinghouses and apartment rentals. Mr. Phelan's seemed the logical place to go.

From the café we drove on over to his house. She left my kid brother and me in the Buick, parked at the curb with the motor running, while she spoke in private to Mr. Phelan. Was what she had to say to him so confidential that she couldn't have involved me? Through the plate glass window at the front of the house, I watched the two of them. They sat opposite one another in my teacher's overstuffed chairs, my mother dabbing her mascara with a tissue, Mr. Phelan leaning forward to offer his hands in sympathy. He was proposing that she and her boys stay with him. And so it happened, until the end of the school year, we lived in the cottage at the back of Mr. Phelan's property.

The four of us celebrated Jesse's sixth birthday with a picnic in the backyard. Mom cooked up a bowl of potato salad, and Mr. Phelan made sandwiches. Although the Fourth of July was over two months away, in the evening Mr. Phelan let us set off fireworks. They were "child-safety fireworks" and pretty pathetic, but it was the thrill of a lifetime for my kid brother. We let him set off most of them. At nightfall we gathered in the silo, in Mr. Phelan's astronomical observatory, and we took turns gazing through his Schmidt-Cassegrain reflector. By then my brother was enrolled in a program for the developmentally handicapped, in what Jesse called "Boring school" for the town of its origin. For the short time of his attendance, he made dramatic improvements. It seemed clear that he understood a little of what it meant to look through a telescopic eyepiece and see bits and pieces of the universe that were hundreds and thousands of light years away. My brother always loved to look up at the stars. He got so he could name the better-known constellations.

After we relocated to California, I kept in touch with Mr. Phelan for a time but we eventually lost touch. The onus is on me because I neglected to respond to his last letters, until they stopped coming altogether. After that, he no longer sent Christmas greetings or a card on my birthday. The end of our correspondence happened around the time I found a few letters to my mother written in his recognizable hand. Each implored her to consider returning to Oregon, to live with him. Whether their relationship had flourished before or after the death of my stepfather, I cannot say for sure. It doesn't matter. Not to me. I confess to a certain voyeurism on my part, reading his letters, reading between the lines and imagining my mother's letters in reply. My reasons for no longer writing to Mr. Phelan were the number of changes happening in my life, not the least of which were entering college and falling in love for the first time. It came naturally to me to end our friendship. In our local newspaper I have since read that he won a national award for teacher of the year. The article included a small picture. He looked the same, and I had to wonder when the photograph was taken. I cut the article out, and I carry it in my wallet. I've shown it to students who ask about where I got my interest in amateur astronomy.

Years ago my mother returned to Oklahoma, to be with "her people," as she put it. Jesse went with her, of course. It was the first time that a thousand miles of geography separated us. But my kid brother did well. I attended his graduation from a vocational school where he received training in mail sorting. He excelled at it enough to make a career out of the United States Postal Service. Within a few months of her arrival, my mother married a man that she had dated in high school, Bud Tucker. I liked him, and at their wedding when she and I danced together, I kissed her cheek and said "Bud's a vast improvement over your last husband." They had a good life together.

After Bud passed away, Mom and Jesse lived in his house near Osage. For no reason other than the miles between us, we saw each other less often. On Christmas and Jesse's birthday, I'd fly down, spend a long weekend, but for the most part we lived lives in isolation. When Mom was first diagnosed, it was Jesse who called and ended up consoling me. I felt guilty for not being there to help out. My kid brother did most of the heavy lifting during her treatments. I visited once in a while and fondly remember the time we picnicked along the Arkansas River when Mom was in remission. It was springtime, and we were full of hope. During my visits, Jesse seemed so grown up and *normal.* There were tale-tell signs of the syndrome— he still has epicanthic folds—but for the most part he was as close to normal as anyone. At our mother's memorial service, Jesse asked that

I do the public speaking. He was afraid he might seize from anxiety despite extra doses of Dilantin. "Public speaking's the biggest fear in America, Dammy." He always called me that, despite years of speech therapy. I gave a heartfelt tribute to my mother. I mentioned her love for "her boys."

"My mother would have walked through fire for us." After I said it I wondered if I believed it. The lives of the dead deserve to be fancied up. We pretty up the lives of the dead for their sake as much as for our own. I mentioned my father because he was there, twice divorced, rich, sitting in the back row. I talked about my mother's midlife love affair with Bud Tucker, their once-in-a-lifetime cruise through the Panama Canal, a trip to Italy. "My mother loved the *Eye-talians*," I said, mimicking her beautiful Oklahoma accent. At her memorial service, I never mentioned Robin Stanley or the months we spent in Strand. I spoke graciously of her faith in Jesus. It had been her hope that I accept Jesus and be "born again." I joked that I was having too much trouble finding the meaning of this life before I accepted getting born into another one. My brother Jesse laughed because, I think, he truly understood.

Through death we forgive transgressions.

After Nicky Jim's death, whenever something bad happened in my life, I reacted as though I deserved punishment for my denial of sin. This was the residue of my mother's religious guilt rubbing off on me. The scales of justice, she would say, need balancing. I don't know for certain whether or not anyone found his body in the waters of Deep Creek or at a confluence further down its course toward the Pacific. That no one knows and nobody seems to care about him is little comfort to me. I am not haunted by his death so much as by my cowardice and passivity in the face of it.

I have settled in Oakland, California, where my wife and I are raising three girls. For the most part, we have survived the natural trials and tribulations of having three children close in age. When my oldest was five, she took ballet lessons at a studio located in an unfamiliar neighborhood. She almost missed her first lesson. I circled the neighborhood for half an hour searching for it, and we arrived ten minutes late, which upset the teacher. On our return home I stopped for gas at a Shell station in the flatlands. As I paid for the gas, I noticed the name of the proprietor over the door. *Greg McDonough.* I doubted that it was Hitch. It couldn't be the same person, could it? I asked the attendant about him, and he said, "Oh, that guy. He was killed six months ago." Murdered in a downtown bar. Some guy knifed him in the heart. "Did he go by the nickname Hitch?" I asked. The gas station attendant had worked for the new owners "only a couple weeks," he said. He'd never met Greg McDonough. There was no way to confirm it was Hitch. I have imagined what kind of man he would have grown into. Most likely not someone I could be friends with for long, not as an adult. I like to think he's still sixteen, living it up in Arkansas, filching Marlboros and swilling the occasional beer in a Plymouth Duster with primer on all four panels.

Acknowledgements

There are a number of people that I would like to acknowledge. I would like to thank Louise Carleton, R.N., B.S.N, and her husband, who provided references and a concise background on FAS and fetal alcohol effects. Those of childbearing age should be informed of and pay strict attention to the risks of drinking alcohol during pregnancy.

While researching evangelism, I found especially informative Kathryn Joyce's article in *The Nation* (Nov. 27, 2006, "The Quiverfull Conviction: Christian Mothers Breed 'Arrows for the War'"). Also, Chris Hedges book on the Christian Right, *American Fascists*, was helpful in framing Daniel's response to Robin Stanley's religious practice. The biblical passages are taken from the New International Version of the Life Application Study Bible, published by Tyndale House Publishers, 1991. In Chapter 15, the idea for the reference to the history of religion is taken from A. S. Byatt's *Babel Tower*, and as far as I know, the exegesis is her invention.

The tune referred to in Chapter 20, has been sung by James Taylor and was composed by Stephen Foster: "Hard Times Come Again No More." Any fan of Monty Python will recognize the quote from *The Meaning of Life*, a favorite of mine. "Just remember that you're standing on a planet that's evolving...."

For his continued friendship and the first edit, I extend special thanks to Peter Hays, Professor of English, UC Davis. I wish to thank my wife, watercolor artist, Leslie Cheney Parr, for her patience and encouragement.

C. Marcus Parr
January 2007

About The Author

C. Marcus Parr's short fiction, poems, and cartoons have appeared in small independent literary magazines in the United States and Canada. He received the Nancy Pickard Fiction Award, and was runner-up for the Pearl Fiction Award. His short story "The Devil Visits Confidence" was serialized and nominated for a Pushcart Prize. His poems "Oppenheimer's Laugh" and "A Thousand Endless Words" were also nominated for a Pushcart.

He lives and writes in Oregon with his wife Leslie Ann Cheney-Parr, watercolor artist. After a career as a medical science liaison, Marcus briefly taught creative writing at Mt. Hood Community College before full retirement to raise chickens and make pinot noir.

www.ingramcontent.com/pod-product-compliance
Lightning Source LLC
Chambersburg PA
CBHW031226020726
47499CB00002B/659